Cpt. Jose 'Pepi' Granado is a graduate of St. Thomas University. He's a retired captain with 36 years of law enforcement experience spanning two agencies, the Miami Police Department and Miami Gardens Police Department. During his illustrious career investigating violent crimes, he established himself as a dedicated, knowledgeable, and tenacious investigator with excellent mentoring skills. These qualities, along with his experience and expertise allowed him to establish the protocols of how investigations should be conducted, as written in his first book, *The Homicide Manifesto*. Under his leadership, the units of the Criminal Investigations Division were highly successful in solving and clearing cases. As an investigator and supervisor with over 800 homicides and death cases investigated, he brings to the reader a real-life perspective of the emotional rollercoaster that a death investigator experiences.

Cpt. Jose 'Pepi' Granado

# CRY TEARS OF BLOOD

AUSTIN MACAULEY PUBLISHERS™

LONDON • CAMBRIDGE • NEW YORK • SHARJAH

**Ordering Information**
Quantity sales: Special discounts are available on quantity purchases by corporations, associations, and others. For details, contact the publisher at the address below.

**Publisher's Cataloging-in-Publication data**
Granado, Cpt. Jose 'Pepi'
Cry Tears of Blood

ISBN 9781638296102 (Paperback)
ISBN 9781638296119 (Hardback)
ISBN 9781638296126 (ePub e-book)

Library of Congress Control Number: 2022915417

www.austinmacauley.com/us

First Published 2022
Austin Macauley Publishers LLC
40 Wall Street, 33rd Floor, Suite 3302
New York, NY 10005
USA

mail-usa@austinmacauley.com
+1 (646) 5125767

I would like to acknowledge the Miami Police Department's homicide unit for giving me the opportunity in 1988 to live my dream as a homicide investigator. To my mentors who took an interest by imparting their knowledge that allowed me to succeed. To the Miami Gardens Police Department, thank you, for allowing me the opportunity to implement strategies and procedures as well as command the Criminal Investigations Division. To those who worked with me, I hope my counsel was helpful. To the prosecutors of the Miami-Dade State Attorney's office and doctors of the Miami-Dade Medical Examiner's office, whose tireless efforts are the reason many violent cases are successfully prosecuted. Lastly, to 'Casavana' restaurant for providing copious amounts of 'Cafecito' that kept me going during long hours and many days of non-stop work.

# Introduction

I am disturbed daily by the memories of the atrocities and despicable acts that humans commit. You see, I was a homicide investigator for an exceptionally large and well-respected police department. It was my job to hunt those killers that would go out daily, with a black heart to inflict pain or injury to another human being. What type of animal, other than a human, goes out to intentionally kill? That I am aware of, none.

It is known, that in the animal kingdom, each species goes out and hunts in one way or another to survive. This is nature at its best. When a lioness kills an antelope, she does this to help feed the pride. Each part of the kill is sustenance for the growth of the cubs. This allows for the pride to grow and flourish. Those animals hunt for a purpose, not for sport or anger. There kill is not emotional, it is essential.

On the other hand, there are times when animals in self-defense will stave-off an attack and in so doing might injure or kill its attacker. There again, one can see that the attacker was searching for prey to survive and the prey was able to defeat its attacker. Something like self-defense. None the less, this act was not personal. No kill in the animal kingdom goes to waste. Once the carcass has been discarded, other species that act as the waste management system of the animal kingdom and nature come in to perform a specific function. In the end, every piece of the carcass that could be used as food is, including the bones.

Now you wonder why the analogy. Well, it is quite simple. Violence in the animal kingdom takes various forms and at times, the result is death. Unfortunately, violence in the human kingdom is one of thought or emotion. Humans kill because of anger or because of a primary/premeditated violent act that leads to death or because of a mental debilitating condition. Humans do not kill other humans because they need to survive. Therefore, all humans need is a motive, a willingness to carry out the act and the opportunity when it presents itself. Unfortunately, we have not been able to eliminate a person's desire to commit such atrocious acts. Law Enforcement cannot forecast when someone is going to commit a crime, "Minority Report" is not real.

Society and all its social programs fail to target the problems head-on. They handcuff law enforcement and make it more difficult to prosecute or convict offenders that have been apprehended. The ills of society will not be remedied by social programs. Instead, other avenues can be taken but are not because they are not politically advantageous. Therefore, law enforcement is left holding the bag of cleaning up the mess. They are always behind the eight ball and the killers are out-there waiting.

I learned these simple lessons early in my career and much has not changed in over 36 years. So, knowing this, I made it my mission to do the absolute best job to apprehend as many miscreants as possible, especially if they were killers. Unfortunately, there are those cases that will never leave you and will keep you up at night. I was once a crusader and felt invincible, able to handle anything that came my way. Then, the unimaginable took place.

What happens when you face evil and see firsthand what it is capable of doing? This is where it started, a moment in time that I wish would have never occurred.

# Chapter 1

To this day, I am still haunted by the memory of an event so unspeakable that it has taken me years to fully understand its effect on me. Many will never comprehend how incidents such as this one can occur, but unfortunately, they are much more common than anyone can imagine.

As a veteran homicide investigator, I have investigated or assisted in over 800 death cases. Some more common than others, as death cases go. But 1994 was a very unusual year for me, I had the misfortune of being a part of several death cases involving children. On a homicide team, caseloads are distributed amongst team members to lessen the burden of the investigative intensity each death case rightly deserves. Unfortunately for me, I was the senior training homicide investigator during this period. Therefore, my primary responsibility was to train the new investigators assigned to the midnight shift as well as being the lead investigator on all death investigations that occurred during our tour of duty.

Remember, I stated that I was the senior homicide investigator on the midnight shift. Well, this was only my fifth year as an investigator, and I was already averaging over twenty-five death cases a year. That is a heavy load and due to the turnover rate within the unit, my responsibilities kept multiplying. Working cases, attend court and make sure that all of the follow-ups were being done properly in order to bring cases to a successful conclusion, besides training the new investigators that were assigned to the Homicide Unit. Not every investigator was going to make it. Some just took the assignment as a status symbol, just to say they were a part of the Homicide Unit. It does look impressive on a resume, even if they had no clue of what they were doing.

So, during this particular year, I was in the process of training two young investigators, John Gonzo and Fred Alvarez, both were filled with a lot of desire but were neophytes to the craft. My supervisor, Sgt. Edward Martin, had homicide experience but it is not like he was a go getter and willing to assist. He allowed me to manage and train the junior investigators as I saw fit. Considering he was a supervisor within an elite unit, his input was minimal at best. He only wanted to be kept informed so that he could brief the command staff when they arrived in the morning. That arrangement was fine by me. It provided me with the latitude to professionally train each investigator in a manner that would best benefit them as well the unit.

There are many incidents, especially death cases that can affect an investigator. Some do not do well with suicides and others do not do well with elderly abuse which results in death. I have always known that children were my Aquila's heel. My reason was quite simple, my first two children from my first marriage were still in elementary school and it hurt that I could not spend enough quality time with them. But during this period, I had two younger children from a second marriage. In total, I had four great kids with ages that ranged from eight to thirteen.

Now, one never imagines how events can change one's perspective, but it does. For me, it was knowing that dedicating so much time to being the absolute best homicide investigator I could be, was affecting my responsibility as a father by sometimes neglecting my children. I was too busy focusing on my career to consider the ramifications. But in my wildest dream, I could have never fathomed the extent of someone's intentional cruelty toward a child. Let alone, one that's two years of age. So, this is how my nightmare began and the path for a devastated mother to heal.

I was dead asleep when suddenly, 560 on my radio's AM dial started blaring and the alarm began to ring. It was March 5, 1997 at 0630 hours, I made sure that the alarm was set to ring early. I hated waking up in the morning, since I have always worked midnights (9pm–6am). Like a vampire, the morning and its sunlight were my times to get some good rest. Such a concept was far and few in-between. You see, the midnight shift is when all the action took place. All the ghouls, miscreants and scourge of the earth come out late at night. With a few exceptions, normal people sleep at night. In police work, if you are out and about at three in the morning with nothing better to do, then you are up to no good. Now, I know that sounds bad, especially in today's world. But if you really think about it, unless your city or neighborhood is open twenty-four hours a day, what are people doing walking around a neighborhood or driving slowly in an area where they do not live. Unless they too are working or up to no good.

Anyway, this was a particularly important day in my professional career, so I needed to wake up early. It was important that I was prepared and ready to attend criminal court. The verdict of a case from three years prior was close at hand. The jury had been diligently deliberating since yesterday evening. You see, closing arguments ran late and the jury went into the deliberating room after four o'clock in the afternoon. Then, they were sent home at six o'clock last night, but I had a gut feeling this verdict would be brought forth today. This case had taken its toll on me, not just the act itself but the fact that I was haunted daily just remembering. I do not think an hour in the day went by where I did not have this case cross my mind. It literally consumed my being. I had been laser focused since that early morning on June 3, 1994. So, it was important to be ready to watch how this case played out. Not just for me, but for the victim and her mother.

It was so early; my two daughters were getting ready for school. They were going about their routine as was their mother. You know, getting dressed, fixing breakfast, brushing their teeth and the typical bickering back and forth like normal sisters. While I was listening to this, I could not help but wonder how my victim would have been behaving on a morning like this if she were still alive. Would her routine have been the same, or maybe a little different. I really could not think too much about it, it was never going to happen.

I quickly jumped off the bed and entered the shower. The warm water began to run down on me like rain hoping to wash away the gut wrenching feeling inside. While dawning my robe and exiting the shower, my oldest daughter brought me a shot of 'Café Cubano', ah yes, the elixir of life, the jet fuel of a midnight homicide investigator in Miami. Once I got that adrenalin rush from my Cafecito, I stood inside the walk-in closet to pick out the proper ensemble for the occasion.

Unlike many Homicide Units, the City of Miami was special. It was a daily fashion show, every investigator dressed impeccably. Every suite was well coordinated, even when wearing the famous 'Guayabera' shirts, nothing was left to chance. As an investigator, you wanted to make sure that others took notice. This unique style had been passed down for many years, from an older generation of investigators to this new breed. It showed confidence and professionalism. An investigator never wants to walk into a courtroom looking like yesterday's hand me downs. Believe me, it is not the clothes that makes an investigator or closes a case but the way one is perceived makes a huge difference.

Choosing a snappy charcoal gray suite, I decided to go with a white shirt and a blue tie with gray accents. Professional, not crazy and a statement that said, "We're winning today."

So, I began to get ready and while sitting at the edge of the bed, my little girls came in running. They each gave me a kiss and ran out yelling, "Love you, Papi. Good luck!"

*Good luck, if they only knew*, I thought.

These two innocent girls had no clue of the type of case I was going to court for, they just knew it was important. As they were exiting the house,

I remember my wife looking at me and saying, "It's the little girl case, right?" I just nodded my head without saying a word. She knew what this case had done to me.

Now, I was finally alone and able to finish my task of getting ready. I started leaving the house just as the clock chimed, it was 8 am. Good, I was making great time. You see, Miami traffic in the morning is brutal and even though I lived less than ten miles from the courthouse, it could take close to an hour's drive to get there. Then, trying to find a parking space, that was another mission.

As luck would have it, I was making surprisingly good time. Therefore, I took a chance by using one of the main thorough fares, Flagler Street, which runs east to west. It was congested going east but moving steadily. Now mind you, the justice complex is located on 12$^{th}$ Avenue NW 12$^{th}$ Street. This area is surrounded by the Miami River, State Road 836, and a bunch of buildings to include Jackson Memorial Hospital. Not everyone that enters this area has an appointment in the courthouse, so imagine driving around for fifteen to thirty minutes just to find a parking spot. That thought was going through my mind, but today, I was not going to sweat it.

Upon approaching a shortcut, and police officers live on shortcuts when traffic is a concern, I came upon a cafeteria, that is a Miami landmark, "El Morro Castle." They made excellent Cafecito and it was open. Named after the Castle located in Havana Harbor, Cuba, this was also a favorite spot for officers to grab a bite to eat or a quick Cafecito. Luckily, as I drove into the parking lot, a space became available and I was able to park my unmarked vehicle directly in front of the cafeteria's service window. As I approached the window, two officers were getting ready to leave but took some time to exchange pleasantries and asked if I thought today, was the day. I shrugged my shoulders and told them, "I hope so," because this was a grueling case. Then just like that, they went on their way and the cafeteria window attendant had my Cafecito ready. Moments later, I found myself behind the steering wheel of my vehicle driving away from 'El Morro Castle', surprisingly making it to the courthouse complex in five minutes, a first.

I must have driven around the complex for ten minutes before finding the perfect parking spot. I looked up knowing that divine intervention was at work today, at least to this point. I exited my vehicle, put on my jacket, grabbed my Bible (a notebook that investigators use) and walked straight to the City of Miami Court Liaison office to clock in before heading to court, you see, clocking in lets the police department know that you reported to your court appointment at the allotted time. When I looked at the clock, it was 8:45 am. That was probably the fastest time I have ever driven to court during morning rush hour. I made it from home, including a quick pit stop in 45 minutes. Well, this gave me enough time to shoot the shit with those who worked in the liaison office, including my good friend Sgt. Iris Mendez. She had known me for years and was aware of how significant today's court appearance was and what it meant to me as well as the Homicide Unit. We spoke for several minutes, then, as I walked out of her office, she wished me well.

The courthouse is a social gathering early in the morning. During this time, officers that work the midnight shift are dragging their assess in to attend morning court and day shift officers arrive for their appointments, except they are on-duty. Attending court during the day was terrible.

Additionally, you have the off-duty officers that have been scheduled for court.

In a nutshell, a bunch of officers squawking in the courthouse hallways until it was their turn inside the courtroom. Thinking about it, those exchanges allowed me to lower my guard and not think so much about what was going to happen shortly. Not that it was a sure thing, I just had a feeling that today the jury would render its verdict. Honestly, the suspense was agonizing.

I rode the escalator and made my way to courtroom 2–3, this was Judge Banks courtroom, who had been presiding over this case. He was a fair judge, strict in the way he managed the courtroom but very approachable. Always had something nice to say but business like. He was a tall, academic individual and if you ever had a question, he took the time to provide you with an answer. I never felt intimidated by him, even though my time in homicide was relatively short (less than five years) but I respected his opinion. Keeping that in the back of my mind allowed me to feel a little better about what the outcome would be.

Upon approaching courtroom 2–3, I peered through the windowpane of the courtroom's door. Inside I could see the judge's secretary getting her area ready and setting up the judge's bench. The bailiff was walking around making sure that everything was prepared before the hearing commenced. I took a deep breath and before entering the courtroom, decided to sit on one of the long benches that were a fixture in the hallway outside the courtroom. Sitting alone, I went over in my mind everything about this case from the moment I arrived at the crime scene. Trying to keep everything in order, I wondered if I might have made a miscalculation during my testimony. I certainly did not because the prosecuting attorney, Randall Reid, would have let me know. But then again, I have never really been able to gauge ASA Randall Reid. Although I had known him for many years, this was really our first major case working together. I felt confident and yet felt a large knot in my stomach. Even though I had testified as a lead investigator on many cases, this was the first time I felt this way. Was my mind playing tricks on me or was it the nature of the case making me have these doubts? "Shake it off, Pepi, it will soon be over," I told myself.

After ten or fifteen minutes, I looked up and saw ASA Randall Reid walking toward the courtroom. As I stood up from the bench, Randall Reid extended his hand, "Good morning, Pepi." After a brief handshake, he told me that he was going inside courtroom 2–3. I nodded and stayed outside for a few more minutes. While standing outside the courtroom, I spoke with several investigators from other agencies. As I was concluding our conversation, out of the corner of my eye I spotted the victim's mother, Lena Miranda, she was approaching the courtroom with her mother, Floria Calvo and ASA Randall Reid's secretary, Patty Macum. I watched them as they approached, Lena and Floria were holding each other by interlocking their arms. Their walk was one of unsure steps, wanting to get closer but not wanting to be here. I thought, *God, I cannot imagine what they must be going through.* All I wanted was the strength to help them through this difficult and uncertain process.

Lena and Floria approached me, Lena gave me a hug and a kiss on the cheek (quite common amongst Hispanics) and Floria put her hand on my shoulder. I was nearly speechless, but I briefly explained to both, in Spanish, what was about to take place today. We waited outside of courtroom 2–3 until the Victim Coordinator arrived to walk them inside the courtroom. Once the Victim Coordinator showed up, I dismissed myself and slipped into courtroom 2–3.

# Chapter 2

Every investigator, like athletes, go through a ritual of sorts to prepare themselves for what is about to occur. I was no different, my custom was unique to me. During the verdict phase of a trial, I would sit on the bench located in the back row of the courtrooms' gallery. It was five rows behind the prosecutors table where I had an unobstructed view of the jury and the defendant. For me, this was a prime spot. Unnoticed by those who entered the courtroom to witness the final moments of this trial. Now, the news reporters were beginning to file in and take their seats, each wanting to get as close to the defendant's table as possible to take that million-dollar snapshot of a cold-blooded killer. You know, the one look that is provided by an individual when surprise or despair sets in. Like vultures, those reporters patiently waited for their moment. Not that I blamed them, such a photograph could be sold for good money.

As one watched the people walking into the courtroom, one could hear the low mumbling of the observers in the gallery, like the steady idling of a diesel engine. Understand, this was one of the bigger courtrooms and it was filling up fast with on-lookers and curiosity seekers. Standing room only, if the judge permitted, but he was not going to allow a circus in his courtroom. Many were inquisitive because of the media presence and others were part of law enforcement or the prosecutor's office. In either case, all were here to observe the outcome of justice. Throughout the courtroom, there was a chill in the air, one could feel the excitement of anticipation, but it was still too early. The courtroom was being prepared, for a judge who was not present, and neither were the defense attorneys.

Silently, I sat on the rear bench intently scanning the courtroom. With its warm and inviting woodwork which had stood the test of time, it was a testament to the carpenters of that period and their craftsmanship. The surrounding panels with ornate designs were honey-colored, so well-polished that they immitted an orange glow. The high ceilings made one think of an auditorium as opposed to a courtroom. The presiding bench was set high, a king's throne, overlooking those who stood before the judge.

Continuing my unrelenting gaze around the courtroom, one in which I had testified on many occasions, I could not help but notice the symbol and quote directly behind the judge's bench. The words were profound, and I could only pray they were true today. "*We Who Labor Here Seek Only the Truth,*" as I absorbed those words deeply and the symbol of 'Lady Justice', a certain calming peace came over me. Looking at 'Lady Justice', I was reminded of her origins which were Greek. She was strongly associated with the Goddess 'Dike' who was depicted carrying balance scales and was said to have ruled over human law. Now, the Egyptians and Romans had their version of 'Lady Justice' but I only remembered the Greek. In either case, I was just certain that justice would be exacted today. Within minutes, the courtroom was almost filled to capacity.

Suddenly, the courtroom became warmer as the large crowd, with their body heat, caused the room's temperature to rise. Even I began to feel uncomfortable, wearing a suite and with the crowd, so close in proximity, I was becoming irritated. But I was a professional, this was a minor inconvenience that had no place today. This case was mine and I needed to see it through, regardless of these minor concerns. While all the commotion was going on around me, I took a breath and nestled back against the rear wall then closed my eyes. I decided to take a cat nap before the bailiff cried out, "All Rise." But it was still too early, it was not even 9:30 am yet.

The commotion was slowly getting louder. It needed to stop, for whatever reason, I just wanted some quiet time to contemplate on today's hearing. How would I approach Little Lilly's family if things did not work out? What would I say to them? Even though I could not imagine that scenario, but when a case is in the jury's hands, one never knows. There is always a chance that a jury does not see things in a manner that warrants a conviction. This case did not fall into that category, still, that sinking feeling in the pit of my stomach was real. As I continued to look beyond the incoming crowd, a couple of investigators saw me and approached.

"Well, Pepi, what do you think? Anything yet?"

Looking at them with a stern face, I replied, "Dude, really!" We looked at each other and chuckled, they knew that at this point I had no clue of what the verdict was going to be, and my response was not meant in a mean way. They found space on the bench in front of mine and sat down. Both were in the courthouse on another case, but like I said, this was a case that drew a lot of interest.

Just then, I glanced up and standing next to me was Sgt. Luis Albuerne. He had been my mentor since my selection into the Homicide Unit. Luis was a savvy, old school Cuban and an excellent investigator in his own right. He did not need to be there, but he knew how much this case meant to me. Besides, he was always interested in how this protégée performed.

For whatever reason, seeing him there gave me a sense of renewed confidence. Which I should have had anyway; this case would have never reached this stage if I had not performed my job the right way, besides, Luis would have never signed off on my report. Luis began walking out of the courtroom and motioned for me to follow, so I did. I left my Bible on the bench as a place holder.

We gathered in the corridor which led to the judge's chambers, behind the courtroom that was located on the second floor. "How are you feeling dude?" he asked.

"I'm doing fine, just a little edgy, the waiting is what's driving me crazy," I responded. Realistically, it should have been driving me crazy, this was my first Death Penalty case and I wanted to make sure everything had been done correctly. It would be unconscionable to lose this case on a technicality or on a misinterpretation by the jury. Having testified in so many cases as I have in a short homicide career, I should have been calm, but not today. Surprisingly, I was amazed how queasy I was feeling today.

Then, with that heavy Cuban accent, Luis knew just what to say, "Dude, you don't have anything to worry about, you did your job." With that, I walked back inside courtroom 2–3 and quietly sat down on my reserved space.

Sitting there, I began to wonder; how did we get to this point? What triggered the events that got us to this place, sitting here waiting on a verdict where the Death Penalty could be imposed. Not too many investigators have investigated cases that merit the Death Penalty, but here I was, to think it was all set-in motion on a relatively noneventful evening three years ago, June 3, 1994 at 3:30 am to be exact. Sitting back, I began to think about that dreadful night and the daily reminders of Little Lilly. From the moment I stepped inside the crime scene of this case, I knew immediately that it was going to stay with me forever. Within minutes after returning to my spot, my mind created an envisioned portal which transported back to that shocking night.

Like if it were yesterday, there I was a Thursday night in 1994, reporting to the Miami Police Department as usual. My shift began at 9:00 pm but I routinely arrived at the station around 8:30 pm. I liked arriving early, it allowed me time to be briefed by the on-duty afternoon team. Based on their briefing I was able to gauge the type of tour my team was going to have. Not that it mattered, in the City of Miami all hell could break lose at a moment's notice.

But here I was hoping this night would be nice and quiet. Having fallen behind on my administrative duties, paperwork, I needed to catch-up. As any homicide investigator will tell you, the initial stage of an investigation is strenuous because investigators need to be thorough and meticulous to ensure that everything has been done correctly. What people fail to understand, the follow-up after the initial stages of any investigation is at times more time consuming than the initial stage, which is when an investigator arrives at the crime scene attempting to decipher the when and why of the violent act.

Now, my system was like clockwork. First, I arrived at the office and checked the 301 Board. This board had the daily memos written by investigators assigned during the Day and Afternoon shifts. If there were any incidents of significance, associated with a death investigation, it was written on a 301 Memo (it resembles an FBI 302 report). Then, it was placed on the board for all to review. This was the board that depicted every significant event being investigated by the unit.

Once the 301 Board was reviewed, I would meet with the on-call team at which time they would brief me on any events that they worked or if follow-ups needed to be conducted by my team on any of their cases. Normally, investigators do not pass on follow-up work to other teams but simple things like, responding to a hospital and checking on a live victim's status was par for course. If the little things were not passed on, homicide investigators would never go home, the volume of cases are just too many to tackle by one's self.

Once my briefing concluded, I walked to the area where Team 5 was situated. You see, Team 5 was my team, and I took extreme pride knowing that every new investigator who was assigned to me was professionally trained. Though my days off were Sunday, Monday, and Tuesday, I was lucky enough to have my desk situated in a great location. My desk was next to a large window that overlooked the north end of the city. At night, the view was breathtaking.

Normally, this area was reserved for senior personnel or senior teams. Unfortunately, seniority was on demand, I mean I was considered a senior investigator with only five years of homicide experience. That was a nice feather in my cap. Now granted, I was averaging anywhere between twenty to twenty-five major death cases a year. There were not too many investigators in the country that had a case load such as this, but in Miami, double digit murder cases were normal, especially for one who was assigned to the midnight shift.

Once my team, which consisted of Detectives Fred Alvarez and John Gonzo, began to arrive, I let them know that we were going to meet in the conference room so that I could review what they learned during the week. Mind you, this was not like a lesson review but there are tasks within a homicide unit that must be completed in a specific manner, no questions asked. Each investigator needs to know their responsibilities during the course of any death investigation, whether they are the lead investigator or part of the support team. Since Fred and John commenced their training, they had performed well. They were eager to learn and did not mind getting their hands dirty. Fortunately, in the short period they had been assigned to homicide, they already participated in several death cases where their performance was admirable. The one good thing that I observed, was how quickly they picked up the habit of taking a ton of notes. Picking up on the Bible concept extremely fast was going to be crucial in their development.

While both were setting up their desks and going over cases, I decided to check the homicide board to see if there were any updates. Not tonight. Let me describe the homicide board. This board, which was twenty feet long, covered the complete east wall of the Homicide Unit. At first glance, anyone who walked into the Homicide office could see how many murders were being investigated, how many had been solved, unsolved or pending. More than anything, this was a status board for the six homicide teams to see which team could claim the best clearance rate.

That was big amongst the homicide teams, to see who could outperform the other. It is not like bonuses were received for closing cases but for a period, it gave investigators some credibility. In the real world, of Law Enforcement, one's credibility or reputation meant everything. Life and Death is our playing field where bonuses and exaggerated salaries do not exist. We perform our jobs knowing that notoriety, fame, or contract extensions are not in the cards.

Only as a professional athlete can you make millions of dollars for playing a game and get endorsements without any real risk. Investigators bust their asses daily, deal with what society refuses to deal with, have a good chance of getting hurt or killed for minimal pay. Let us not even discuss and consider that marriages suffer yearly. A small percentage of investigators can say they started their career married to one person and finished still married to the same one. That is sad and a piece of information that few want to talk about. Added to these facts, PTSD (Post Traumatic Stress Disorder) comes into play. This silent disorder is a main cause of suicides in LE.

Homicide investigators are confronted with traumatic events daily, but the 'Macho' syndrome will not allow for investigators to vent without being ridiculed. So, the next best thing is a lot of drinking and smoking. In my case, I only smoked cigars when investigating a decomposed body or a stinker as we call them. I was never into the drinking but did develop a habit of writing poetry. It was dark stuff and not too many people appreciated it because of their morbid views.

So, the night was moving right along, I went to the coffee station and prepared a fresh pot of coffee. Fresh coffee is a must, this is a team's go-go juice to work throughout the long night. While the sweet aroma of coffee was in the air, in waltzed Toya Bames, our Victims Advocate. She was one of the absolute best V/A's in the State of Florida and worked closely with the Homicide Unit. The great thing about Toya, she was older than most of us, had a very colorful history and was able to take a joke. We were always playing jokes on her. Surprisingly, she loved it and dished it out just as well. As I took a moment to speak with her, she let me know that she was going to be leaving early but if anything came up to give her a call. She had been working throughout the day on a sexual abuse incident of an elderly female and was tired.

Once the coffee stopped brewing, everyone in the office scrambled to get a cup, they were like vultures. So, I told them, "The next pot better be made by somebody else, everybody drinks coffee, but they refuse to clean or set up the next pot." Just imagine that event, especially with a bunch of cocky homicide investigators. They looked at me as if I were crazy, which was followed by some smartass comments, and laughter, before continuing with their business. Typical!

Well, with a fresh cup of coffee in one hand and my Bible in the other, I walked toward the conference room with Fred and John. Once we settled in, I began going over the events of the past week while reviewing the specifics of each investigation in which we were involved. Each investigator had already investigated various types of Natural death cases and a few Accidental deaths. I was confident that they could investigate these types of cases on their own. Fred was the more serious of the two, John enjoyed joking around, that was not to say that Fred was better.

On the contrary, it was my opinion that John would make a better homicide investigator, but time would tell. You see, chasing skirts was his forte. While in the middle of our briefing, Sgt. Edward Martin walked in, "Hello fellas, how's everything going?" I let him know that everything was fine and if he was going to stick around for the briefing, to which he replied, "Not this time."

Edward then walked away, as we looked at each other and laughed. "Does he ever stick around?" they asked.

"He's alright," I replied, "he's not really a midnight person," I continued. We just kept laughing and finished our meeting. I ensured that all of us had our assignments issued and walked out of the conference room. As we returned to our work areas, I needed another cup of coffee, so I made another pit-stop and filled up my cup.

Once at my desk, I put my Bible down and walked to the other side of the fifth floor to meet with Detective Jane Freedman who worked Sexual Battery. Her mouth was worse than a sailor, but she was one of the best Sexual Battery investigators that I had ever worked with. It was common during a midnight shift, for the Sexual Battery team to assist Homicide if needed. They were the closest unit to document an investigation as if it were a homicide. They were a great source to use as a support unit and much needed, especially during the midnight shift.

While in the Sexual Battery office, I discussed with Jane where we would be eating this evening. Usually, this was not a problem, whatever was open would be the spot. But with such a big group, we figured we would meet at Wolfie's diner. This was a classic, iconic restaurant on Miami Beach where everyone went to eat after they got out of the clubs. The great thing about Wolfie's, the sandwiches were huge, and the desserts were off the chain. Once we decided on Wolfie's, we figured that we would meet there around 2:00 am. That was a perfect time, not to crowded and the service would be faster. "Well, that's done," I commented to Jane.

"We'll see you guys there," she replied.

Since I have always been a very social type of person, I needed to make stops at the information desk (this was a place where our teletype operators worked) and communications to let them know that Team 5 was on-duty. After several minutes, which in all actuality was about an hour and a half, I returned to my desk and began working on completing my supplemental reports of my closed cases before depositions were set. It was early in the month, but I wanted to make sure that I did not fall behind on my stats, even though they were due at the end of the month.

While sitting at my desk, I began to work on a report reference a four-month-old baby that died from being pinned while sitting on a reclining chair. The baby was left, unattended, on the recliner by the mother and when the mother returned, the lever had accidently changed positions. As the recliner went into the rest position, her baby became wedged between the seat and the armrest. I was reviewing the autopsy report, and, in my head, I kept thinking, *how can parents be so carless with their children?* The more I read the Medical Examiner report, the angrier I got. Here I was, working like an animal to be able to provide for my children, that I hardly saw, and could never think of being so careless with them. One would think that you want to protect such a valuable commodity. I guess some people just do not see it that way.

Once I finished reviewing the Medical Examiner's report, I began to set-up the case file. Every death case has a case file, and each file must be set-up in a specific manner. Granted, for a simple investigation, such as a Natural death, all that is needed is a legal folder because the investigation is minimal. But, if the case becomes more complicated, the case file will naturally become larger. I have had investigations that filled up banker's boxes. That is huge and very time consuming. The other thing to keep in mind, each case file had to be secured in a special room we called the 'Bowling Alley' or 'Vault' due to their sensitivity.

In the 'Bowling Alley' or 'Vault', every case file from the early 70s through the present and a few cases from the 60s were stored. Therefore, investigators had to constantly walk into the 'Bowling Alley' to retrieve case files from cases they were investigating. That took time and our unit was not computerized yet, so investigators would type their supplemental reports or dictate them to a stenographer that was on-duty, assigned to the homicide unit. We had those back in the day. It made our life easier, especially if someone, like me, was not a good typist. Well, enough with the clerical responsibilities.

Tonight, was somewhat strange, there were a lot of nutty calls for service but nothing major. In other words, units were running from call to call but nothing significant. It was Thursday going into Friday, I thought, *this was how this night was going to be*, so I kept working on my report.

In between my report writing and getting up for coffee, there was John and Fred. They would interrupt me constantly, mostly bullshitting around to pass the time. They were hungry and wanted to desperately get out of the office. I understood, but I knew how the weekends are in the City of Miami, in a blink of an eye things can happen. Although I told Jane that we would meet her at Wolfie's, my gut was telling me not to stray too far. By now, the guys had been whining about dinner for a while. This was driving me crazy as they were worse than my kids.

Finally, after much grumbling like bratty kids, John and Fred convinced me and I gave in. "Dudes, okay, let me put my things away and we can leave, but let's go in separate cars just in case." Both looked at me kind of funny but continued getting ready. Truly, I did not feel like leaving the station tonight, besides, it was cloudy and very humid. Just stepping outside the building, one began to sweat. Miami is nice, but the humid weather year-round always got to me.

Looking down at my watch, I suddenly realized it was 1:00 am and it was now Friday. Hopefully, this night would stay quiet so that I could finish with my report. Well, I called Jane and told her that we were ready to leave and would wait for her on the ramp that goes to prisoner processing. Jane acknowledged and said she would be down in a few minutes. While we were waiting, a bunch of officers were about to leave the station and return to their sectors. One of them was Ofc. Rocker, affectionately known as 'Rocky'. He was always pleasant and had an incredibly good demeanor. He enjoyed working patrol and never considered applying for an investigative position. Some officers genuinely enjoy working the road. After a few minutes, Rocky began to leave but before departing he asked if we were going to meet for 'Cafecito' at 'Las Palmas' later. Las Palmas was a restaurant that was open 24 hrs. and made excellent Cafecito.

It was an officer's hangout between calls, especially if you were assigned to the South District. Plus, there was no other place open late at night. Slowly, everyone began to walk toward their vehicles. I stayed on the ramp waiting for Jane. As she exited the prisoner processing area, I asked what took her so long. In typical Jane fashion, she answered, "What the fuck, are you my mother now?"

I just laughed and walked away. I could hear as she continued yelling obscenities, I just did not pay attention. I entered my vehicle, then listened to a call for service being dispatched as I sat behind the steering wheel. While changing the dial on the radio, I could hear that the previous dispatched call turned out to be a group of males arguing in the middle of the street.

The call was in 'Little Havana', which was routine to have guys drinking and arguing. I slowly drove out of the parking lots west gate and made my way onto 5th Street to drive toward Biscayne Boulevard. This was the fastest way to get to Wolfie's, which was located on famous South Beach. I loved driving toward Miami Beach on the MacArthur Causeway, passing all the cruise ships and looking at the mansions on Star Island. This drive took my mind away from all the daily bullshit one had to deal with. Not just work but many times there were personal issues at home, but that could not interfere with one's responsibilities. Minutes later, I arrived at my destination and as luck would have it, a vacant parking space right in front of Wolfie's entrance. *No one was going to get it, it was mine*, I thought, while turning onto 16th street from Ocean Drive.

# Chapter 3

As I made the left turn at the light, there it was, surprisingly the parking space was still empty. Upon maneuvering my vehicle into the parking space, I glanced at my watch. To my surprise it was only 1:25 am. Not too bad, maybe we can literally sit down and have a nice meal. While exiting the vehicle, I could see Jane pulling up next to me and in typical Jane fashion yelled, "Make sure you fucking get us a big table, the others are right behind me!" After locking the car, I made my way to the entrance of the restaurant laughing and met with the night manager, Larry. He made it a point to take care of the police officers, making them feel special by sitting them in the VIP section. It was located toward the rear of the restaurant, out of sight. Larry kept this area closed to the public unless you were a VIP. He was a smart guy, free protection from the late crowd that sometimes-got rowdy, but not while we were there. Heck, the owners knew that the cost to the restaurant was peanuts if one considers the rate of an officer working off-duty. Also, those who patronized Wolfie's felt safer because officers would swing by at any given time to eat.

Finally, all of us made our way to the big table and before we got comfortable, our waitress had the Coleslaw and Pickles ready and set. She made sure that our table was set and drinks on the way. This place was great, a reminder from an era long gone. There was so much on the menu to choose from that sometimes it was difficult to decide. Today was no different, so I ordered my usual, turkey sandwich on whole wheat bread but started the meal off with a split pea soup. What a weird choice, soup, considering it was hot and humid outside.

This meal should take me all the way through my tour of duty. I knew a meal like this would hit the spot, especially since I still had a lot of administrative work remaining. Besides, there was no telling if I would get another chance to leave the office and eat. Sitting at the huge table, I watched as the others dragged themselves into the restaurant. Moments like these were great for team building. Besides, it allowed all of us to take our minds off work and enjoy the present. Officers never know what lies ahead, so these moments had to count. It gave all of us on the midnight shift time to just sit back and shoot the shit. We joked, poked fun at each other and generally kept it light. You see, investigators who work Violent Crimes need a little levity to stay somewhat well-balanced. We are exposed to so much horror and anguish that if we do not keep our wits, eventually one can become affected.

People think that investigators like us are impervious to emotion, understand, we do not have the luxury of being outwardly expressive while investigating our cases. Unfortunately, we carry the burden of those inexplicable acts forever. Unless you have been exposed to such atrocities, you will never realize what investigators go through. It is for that reason that we have such a morbid sense of humor and at times we stick out like sore thumbs, especially when command staff is around. When you hear them come up with theories and suggest ridiculous ideas while one is in the middle of working a double homicide where blood is all over the place, their ideas take a back seat. Honestly, one does not want to be disrespectful, but they have no clue as to what we deal with because many have never dealt with such events.

But tonight, the waitress was firing on all cylinders. Our service was great, and the food was brought to us quickly, considering that both the Sexual Battery team and my team were eating together. I should have been content sticking around with the group since this felt too good to be true, but I just needed to leave and return to the work that was left pending on my desk. Like I said, we ate and joked around for a few more minutes and by 2: 30 am, after leaving the others, I decided to drive to Las Palmas for some much-needed Cafecito. Las Palmas was an awesome, all-night cafeteria, where officers hanged out between calls and relaxed, even if only for a few minutes. With that in mind, I quickly entered my vehicle and turned the engine on.

Man, I could taste that Cafecito so much, my mouth was watering. The great thing about working midnights was traffic, there was none. One can drive from one end of the city to another in less than 15 minutes, especially after midnight. Now, I was turning the steering wheel to pull out of my VIP parking spot. While driving away from Wolfie's, I decided to take the scenic route and cruise south on Ocean Drive. This was a stretch of Miami Beach where everybody looked good. Beautiful exotic looking women and men with their chiseled bodies. Plus, the massive amounts of expensive cars driving around trying to catch as much eye candy as possible. Every club was hopping, people having a good time and here I was just driving through. In the back of my mind, all I could picture was a scene from *Miami Vice*, the iconic show that showcased Miami. The one thing missing was the background music of *In the Air at Night* by Phil Collins. With that in mind, I began to laugh while air drumming his iconic roll at the beginning of the song.

As I drove away from Ocean Drive, Alvarez called me on the police radio, "Are you enroute?"

"Yeah, give me a few minutes," I responded. While stopped at a red light, my eyes kept wondering when suddenly this gorgeous girl approached my vehicle.

Her youthful body was now two feet from my lowered window when she realized I was a cop and said, "Too bad you're working." I just smiled, chuckled, and drove off once the light turned green. Driving away slowly, I thought to myself, *she must be blind or had a few to many drinks while partying*. Nonetheless, the gesture felt good and it sort of stroked my ego, even if it was just for a few minutes. As my window was closing, the last bit of ocean breeze entered the vehicle.

Traffic was light which allowed me to get on the Venetian Causeway fairly quickly, and that Cafecito was getting closer. While driving toward Miami, across the bay, I could see the mansions of Star Island against their background lights. Even in the dark of the night, those houses looked awesome, even Al Capone's old mansion looked equally good in comparison to the ones surrounding it. During my drive, I could not help but agonize about this constant heat and humidity 12 months out of the year that felt brutal. The thing that made it tolerable and worthwhile, was Miami has some fantastic views, with a tropical breeze whipping from the ocean that no wonder people feel this is paradise. Obviously, for those who do not live here year-round and just visit for a few days to get away from the freezing north, it would be paradise. Who could blame them, visiting such a robust location filled with many flavors?

Continuing this scenic drive on the Venetian Causeway, my mind went adrift thinking about my kids. How much longer would I be stuck with Sunday, Monday, and Tuesday off. I really wanted a resemblance of quality time with the kids, unfortunately, with a career as a homicide investigator, quality is always in high demand. Realistically, very few people understand the sacrifices that violent crimes investigators make, including significant others. I kept justifying my career path by saying to myself, "The kids are small, there will be plenty of time on the backend." But in police work, tomorrow is not promised just like the next minute is not promised.

Finally, there it was State Road 836, the Dolphin expressway. This strip is a major highway that runs east to west from downtown Miami all the way to the Florida Turnpike. Enjoying the drive, I passed the legendary Flagler Dog-Track, with its neon red letters illuminating the night. This facility was a reminder from back in the day when it was hopping with pari-mutuel action and gangsters from all over the country. Now it was just an iconic venue in Miami from years past, run-down and in great need of repair. It was unfortunate but it would never return to its glory. Soon, the neon lights were well behind me. With the Cafecito getting closer, my lips could taste its flavor.

Suddenly, the police radio went wacky as the dispatcher began dispatching multiple units to a bar near the Miami River on 27 Ave NW 16 Street. I only caught bits and pieces of the transmission, but thought I heard something about a baby, which piqued my interest. Several patrol units answered the call and advised they would be responding. Well, one of those units was my friend Rocker, who was a seasoned veteran and if there were any issues, he would certainly give me a call. So, I continued driving toward my destination, Las Palmas. Unexpectedly, an uneasy feeling about the dispatched call began to creep inside me, which to this day, I could not tell you why. Just as I was approaching my Cafecito, I decided to turn around and head toward the call at the bar. Not for any particular reason, I just needed to know why a reference of a baby was made.

Driving quickly toward the bar, I radioed Rocker and asked, "How close are you to the call on the river?" He told me that he was not that far and would be there in about five minutes. That was perfect, by the time he responded, I was on the highway speeding toward his location. With such little traffic, we would probably arrive at the same time.

# Chapter 4

Just as I thought, while exiting State Road 836, three marked patrol units were heading toward the river at warp speed, no sirens, just their red and blue lights illuminating the night. The desire for Cafecito had faded and now I was in focus mode. Not that anything had happened yet, but patrol units had had problems in the past at the location where they were responding, "Del Rey Cafeteria," known for narcotics being sold by customers and a rowdy crowd during the weekends, especially late at night. It would not be unusual to respond to violent fights at this establishment, just like it would not be unusual that some waitresses would be involved in disputes with patrons.

Upon arrival, I watched as the uniformed officers took charge while I stood back and listened. The complainant was Lena Miranda, a 21-year-old Honduran national. She was a good-looking girl, who spoke no English, was very agitated and trying to talk to the officers as fast as she could. So fast, that one could hardly understand what she was saying. Her state of mind was of desperation, speaking a form of Spanish from her native country. The patrons and other waitresses of the restaurant were now outside witnessing her hysteria. While Lena was speaking in a loud tone, every time she mentioned 'Laudin', her waitress friends would interject in Spanish saying, "He's the one that was here causing a problem."

*What problem were they talking about?* I wondered Did he brandish a weapon or get into a fight? Nobody was responding, they were just speaking loudly and talking over each other. It was as if they were speaking in tongue. It got so hectic that the officers began to disperse the people that were not needed and separated Lena to properly question her to extract additional, vital information needed to follow-up accordingly.

I could tell by her demeanor that she was very distraught, almost desperate, but nothing could be done until information was gathered by the officers. While the officers were performing their duties, something in the back of my mind, instinct, suggested that this was not going to be your typical police case. For some unspecified reason, maybe intuition, the hairs in the back of my neck stood up. It is my belief that years of experience contributed to this reaction. While the officers were attempting to extract information from the complainant, I began to wonder, who was Lena Miranda and this Laudin? These seedy bars had a way of attracting strange people.

What kind of history did they have that would lead to this event at the 'Del Rey Cafeteria?' The answers to all these questions had many layers, like an onion. For many illegal women, desperation, necessity, and survival was a driving force in working at dives like 'Del Rey Cafeteria'.

As for Lena Miranda, she was a young girl from Honduras. Poor, she lived in a small town outside of San Pedro Azula, Honduras. There, she was raised by her mother and father. They lived a quite simple life in a rural part of the country. Her parents tried to make ends meet, as they worked menial jobs doing whatever it took to provide for their family. Unfortunately, for Lena, because of her family's financial circumstances she was unable to get ahead. Mostly living on scraps and barely going to school, her destiny was already laid out for her long before her 15th birthday.

There was no hope for Lena or her family in Honduras and she knew it. In their country, the ability to move ahead was unimaginable. As peasants, they were not close to affording the possibilities of living a decent life. They were simple country folk with simple means and all though Lena was a bright girl, she was unable to attend school enough to excel. Her life was one of hard work, hand me downs and dreams that would never be fulfilled while living in her misery. A life of poverty was all Lena knew.

Regardless of how much they tried, her family was never able to progress. During her formidable years growing up, she watched her father become an angry drunkard, bitter at what he had become and disillusioned at the world. He barely provided the basic needs for his family and what little money he earned; he would spend on cheap liquor. Anguished, she watched him come home drunk, proceeding to beat her and her mother for no reason. This was her education as a young girl. Shortly before her fifteenth birthday, her father, tired of their situation and unable to deal with his lack of responsibilities, left Lena and her mother to fend for themselves.

Not having her father around was not the worst thing, as a matter of fact, maybe it was the break her and her mother needed to move forward. For months they were able to scrape enough money to survive. There were times when they went several days without eating a regular meal, just a piece of bread and maybe some milk, if they were lucky. Lena could see the sadness in her mother's eyes daily, but she was glad they were not on the receiving end of the senseless beatings from her father.

Lena, like any other teenage girl was a dreamer. Dreaming of another type of life did not cost anything and kept her spirits uplifted. She wanted to become somebody respectable, longing for an education and a chance to attend a good university. But these were only dreams. Deep down inside, she felt as if she was on a road going nowhere. She did not want to wind-up like her friends who were running around, prostituting themselves with the local men in order to survive.

You see, in the town where Lena lived, only young pretty girls had a chance to leave, maybe go to a big city like, San Pedro Azula or Tegucigalpa, the capital of Honduras. Her chances were as good as any, even if it meant being with a man she did not want to be with. In her mind, having a chance to leave her miserable world was a price worth paying. What else could she do?

Now Lena's mother, Floria, did everything she could to keep her young daughter under control but soon after her sixteenth birthday, things began to change. Lena barely finished school, even though she was smart, her dream of a higher education faded. Unfortunately, because of her family's situation, there were many days where Lena did not attend class. Not attending classes bothered her because she knew her future and dream of success was slowly evaporating.

On many occasions, while at home, she would find her mother in a corner of their rundown shack trying to hide her crying. Who would help them get out of this situation, Lena would wonder? For her, it was just not meant to be. She was going to be stuck in this little town, eventually get pregnant and contributing to a vicious cycle of despair. This nightmare she feared was materializing right before her eyes. Desperately, she longed to change her current situation before finding herself in the same situation that her mother did, watching her father come home drunk and beating them because of his impotence to thrive.

As days and months passed, things were not getting better for Lena and Floria. Family members that were helping them stopped, not because they wanted to but because their situation was not any better. So, a year after her father walked out on her and her mother, Lena convinced her mother that they should attempt to immigrate to the United States. They had been told by friends that those who made it to the border had a good chance of sneaking into the United States and finding work. Considering how badly things were going, Lena and her mother felt that immigrating was the only way to survive. Instantly, they looked at each other and immediately decided to leave Honduras, attempting the long arduous trek for the greener pastures of the United States.

Their goal was clear, leave Honduras and the horrible conditions they were subjected to. The decision to leave their homeland was difficult but necessary. On many nights, Lena would find herself continuously crying, wondering why her but there was no more time for tears. Lena would keep telling herself, things were going to be better in America. There, everyone has an opportunity to get an education, find a job and at the very least, live better than how she had been living with her mother. Besides, they would receive assistance that Honduras did not offer. Before long, two years had passed, and things only got worst. Doubts regarding her decision to leave lingered.

This was not the way for an eighteen-year-old girl to be living, constantly worrying where she was going to find her next meal, and surely, she should not have the responsibility of caring for her mother. Why was this burden of responsibility falling on her? She feared winding-up pregnant like many of her other friends or prostituting, surely God did not intend for this to happen.

Unfortunately, in Lena's world that is exactly what she had to do to fend for herself and be responsible for her mother. Every day was a struggle and treacherous, and they were not getting closer to America. The squalor conditions that she was living in were unbearable. There were few options for a girl without an education or a stable family. Although she did not want to go down the road of selling herself to live, it seemed inevitable. Soon, spreading herself became common place, if only to survive.

Every time Lena looked at her mother, all she felt was anger and resentment. *What mother would ever put her child in such a position?* she wondered. There was no way, if she ever had a child that she would allow for such things to happen. It would live better and be happier than she ever was. Deep down, Lena knew that her mother was a casualty of circumstances beyond her control. Very few peasants in her country escape the conditions that they are brought up in to make something of themselves. Only those with a good family pedigree go on to rule those less fortunate.

It was in that instance when the decision was made. This manner of living was not going to continue, Lena vowed to change her stars and realize her dreams one way or another. For them, luck was not an option and they knew it, they prayed that God would not let them live out their lives like this. Thus, her grueling quest began. Her resolve was now unwavering, she was going to take matters into her own hands regardless of its outcome. Her focus was on the prize, reaching the United States.

So, in late 1990, Lena did not remember exactly when, she met a young man named Antonio. They were smitten with each other and like many young eager men, he wooed her with his promises of a better life. As things worked out, they stayed together for a short time before he too became abusive toward her. This brought back sad memories of her past. The relationship was one of constant disrespect and physical abuse. For Lena, there was no light in sight, she had fallen back into the vicious cycle of her past, except this time she was the one being abused by a man. Especially one that was not her husband. Not that Antonio was bad, she justified, he suffered from the same ailment as all the others, little education, no skills, and an insatiable desire to get drunk whenever he could. Such was the coping mechanism for men such as Antonio.

As I listened intently to Lena's account, there was a genuine fear in her voice. Yes, she was speaking in a loud tone, stern, but not yelling. Her voice kept cracking, but one could sense panic. The officers who were handling the call were trying desperately to get information, so much so that they were not really listening. For Lena, this moment was gut wrenching and chaotic, still, the feeling of despair emanated from her voice. The hopelessness and fear were quite evident.

You see, Laudin had come to her place of employment, created a disturbance and when she refused to leave with him, he tried to force her into leaving. That is when the manager came to her defense and convinced Laudin to leave the premises. According to Lena, Laudin yelled obscenities at her, saying that if she called the police, she would regret it. Upon realizing that the police were present, Lena became hysterical. Why? What were her reasons? So far, the only thing that we could make out was that a jealous boyfriend came to her work, began to drink, possibly got agitated when he saw that men were speaking to his girlfriend and lashed out.

Then out of the blue, Lena made the comment, "My baby, I'm afraid for my baby." Upon hearing the distress, I told the officers that a well-fare check should be conducted where Lena lived. The officers asked Lena if the baby was home, she responded that it was home with her mother.

Once we heard that her mother was with the baby, we all took a collective sigh of relief thinking everything was going to be fine. Lena proceeded to tell the officers where she lived. With information in hand, Ofc. Rocker placed her in the back of his marked unit and began to drive her home. The other officers cleared from the Del Rey Cafeteria and followed Ofc. Rocker and Lena to her home which was located in the middle of Miami's Little Havana neighborhood. She did not live too far from her place of work, so it should not take the officers more than ten minutes, especially at this time since there was hardly any traffic. *They should be alright,* I thought to myself. They will get there, check out the home and advise over the police radio that everything was QRU (that is everything is fine in police jargon). As the units left the area, I heard over the police radio's airwaves Ofc. Rocker advising, he was going to transport the complainant to her home. They were going to check on the wellbeing of her baby. He also told the dispatcher that other officers were responding with him as back-ups.

Watching them leave, I began to walk slowly toward my vehicle. I entered my vehicle, turned on the dome light and began to write some notes in my Bible. I vividly remembered my last entry, all is QRU Boy/Girlfriend dispute, BF GOA. Upon closing the book, that inside voice whispered, "Something doesn't feel right." Immediately, I started the engine and shifted the gear into drive. While driving away from the 'Del Rey Cafeteria' and again heading toward Las Palmas, a change of heart came over me. Instead, I found myself driving toward the home of Lena Miranda. The officers had yet to arrive at her house and I was about five minutes behind them. For the time being, Las Palmas could wait. There was something about this particular call that did not feel right. It was probably nothing, but there was something in her voice that was compelling.

Suddenly, I felt my leg being bumped, a dull thud. It snapped me out of my daydream and slowly I looked up; somebody was trying to enter the back row where I was seated to sit down in the only available space. "Excuse me," they said, "I am just trying to sit down, the courtroom is getting packed." Sure enough, I looked around and realized the courtroom was full. I must have been out cold because the courtroom filled without me noticing. I was pleasantly surprised seeing such a full house on one of my cases. But then again, this one had made all the local news releases and there was a genuine human interest in seeing what would happen to a monster.

Looking around the gallery, I noticed the bailiff who had just stepped out of the courtroom and entered the corridor that led to the judge's chambers. We were getting close; curtains were about to go up. Off to my right, there was Lena and Floria entering the courtroom with the Victim's Coordinator. They had a special section reserved behind the prosecutor's box. The coordinator looked at me and asked if I wanted to be with the family. "Maybe when it gets started," I replied, I still needed some me time to process what was happening. I did not want to be next to Lena just yet. My heart was racing anticipating an end to an unwanted nightmare.

There were no words that I could muster to provide any comfort for this still grieving mother, not now. I wanted to say something perfect, words that would be meaningful. Unfortunately, there is never a perfect sentiment to convey. The family just needed support, but who was going to support me? True, Lena's horror will live with her forever, that was her child.

The sad truth, this horror will be engraved in my memory until the day I die, and this child was not mine. I needed to cope with this feeling before being able to provide comfort to Lena or Floria. Then, as if by divine intervention, there stood Luis. Boy, I needed someone that fully understood what I was going through and there he was. I got a hold of his arm and said, "Cafecito." Well, that was a no brainer, within seconds we were off to the cafeteria located in the first-floor lobby. We did not say a word to each other as we rode the escalator down. We got to the cafeteria and I requested two Cuban cafes. Once our cafés were served, Luis turned to me and said, "Dude, don't worry, you did a great job with this case, it's going to work out."

I listened to the words but did not respond, probably one of the very few times I have ever been speechless. We sipped our café and as we exited the cafeteria, Cecy, who was an attorney's assistant bumped into me. She had just come down from the courtroom and said, "The judge called a recess, it's been rescheduled for 11:30 am."

My response was priceless, "What! I was not gone but 10 minutes and the courtroom had not been called to order. Besides, the defense attorney was not in the courtroom." Maybe that was it, an emergency, that had to be the reason.

*Lena must be going crazy*, I thought. I thanked Cecy and headed back to courtroom 2–3. There, standing in the hallway was Lena and her mother, they had just stepped out of the courtroom. In Spanish, Lena asked me what had happened and did anything go wrong. I assured her that these things happen from time to time, most likely an emergency came up and I was going to find out. The tension in her voice was totally understandable, also, she was feeling anxious and a little angry. There had been little or no emotional expressions from Lena or her mother Floria, to this point considering the situation. In reality, they had composed themselves like super troopers. I could not imagine how any mother could stand such emotional pressure.

We spoke for a few minutes, during which time I comforted her and her mother. I did not want them to stay in the courthouse during the delay, so I escorted them to the State Attorney's Office building which was across the street. Entering the building, we ran into Cecy again, and I asked her if she could assist Lena and Floria until I found out what happened. Cecy said she would and was going to place them in the conference room located on the 3rd floor. I thanked her for helping and immediately returned to the courthouse.

Entering the courthouse again after a having left 10 minutes prior, the security guard waved me through. Heck, he has known me for years, besides, he is the one that checked me in earlier. Finally, I made it to courtroom 2–3 and ran into the prosecutor. We discussed the case and how we felt about it. Knowing he felt good made me feel better. When I asked him about the delay, he told me that the defense had a personal emergency which needed his attention. Whew, a sei of relief came over me and suddenly I felt a rush of energy that had been missing. I then thought to myself, *Okay Pepi, this was just a bump in the road. We are back on track.* With that, I turned and walked back to the State Attorney's Office. It was my responsibility to make sure that Lena was kept informed of everything and she needed to know what I had just learned.

I entered the State Attorney's Office and immediately got into an open elevator. I decided to stop on the 2nd floor to meet with Cecy, she had been a great help to me, and this case was not even assigned to her. She was one of those secretary's that always went out of her way to help and I appreciated her for it. After meeting with Cecy, I scampered up to the 3$^{rd}$ floor conference room. Sitting at the big table was Floria and pacing by the picture window facing the courthouse was Lena. She did not even notice when I had entered the room, that is how out there she was. Her mind had to be racing at a million miles per hour. Whatever she was thinking, she did not express to me. I tapped her on the shoulder, she turned and with watery eyes asked if we were going to win. I got a lump in my throat the size of a basketball, suddenly I found myself telling her in Spanish that everything that could be done had been done and I was very confident that the outcome was going to be in our favor. After telling her what she needed to hear, I cringed.

A Cardinal rule was to never guarantee victory or outcomes, that will set you and family's up for disappointment. I got caught up in the moment and wanted to make Lena feel good. I thought, *God, did I do the right thing in assuring her? I hope I did.* In the back of my mind, I figured no jury with common sense that reviewed all the facts could possibly come back with a Not Guilty. That would be unconscionable. Nonetheless, this was Miami, and anything could happen with a jury.

I asked them if they needed anything and they replied, "No." I told them that if they did, they were to notify me immediately. They thanked me and I began to walk away.

Just before I reached the door, Lena, in a soft voice asked me, "Why did he have to do it?" at that moment, there was nothing for me to say, I had already said enough. I shrugged my shoulders, slowly opened the door, and walked out of the conference room.

Boy, I had to get out of there quick. Emotions were running high and I needed to get grounded fast. So, how could I do that? The best thing for me was to walk around the hallways that led to the various state attorney's offices and begin to contact all those who were still working and just shoot the shit. Besides, one must be social if they want to get ahead. Detectives just cannot walk around thinking that their shit does not stink. They need to socialize with everyone who works at the State Attorney's Office, if they want to get things done. In reality, it is not the attorneys that move and shake, it's their secretary's. They have more pull than one could imagine, believe me. So, for the next hour, I was Mr. Social Butterfly. There was nothing better than walking around and being recognized by everyone, attorneys, and secretaries alike. It seemed that everyone's goal was the same, teach and prosecute good cases.

None of this, I don't have enough crap or I need more or I can't bring this case to trial was acceptable. Today, investigators need a weapon, confession and a hundred witnesses and even then, there are attorney's that will not prosecute. I know I am being a little exaggerated but early in my investigative career, attorneys were more go-getters, not that they were better, they just had a bigger fire in their bellies. They had a passion that was contagious. These types of attorneys were the ones I enjoyed working cases with because they made me better. They forced me and other investigators to really understand the law and to fight for the victims. It was all about the details in preparation for a trial.

Once 11:00 am came around, I went to the Victims Coordinator's office. I told her that she should bring the family over to courtroom 2–3 around 11:15 am, because I did not want them to be sitting inside the courtroom any longer than they had too. Upon concluding with the Victim Coordinator, I began walking toward the courthouse. Along my walk, Luis caught up with me and we both entered the building. We struck up a conversation about our kids and how they were doing. Luis was great, he knew how to get my mind off this case, at least for the moment.

We rode on the escalator to the second floor. He told me that he was going to the Court Liaison office and would return. I nodded my head and went straight to courtroom 2–3, eager to return to my place in the back row. Entering the courtroom, a small group of people were floating around, mostly from the media. One reporter approached me and said, "What do you think detective?"

"It is going to be fine," I replied. What else was I to say while working my way toward my spot on the last pew. Finding my place, I immediately sat down and got comfortable. This time, I did not want to drift off. I just wanted to stay in the moment. This was no time to do the What If thing. That train had left the station three years ago. If I did not do it then, certainly it was not going to be done today. *Too late, Pepi*, I thought. What had been done could not be changed.

# Chapter 5

While sitting on my pew, the same spot as earlier, I thought *déjà vu*. I chuckled knowing that I was about to go through my entire routine as if for the first time, but it was not. Looking around, the clock above the courtroom entrance, read 11:15 am, Lena and Floria should have been making their way toward the courtroom by now. Hopefully, the reporters who were standing by will not notice them as they enter the building until it is too late. This will allow Lena time to make it inside the courtroom. Some reporters are good, but some reporters violate people's space by getting in their face, especially for a sound bite. Unfortunately, these local news correspondents wanted to capture a moment that will be immortalized, even if it is at a grieving family's expense. Surely, on a day like today, Lena did not need any additional drama.

I sat comfortably and leaned slightly forward to observe when the jurors were seated but more than anything, I wanted a clear view of 'Laudin'. He was the reason all of us were here. Then, Assistant State Attorney Randall Reid entered the courtroom. He gestured to me and immediately focused on where he was going. Following Reid was his second chair, a young attorney who was learning the ropes.

Much of the work and preparation was done by Reid, all others who assisted were merely 'go-for'. But this was my case and Reid kept me engaged, he knew how badly I wanted to win this case. It was not for me; it was for our precious victim and her mother. I was getting fidgety and kept looking at that clock, which now read 11:22 am. Damn, time was moving way to slow. *When was this show going to get on the road?* I wondered. I knew Judge Banks enough, but I did not think myself to be so bold to go into his chambers and rush him. Having that thought pop into my head caused me to chuckle, then reality set in.

Hell no! I would have been held in contempt, removed from the Homicide Unit, and probably given a hefty reprimand. Well, I was not going to worry about doing something stupid, even if I felt like doing it. Oh my gosh, that would have been a spectacle in and of itself. Better heads prevailed I thought and silently continued chuckling.

Just as I leaned back, Lena entered the courtroom with Floria. They walked right past two reporters that were looking the other way. They found their place and sat down. Reid, seeing that both were seated behind him, extended his hand, and placed it on Lena's forearm, a comforting gesture. I watched as Floria whispered something to Lena who immediately bowed her head. *What did Floria say?* I wondered. Hopefully, it was something positive considering she had been a ball of nerves since the beginning of the investigation.

I could not help but remember that every time I set up an appointment with her to take her sworn statement, she was always too nervous or would verbally say what she knew but would never go on tape. My feelings toward her were mixed, I felt a lot of her trepidation was due to a mixture of emotions, mainly, a lack of trust in the police. Maybe it was not understanding our justice system. For whatever the reason, who knows, she never gave a formal statement until late in the investigation. Her statement was basically a filler, good for a background exam of a monster.

Finally, 11:30 am, let us get the show on the road. This waiting around was exhausting. Suddenly, the defense attorney entered the courtroom and said something to the bailiff. The bailiff left the courtroom through the judge's hallway as if he were going to let the judge know that both councils were present. Everyone in the gallery was seated, one could hear a slight murmur from those who were whispering and clanging from the metal of the camera man's equipment.

Suddenly, the courtroom's rear door swung open, Laudin, who was being held in the prisoner holding area entered and made his way to the defense table. He was escorted by two correction officers. He was wearing a gray suite, white shirt, and black tie. His once chubby face was pale and drawn. One could see his metal jewelry peering from his wrists and feet. A much-needed precaution, especially for an individual such as this one. Still, his stoic expression was consistent.

This had been his look throughout the trial. The fact that he was wearing a suite, probably the only time he had ever worn a suite in his life. Obviously, the dress was a term of respect for the court, orchestrated by his attorney. He sat down next to his attorney, leaned over while his attorney whispered something to him. Laudin immediately faced forward, avoiding any temptation to look in Lena's direction. Lena, with piercing eyes was staring him down as she had throughout the whole trial but was always composed. As for Laudin, eye contact was never made with anyone associated with the victim's family. He maintained an indifferent expression as if nothing bothered him. His I do not give a shit demeanor was bothersome, such lack of respect infuriated me. But why would this monster respect anyone, he already proved that did not exist.

In another place and another time, this miserable human would have never made it to trial. Nobody would have cared but we are in America, due process is our way of life. We, as a society need to understand its importance if the rule of law is to rein. Vigilantism is not the way to go!

Moments after Laudin looked forward, the jury door opened and in marched the jurors. This was a mixed group of people, some young, the majority older more experienced. There were women, Hispanics, Anglo and African American. This pool of jurors was very much into the trial, they listened, took notes, and seemed to have a genuine interest in this case. Who wouldn't? This was a once in a lifetime trial.

Several minutes passed and the door to the judge's hallway opened. As the judge walked through the door, the bailiff spoke in a loud voice and said, "All rise!" The court was now in session and the judge took his place on the bench. Judge Banks apologized to everyone for the delay but gave a brief explanation.

The bailiff then said, "You may be seated!" Judge Banks greeted the attorneys and the court reporter. They exchanged pleasantries which was followed by an off the cuff comment that got a laugh from everyone. Whether intentional or not, it broke the chill in the air and this session returned to order.

Assistant State Attorney Randall Reid stood up and asked the judge if he could approach the bench. The judge acknowledged by saying, "you may approach," that was followed by the judge asking the defense attorney to approach the bench as well. All parties spoke during this in prompt to sidebar, but it did not appear to be anything serious.

A few minutes later, each attorney returned to their places and Judge Banks began to read some instructions. The courtroom was like a tomb, one only heard the judge's voice as it resonated off the walls. While he spoke, Laudin kept looking down. *What a coward*, I thought, watching his pathetic demeanor.

I barley paid attention to the judge, or the jury instructions he was reading. During the reading, I was intently examining Laudin's behavior. Was he ever going to show any emotion regarding this case? Was there anything human about this evil man? I could not help but wonder if he ever cared enough about Lena. Truly, I was still shocked questioning how she ever found him to be remotely viable as a companion or possible husband, let alone responsible enough to be a father to her little girl. Surely, there must be many women dealing with such issues around the country.

Soon this phase of the case was going to be over, and I still could not put my finger on Laudin's character as a man. Truth be told, he was not much of a man. Anyone who would do what he did could not possibly consider themselves a man. Slowly, I stood from where I was seated, walked toward the pew behind Reid and sat down next to Lena and Floria. They were worn and beaten; reliving the incident during this trial had taken an emotional toll on both but it was not over yet. *Just a few more hours,* I thought. Suddenly, Lena took hold of my hand as if squeezing an orange but never looked up. Now, examining Laudin from my vantage point, my thoughts were only of that dreadful night and how its impact brought all our worlds together. Somberly, I looked down at her small trembling hand as it cupped mine. Taking a deep breath, the eeriness of that early morning of June 1994 returned.

# Chapter 6

I remember driving toward the apartment where Lena was living. As I approached Flagler Street, my only thought was "God please let it be nothing." Still, I could hear a mother's shrieking voice saying, in desperation, "My baby!" While hoping for the best, my foot began pressing harder on the gas pedal. Any harder and my foot would have gone through the floorboard. A sense of urgency was felt in my gut and my only thought was to get there faster. While navigated through the roads of Miami's Little Havana neighborhood to find short cuts, my mind kept playing something unimaginable. The harder I tried to find short cuts, the more it felt like dead ends were around every corner. It is crazy how time stands still when one is anxious. That night was no different.

Eventually, I made my way onto 'Calle Ocho' which is a famous strip in the middle of Little Havana where the yearly carnival is held. This carnival is huge and usually draws about a million party goers from all around the nation, south, central America and the Caribbean. This festival is great and is recognized for the food, dancing, and entertainment. Unfortunately, this was not like a night for entertainment, at least not festive.

Just as I approached 5th Ave and SW 8th Street, I heard Ofc. Rocker announce his arrival at the location. His voice became deeper and deliberate when he informed the dispatcher that he was advancing from the corner but was going to drive by first to see if anyone was outside. This transmission was not just to inform the dispatcher but to advise everyone in his crew, who was monitoring the radio, of his intentions. Just as he was turning his vehicle around, I drove up behind him. Another two officers were stationary on the corner adjacent to where Lena lived. With Lena sitting in the back of the police car, Ofc. Rocker slowly drove up, stopping in front of the one-story apartment building and parked his vehicle. I too parked behind him and exited my vehicle.

Walking toward Ofc. Rocker's vehicle, I suddenly felt a strange sensation in my stomach. There were no sounds within the complex, everything was deftly quiet. Visibility was good enough to see the courtyard of the apartment building with its five apartments. Several of the porch lights were turned on, including the one at the entrance to Lena's apartment. I spoke with Ofc. Rocker for a few seconds as we waited for the other two officers to approach. He began exiting his vehicle and told Lena that she was to stay in his police vehicle until we could check and secure her apartment. We left one officer guarding her as we began walking toward the apartment. Unexpectedly, her apartment door flung opened and rushing out was a man, short, stocky with short uncombed hair and flailing his arms. He began to yell but we could not make out what he was saying. Our pace quickened as we advanced. Suddenly, we heard those chilling words that I would never forget. Enraged, the man said in Spanish, "Lena, I told you that if you called the police, you were going to cry tears of blood!" His anger manifested from deep inside, brought forth like something I had never experienced in all my years as a police officer. Spontaneously, we knew we had to act quickly before something dreadful occurred.

As those words began fading, he quickly turned, disappearing into the apartment infuriated and screaming obscenities. Then, a cold chilling silence fell over the complex. Rocker and I looked at each other in disbelief, since this was something we had never encountered before. Our pace quickened to an all-out sprint. Suddenly, Lena's screaming in the background pierced the nights silence, as her shrieks were permeating from inside Rocker's police car. We continued our pace, almost colliding, to make entry into the apartment. The door was slightly ajar, and we instinctively burst inside with our guns drawn. The apartment was pitch dark and full of people sleeping everywhere. Now, our concern was officer safety as well as for those who we encountered inside this dark apartment. Upon adjusting my eyes to the surroundings, I noticed a glow. There was poor lighting emitting from the kitchen, so we had to use our flashlights to get around.

We searched the living room and the kitchen, nothing. Laudin had disappeared into the only bedroom, according to an elderly lady (Floria) that was sleeping in the kitchen with her husband. "Where did Laudin go?" I asked sternly.

"He ran into the bedroom screaming something," replied the old lady. Another man who had been sleeping on the floor inside the apartment said he heard, "tears of blood." These next few minutes were intense and stressful.

We set-up tactically in front of the bedroom door and attempted to make entry but the door had been locked and wedged from the inside.

While we quickly were coming up with a game plan, Ofc Rocker forcefully called out for Laudin to open the door. Then, he gently asked for the baby to be brought out but there was no response. Seconds seemed like minutes and minutes were like hours. The elderly lady's husband came to the bedroom door and tried to reason with Laudin. Apparently, he had done this in the past, but this time there was no response. Less than two minutes passed when the decision was made to execute a forced entry into the bedroom. Our immediate concern was for the baby's well-being, but at this moment, Laudin had the tactical advantage.

If he was armed with any type of weapon, he had the drop on us. I made quick work of questioning those inside the apartment about firearms. They stated that there were no guns inside the apartment. While continuing my questioning, the officers were attempting to knock down the bedroom door. Every time the door was struck, we would call out Laudin's name and ask him to open it, but he would not. There were no sounds coming from inside the bedroom. Those two minutes were an eternity and without any type of breaching tools, we were relegated to kicking and ramming the door with our shoulders. During this period, I kept thinking, *This Laudin guy was a fucking idiot, he better open the door. If he did not open the door soon, he was going to be in a world of hurt. Besides, who was this character? What did he mean by 'Crying tears of Blood?'*

Unknowingly, we were going to be faced with a decision that was going to alter our careers if not executed correctly. The worst nightmare scenario was taking place while we were inside the apartment and we had no idea what the outcome was going to be, either for this man who had barricaded himself with a baby or us. The audacity of this madman not opening the door.

But to know Laudin, one would have to try and understand his persona. He was a shallow human being. But how or what caused him to become such a selfish, loathsome individual? Well, I was going to get that answer soon enough. After a few minutes, finally, the officers were able to breach the bedroom door. With weapons drawn and as the bedroom door was forced open, there stood an overweight, wimpy, disheveled looking man. We immediately rushed in to detain him, his eyes were bugged out and hands were in the air. A quick look at his hands let us know that he was not armed. I observed something on his hands, but with the visibility being so poor, I could not be sure what it was. Once Laudin was secured, he was handcuffed and escorted out toward the courtyard of the apartment building.

As the officers escorted Laudin first, then the other residents out of the apartment, I immediately entered the bedroom. Making my way around the bed that was nestled against the west wall, I could see a young child's body, it appeared lifeless. But I needed to verify her condition before fire-rescue, who had been requested by the dispatcher, entered. Deep in my heart, I already knew the answer but proceeded to check her nose and mouth. There was no need to go any further, as I examined her closely, a deep wound was clearly visible. This moment would forever be engraved into my memory. Knowing I had a job to do, my emotions were put in-check as I exited the bedroom. This was not the time to show emotion, but in the end, we are all human.

I remember exiting the apartment and sitting on the stoop. There was a deep void left in my being which begged the question, why? Considering all the cases I had investigated during this past week, I just could not believe this one was mine. After a few minutes' past, Ofc. Perez who was one of the officers that entered the bedroom approached me and in a low tone said, "Pepi, are you okay?"

I looked up and replied, "He should be dead! There is no reason for him to be a part of the human race!" Ofc. Perez put his hand on my shoulder and shook his head. We both knew that Laudin came within seconds of being shot, had it not been for his empty hands when we breached the bedroom door. Finishing that thought, I stood up and vowed that this guy was not going to get away with this monstrosity.

Looking at Ofc. Perez, I instructed him to transport the subject to the homicide office and place him in one of the interview rooms. I then advised Ofc. Carmell who was another back-up to make sure that the other witnesses were transported to the homicide office and placed in separate interview rooms to be interviewed by one of my detectives. My feelings were nonexistent, there was an investigation that needed my complete attention and no time for wallowing in emotions.

With a renewed sense of purpose after composing myself, I knew what my responsibility was. I would not allow these emotions to play a part in my actions. With that aside, I contacted Det. Gonzo who had yet to respond to the crime scene via the police radio and informed him to notify the on-call Assistant State Attorney and Medical Examiner. Just as I finished with Det. Gonzo, I watched as the two crime scene technicians arrived on the scene, it was Bonny and Jefferson. CSI Bonny was going to be the lead technician on this case. A sense of trepidation came over me when he stated that he was going to be the lead crime scene technician. Sheepishly, I smiled.

Not wanting to get ahead of myself, let me return to Laudin. To begin to understand this monster, one must try to understand his past. It was not a past filled with accomplishments or a promise of a bright future. It was one of struggle, lies and deviancy. But not everything can be served up so easily or was this individual a psychopath. Instead, Laudin was this 26-year-old who had been in the United States for over a year. He entered the United States illegally from Honduras. He worked odd jobs to make ends meet, which enabled him to make his way from MacCallum, Texas where he originally entered and finally, Miami. Miami was a perfect place for Laudin to begin his new life, this is a city with a vast Latin population, mostly Cuban but the cultural landscape was slowly changing. While civil wars were being waged in Central and South America, many men from those countries were forced to flee to avoid getting caught up in the unrest.

So, they fled to the good ole U.S. of A. especially Miami where they could easily blend in and no one was going to question them. Miami had become a haven for those individuals fleeing civil war, gang violence, poverty, and a general lack of opportunity. Unfortunately, many men make their way to the United States without skills or a basic education to assist them. As these men trudge about Miami, work was difficult to come by for many, but some managed by picking-up menial labor from savvy contractors who would pay them half wages in cash that went unreported. Well, Laudin was one such man.

From the time he set foot in the United States, his sole purpose was to make money, by whatever means. His purpose was to send it back to Honduras to support his family. He had no intention of assimilating to the ways of America, or its way of life. Years earlier, he bought into the lies that streets were paved with gold and money grew on trees. So, why would he want to assimilate? He figured to make it by any means, doing what he was familiar with, scamming and bamboozling others. His intentions were never to make something of himself, merely to leach and get by with minimal effort, taking advantage of a generous community. Unfortunately, the United States, especially Miami is loaded with many men that provide no positive value. They quickly become a burden on the country and community. This was the payback for a weak, ineffective immigration system. A bill paid with the blood of an innocent child.

*What a waste of human being*, I thought, watching Laudin sitting in the back seat of Ofc. Perez's patrol vehicle. Only a selfish, evil individual could be in such a great country and provide nothing positive, just misery. Much of the Latin community sympathizes with men like him because they are well familiar with how it feels to flee their native lands to escape persecution. As I watched the patrol

71

vehicle drive off, Laudin just lowered his head. Maybe he did feel something.

Standing on the sidewalk, I watched until Ofc. Perez's vehicle turned the corner. My immediate thought was to begin the on-scene investigation before returning to the homicide office. I wanted to have enough information to conduct a great interview of Laudin. A full confession from this monster is what was needed to better understand the why. Even then, how could one understand this despicable act. While gathering my thoughts, out of the corner of my eye, I observed Lena Miranda crying. The dim yellowing light from the light pole across the street was caressing her. It exuded that of an angel hugging her.

Ofc. Rocker, who was standing next to her appeared nervous, not comfortable in this situation. How could anyone who has never dealt with such an incident feel comfortable. Even seasoned investigators can be struck by the raw emotions that an incident such as this one conveys. I deliberately walked slowly toward Lena Miranda, which gave me time to gather my thoughts before approaching. How does one begin to console a mother who has just been exposed to the brutal reality of knowing her only child was murdered? At this precise moment, I remember asking God for the strength to endure the following task. Still, I needed to speak with her to let her know how much her assistance was required. This was a daunting request, but it had to be made. Soon there would be time for consoling, but not now. Now was about exacting justice.

Finally, there I was, standing next to her diminutive frame that looked fragile, more than it did earlier. That short walk seemed like an eternity. I took a long hard look at

Lena, wanting to see if there was anything out of the ordinary. There was no way of knowing at this point in the investigation, or if she had any part in this gruesome act. Not that I could imagine her being a party to this abominable act, but there have been many instances where the unthinkable becomes reality.

Lena, who was still wearing her tight-fitting black waitress uniform hung her head. The light from the streetlamp was now reflecting its dull glow off her jet-black hair. Without raising her head, she passed her hands through her hair until they came to rest in front of her eyes. Standing close, I could hear her whimpers and sighs. In a low tone and under her breath, I could hear her saying in Spanish, "Why me? What have I done to deserve this?" Listening to her pleas, I instinctively and gently placed my hand on her shoulder. That was the least I could do for now.

An awkward silence fell while trying to figure out how to begin my conversation. Finally, I mustered up the courage and told her, "I cannot imagine the pain you're experiencing, but I will do everything possible to ensure justice is served." As I formally introduced myself, I told her how her assistance was going to be crucial and that she needed to stay strong. What else could anyone have said in such a moment? The intention was to console a mother who was unaware of the brutality which had recently been committed on her little girl. That image was still fresh in my mind. It took everything I had and learned not to break down emotionally.

That is when you question yourself. "Why would I breakdown? I am a seasoned homicide investigator; guys like me are supposed to be void of emotions. That is the biggest crock one can imagine and dangerous."

You see, these types of cases can break any investigator who is not mentally prepared, especially new ones. *We say we are dealing with a case like any other. That there is no reason for feelings, heck it is not a family member or friend,* I thought, trying to psych myself. Unfortunately, cases like this one leave scares that become permanent stains on our soul. Frightful emotions will manifest out of the blue. Now, I gently placed my hand under her chin and propped it up. Seeing her tear-stained eyes, watching her tears flow down her cheeks caused a lump in my throat. Softly, she spoke and said, "what am I going to do now?" Seizing the moment, I asked for her consent to search and process the apartment.

As I was explaining why her consent was required, she interrupted and without hesitation replied, "Yes, whatever I have to do to help you." Once her consent was obtained, I helped her enter Rocky's vehicle then watched as they drove away.

# Chapter 7

While replaying in my head the occurrence of that dreadful night, I studied Laudin. There was nothing close that resembled a man feeling remorse. He had a stoic look about him; he deliberately made no eye contact with anyone related to this case. His head hung low and what little communication he had, consisted of his attorney whispering in his ear. I continued watching Laudin, while Lena kept squeezing my hand, but she never looked up. Her mother, Floria, spoke to her about God's plan and how one day justice would be had for the family. Her words were comforting but Lena was not paying attention. Suddenly, she squeezed my hand tighter, turned her head toward her mother and said in a low stern voice, "You're never going to understand." The response cut right to the core of her feelings. Were those words said in anger or resentment?

Her response was chilling but I dared not look their way. This was an internal conflict between a resentful daughter and a mother filled with guilt, so who was I to interfere. Understandably, the emotions of both mother and daughter had to be at an unimaginable level. One that cannot be understood without dealing firsthand with the suffering of a grieving parent. Guilt on behalf of one for the inability to protect her own and impotence on the part of the other for having failed again. These sentiments are often seen in tense and excruciating trials. They are raw and unfiltered. And to be honest, I was still amazed at Lena's composure. Listening to both, I thought, *God help any parent that goes through an event such as this one, continuously having to live through the nightmare.* Unfortunately, both women lacked the basic knowledge and intellect to completely comprehend or make sense of their dilemma. They too became collateral damage.

I slowly peeled Lena's grip from my hand and stood up. I knew that staying with her any longer would frustrate me more because of my own bottled-up emotions. Looking down, I told her that I would return shortly. While exiting the courtroom, I could feel that the tension building inside of Lena was being transferred to me. How much longer was she going to hang on? There was no doubt in my mind she was going to be an emotional wreck long after this trial. You see, while she kept a strong front, her demons were eating her up inside. Surely, at some point she was going to explode emotionally, to whom that burst of energy would be directed was anybody's guess.

Unable to provide her with any assurances made me feel incomplete as an investigator. This, being one of my most difficult cases tested my resolve as an investigator, father, husband, and human being. Emotionally, I knew this case would stay with me for a long time because the horrific act was continuously replaying in my mind. No matter how much I tried, snippets of the crime scene and its violence would appear without request. Now, here I was, standing at the courtroom's entrance preparing to move out of the way of those wanting to enter. Once outside the courtroom, I commenced my routine. While pacing the entire length of the crowded second-floor hallway, I managed to work my way toward the escalators. Suddenly, I was on my way toward the main lobby of the courthouse. My tie felt tight around my neck, but I just needed to get away for a few minutes to gather my thoughts. During my trek to nowhere, many of my colleagues wished me well but they were all a blur. My mind was in another place, questioning.

The more I vacillated over this case, the angrier I became not having ended Laudin's miserable existence on that dreadful night. *It was divine intervention on that night that did not allow us to take justice into our own hands*, I thought. Then, like an epiphany, I knew the right thing was done. Besides, what good would have come of doing something stupid. It was not going to bring back the victim and my life as well as that of my family's would have been turned upside down. But doing things right does not always mean that one is devoid of the impact it presents.

Navigating through the crowd, I continued tuning out the hellos from other officers, and finally got a clear path to the cafeteria. The familiar aroma of Cuban café was in the air and getting stronger as I approached. My focus was on Cafecito, not idle chit-chat. This was not the time or place; I was in a zone and officers that knew me would understand. *If not, fuck them*, I thought. My immediate goal was to get through this day, too many years had passed, and I could sense an end to this emotional roller coaster. The officers who called out to me earlier were now standing next to me. I heard one say, "Really Pepi."

I replied, "Sorry dude, my mind is somewhere else."

I bought a round of Cafecito and smiles immediately appeared on their faces. All was forgiven, they knew exactly what I was going through. Hell, there are very few officers that will ever be a part of a case or trial like this one. Silently, we stood at the cafeteria counter sipping our Café. Then just like that, we each finished our shots, threw away our cups and walked away from the counter. As we walked away, one of the officers said, "Good luck, Pep, I'll see you tonight." No reply was necessary, as I went about my business. My thoughts were on this case and its conclusion. Still, while walking back to courtroom 2–3, I continued reliving that night. Years later and the haunting persisted. Remembering how I watched Ofc. Rocker drive away from the scene with Lena, replayed in my mind as if on a loop. His police vehicle driving away slowly and me turning to walk toward apartment #3. Like a nightmare, there I was again gazing at the complex.

As customary, I stood still on the sidewalk and noted the time that Ofc. Rocker transported Lena from the scene to the homicide office in my Bible. I began writing notes regarding weather and lighting conditions for this day, plus I drew a diagram, not to scale, of the location and how it appeared to me. This was important so that I could make comparisons to the official crime scene report. Also, it allowed me to have a reference of where items (evidence) were located. Now, standing next to me was Det. Alvarez, being new to investigations, it was my responsibility to train him and Det. Gonzo. My emotions had to be set aside to deliberately explain to Det. Alvarez why certain protocols must be followed. Watching him as he mimicked everything, brought me a much-needed smile. Once he completed writing what he observed, he was told to shadow me and write down everything. Later in the night, we would go over his notes at our briefing.

Upon completing my explanation to Det. Alvarez, I observed CSI Technician Bonny drive up in the familiar Miami Police Crime Scene van. With him was CSI Technician Jefferson, who would be assisting with the processing of the crime scene. I walked to the crime scene van and met with Bonny and informed him that I would need a few minutes to get everything ready. Also, it was first necessary to do a cursory walk-through with Det. Alvarez. Then, I told Bonny, "I still need consent from the subject."

Bonny replied, "Okay, not a problem."

Knowing that Bonny was going to be the lead CSI technician was not a confidence booster for me. He was a nice guy, adequate on simple cases, but this was not a simple case. This was a major crime scene that needed someone who was extremely meticulous and willing to go the extra mile. Unfortunately, Bonny developed a reputation as a CSI technician that needed extra supervision, now I owned him on this case. Based on the current information available, I briefed him on what was going to be required to ensure that this case would not be lost. We could not have a crime scene error, or a technicality destroy this case. Bonny gave me a harsh look, unmoved by his response, I told him, "Listen, it isn't personal, but I will be all over this crime scene, so you better do your job right!"

To that, he just shook his head and dared not reply. Bonny knew I was not going to stand for any shortcuts or bullshit excuses. There was no way that a crime scene technician was going to ruin this case. With that out of the way, I turned away from Bonny and continued jotting down my observations. Taking a glance at him, he was returning to the Crime Scene van. As he walked past CSI Jefferson, something was said to her, but I was too far to make out what he told her.

Next thing I knew, Jefferson was standing next to me with a smirk on her face. "What's up?" I asked.

"Nothing, Bonny just told me to be ready for anything," she replied. "He must not know you as much as he thinks, I know exactly what you are going to need," she whispered.

Immediately I told her, "He better be ready, if not, I'm going to your supervisor on his ass." Jefferson totally understood what I meant. Knowing how I was trained and who trained me, she stepped back and watched as I began to draw a rough diagram of the exterior scene.

While drawing the sketch, I could not stop thinking of what was waiting for me inside the apartment. I really did not want to give it another thought until the time came. Just as I was noting the number of each apartment and their correlation to the exterior scene, Det. Gonzo called me on the police radio. "3162 (his unit number), can you have 3161 go to the tactical channel?" Upon hearing the request, I did not wait for the dispatcher, I just advised that I was switching to TAC (short for tactical channel). Once on the TAC channel, Det. Gonzo informed me that both Lena and Laudin signed the Consent to Search form. Great, this was something less to worry about for this was crucial to proceed with the search of the crime scene, its processing and collection of evidence.

Det. Alvarez, who had been standing at the entrance of apartment #3, where the incident took place approached me and asked, "Is there anything I can do?" Not answering his question, I asked to see his Bible, it was to check if he had been writing down his observations. He handed me his book and I began to thumb through the pages, not being critical, this was not the time. Being satisfied that he had written down information crucial to the case, I told him to respond to the homicide office to assist Det. Gonzo.

"You don't want me to stay here?" he asked.

"Not this time dude, I need to manage this scene before interviewing the suspect," I replied.

Det. Alvarez left the crime scene at almost 4:30 am and the on-call Assistant State Attorney had yet to arrive. There was only so much I could do; I did not want to start any of the processing before the Assistant State Attorney's arrival.

As Det. Alvarez walked away from the scene and nearing his vehicle, I took a deep breath and sighed. This was not the most difficult case to work but the sheer dynamics of it was taking an emotional toll and I had yet to enter the main crime scene. Before Det. Alvarez drove off, I told him to confirm that the Consent to Search forms were signed and to call me when he verified that they were. Det. Alvarez nodded his head and drove off.

While mentally going over my game plan, I found myself pacing back and forth on the walkway in front of the complex's apartments. To the untrained eye, I must have looked like someone on some type of medication. But in my world, I was formulating a game plan and mentally preparing myself for what was about to be encountered. It was a preparation of sorts to avoid surprises.

You see, all investigators have a ritual that they stick to prior to conducting their investigations. Not all rituals are the same, some are quirkier than others. Still, investigators must manage to garner their inner strength, especially while investigating challenging cases. This is how my psychological preparation was conducted. Upon reaching the end of the walkway, I turned and began walking toward my vehicle to change the battery of my police radio. No sooner did I enter my vehicle, that is when I noticed the on-call Assistant State Attorney, Ruby Sole, parking her vehicle behind mine.

I switched batteries, stepped outside of my vehicle, and walked toward Ruby. She was an incredibly wise and excellent Assistant State Attorney; we had worked several homicide cases together and today she had on-call duty. "Good morning, Ruby," I said in my typical jolly voice, as I opened her vehicle's door.

"Hi Pepi, how are you doing?" she replied.

"Well, everything was going great until two hours ago," I replied. I waited for her to exit the vehicle before going into the particulars of this incident.

Her first words upon exiting her vehicle were, "Are we going to need a search warrant?"

"No, we've got consent," was my short answer. Knowing that Lena and Laudin gave verbal consent, but I was waiting for confirmation that they had signed the form.

Stepping aside allowing Ruby to exit her vehicle, I wondered how much longer before Det. Alvarez calls me with the confirmation I requested earlier. Ruby began by speaking about one of our previous cases that was getting ready to come up for trial. Paying no attention to the particulars of the case or what she was saying, I replied, "Oh yeah, let me know when you schedule the Pre-Trial conference." I guess she got the hint because she did not respond. Now that we got the idle chit-chat out of the way, I began to brief her on what I had learned. She began writing in her version of the Bible what I was telling her. Like all investigators, Assistant State Attorney's need to take notes as well. It is amazing how everyone involved with an investigation must take notes, not just the investigator.

Ruby was just about to finish, when finally, Det. Alvarez raised me over the police radio, "3163, can you have 3161 go to TAC." I keyed the mic and advised, "3161, show me on TAC." Once I switched to the TAC channel, I was able to ask Det. Alvarez if Lena and Laudin signed the Consent to Search form. This was crucial for the investigation to proceed. Det. Alvarez immediately responded that both had signed the form. A complete sense of relief fell over me.

I did not want to take longer by drafting a Search Warrant, that would have added at least two hours to the investigation. Thank God everyone had been cooperating. Then, Det. Alvarez let me know that Dr. Prince, the on-call Medical Examiner, would be responding to my location. I asked Det. Alvarez if the doctor gave an estimated time of arrival. He informed me that no time was given.

Well, since I had to wait for the Medical Examiner, this was the perfect opportunity for me to brief Ruby and give her a quick walk-through of the scene. I told her how this entire incident began with the patrol units being dispatched to a disturbance call at 'Del Rey Cafeteria', located on 27th Avenue NW 19th Street, near the 27th Avenue bridge. I told her what I heard and saw during my time at the cafeteria and what led to the police responding to this location. Once I concluded my synopsis of the incident, I asked if she wanted to do a walk-through of the crime scene. There are many state attorneys that would have shunned from this walk-through but not Ruby. She was a veteran prosecutor, as tough as they come, and she wanted to get a good sense of what we were dealing with.

We began by walking the exterior of the crime scene, with its yellow police tape cordoning off the entire front of the apartment building. We then walked toward the parking lot where Laudin's pick-up truck was parked. It was yet to be searched but both CSI technicians were already beginning to process the scene by taking photographs that would later be introduced as evidence during the trial. "Make sure you photograph everything," I told Bonny. Intently, he just glared at me and waived his hand. I knew that he was doing his thing, I just wanted him to understand that I was being vigilant. Jefferson, who was taking measurements just smirked.

Now, my next task was how to prepare Ruby for what she was about to witness? There was no easy way, but she needed to fully understand in order not to be shocked. Slowly, we made our way toward the entrance of apartment #3. The officer who was securing the entrance stepped to the side. "Are you going in?" he asked.

"Yeah, this will be quick, I am showing the State," I retorted.

The officer's next comment made me pause, "Better you than me, that's why I would never want to work homicide." In a strange way, the officer was right. I would not blame any officer who did not want to be a part of the homicide unit after a scene like this one.

As we entered the apartment, Ruby and I stood in the dimly lit living room that was being used as a sleeping quarter for the multitude of people living here. I explained how this apartment was overcrowded, and many of the inhabitants were illegals, primarily from Honduras. Heck, even with the over crowdedness, to them, this was the Hilton compared to how they were used to living in their country. From the living room, I showed her where the kitchen was located and explained that this was where Floria, the victim's grandmother was found. She had been sleeping there with her husband. Now, I found myself delaying the inevitable and it was evident as Ruby asked, "Pepi, when are you going to show me the bedroom and the victim?"

"In a moment," I replied. My trepidation was more than evident. I had already witnessed the unimaginable. Now it was someone else's turn and there was no getting around it. I was puzzled why she was in such a haste to enter the bedroom.

There was really no rush, at least not for me anyway. She just wanted to see the crime scene and leave, while I on the other hand knew what was in stored. "Sorry Ruby, I'll show you in a second, I know you're in a hurry," I said.

"No problem Pepi, I know it's tough," she replied. Well, at least she had a good understanding of what this scene would be like, after my explanation. I could not have been any more graphic in my description of the crime scene.

During this whole time, Ruby, just like me kept writing notes in her respective Bible. "Ready?" I asked.

She nodded her head and said nothing. The silence was eerie as we stood at the threshold of the bedroom door. There was a small lamp on the floor in the corner of the room, opposite of where the victim was laying. The glow of the light cast a shadow on the room as it struck the various furniture pieces. There was enough light for one to observe the victim. Ruby stood at the entrance, frozen. "We haven't searched the room yet; do you want to go inside?" I asked.

Without saying a word, Ruby shook her head declining, then quickly stepped away from the door. The anguish was evident, what little she saw visibly upset her. Wisely, by walking away, she spared herself of the unthinkable. I could not blame her; this was one of those cases that no one should have to investigate.

We gingerly walked through the darkness of the apartment before exiting. Once outside, we stood on the steps in silence, the same ones I sat on when I first witnessed the scene. Ruby continued writing more notes in her pad and began walking toward her vehicle. "Hey, leaving just like that, not even goodbye," I said.

"Sorry Pepi, I'll see you later, call me if you need anything," she replied. Nothing else had to be said, her body language painted the picture while walking away with her shoulders slumped and head bowed.

Watching her walk away, I could not help but wonder how she really felt. It did not matter how seasoned or experienced one is, there are just some incidents that hit you harder than others. This one was a perfect example. The atrocities that man can inflict on others at times is unimaginable. Unfortunately, in my experience many violent crimes committed by men from Central and South

America were vicious in nature by using weapons such as knives, machetes, or axes. Many of the victims were defenseless and terrorized prior to being assaulted. These images are frightening and inexplicable, it is no wonder that few officers want to join the Homicide Unit.

# Chapter 8

Once Ruby departed, I returned to the grim apartment for the purpose of re-examining the ghastly crime scene, double checking my notes based on my observations. CSI technicians Bonny and Jefferson were still photographing the exterior of the crime scene and taking measurements. While they were doing their job, I walked to Laudin's pick-up truck and looked through the driver's side window to see if any weapons were visible. I took a step back and shined my flashlight around the door handle on the driver's side. Would I be able to detect any foreign substance such as blood? That would have been great for the investigation, but no luck.

There is nothing worse than trying to kill time while waiting for others to arrive at the crime scene and that was my situation. *Damn, where the fuck is the Medical Examiner?* I wondered. Dr. Prince should have been here by now. It would have been better had the Medical Examiner and Assistant State Attorney been together during the walk-through, this way, any questions could have been asked and answered. Unfortunately, that did not occur on this night.

While walking away from the pick-up truck, I saw the familiar white SUV of the Dade-County Medical Examiner's pulling up to the swale. *What a relief,* I thought. looking at my watch, I was surprised to see that it was 5:15 am. Two of the longest hours had passed, and I had yet to enter the primary crime scene to perform the on scene physical examination of the victim. That is an unpleasant task but one which had to be done, along with writing additional notes before returning to the homicide office. You see, it was vital for me to have as much information as possible before attempting to interrogate Laudin or interview any of the other possible witnesses. There is no way any investigator in their right mind could conduct an interview of any sort without having pertinent information available. That is why investigators must be meticulous when documenting their observations.

While Dr. Prince was still inside of her vehicle, I decided to communicate with Det. Gonzo over the police radio and asked him to return to the crime scene. He acknowledged and advised me that he would be leaving the station in a few minutes. I wanted him to be with me, it was important for him to observe what procedures are considered necessary on a case such as this one. If he hurried-up, he probably would be present for the on-scene physical examination of the victim. This would be essential for an inexperienced investigator, heck, it would be important for any investigator. Being exposed to a variety of incidents is crucial in building one's toolbox of knowledge.

Unexpectedly, I found myself killing time again, in the hopes that Det. Gonzo would show-up before Dr. Prince began her examination. While waiting, I met with Bonny and Jefferson and asked if they were able to observe any evidence of value around, on or inside the pick-up truck. Jefferson quickly answered, "No Granado, nothing yet." I was glad to get such a quick response because Bonny was still gathering his thoughts.

"Thanks," I replied. I wanted to make sure that the CSI technicians completed as much of the exterior of the crime scene as possible before proceeding to the main crime scene. *Thank God a Search Warrant was not required*, I thought. Although, search warrants are always better, Ruby felt comfortable knowing everything was covered when the consents were granted by all parties involved.

Finally, Dr. Prince concluded what she was doing and exited the vehicle. We walked toward each other and when I got close, greeted her cordially, "Hey Doc, glad to see you again." Dr. Prince was chipper, considering the time it was and I told her as much. She apologized for her tardiness but told me that she had responded to two other calls before this one.

In a soft voice she exclaimed, "Sorry if you've been waiting long, it's just been one of those nights!"

"Not to worry, Doc," I replied. I figured as much since I had been hearing the radio transmissions from Dade County PD and their units were hopping from one priority call to another throughout the night.

After exchanging pleasantries, we walked to the front of my vehicle, which was under one of the streetlamps. Still hoping that Det. Gonzo would make it, I called for Bonny and Jefferson to join us. They stopped what they were doing and walked toward my vehicle. Giving them time to approach, I began providing Dr. Prince with the basic information, case number, exact location, time of dispatch, victims' and next of kin information, regarding this incident. This information is important for a medical examiner prior to them beginning their field processing. They must have as much basic information as possible before departing any crime scene. Medical examiners are aware that sometimes the medical examiner's report prepared by the lead investigator can take several hours to complete and be submitted for review. Therefore, it was crucial for them to receive the information while on the scene.

Upon providing Dr. Prince with the initial information, Bonny and Jefferson had already arrived at my vehicle. I could not wait any longer for my neophyte detective, therefore, I decided to brief Dr. Prince on what had been learned up to this point. During my briefing, I could see that both CSI technicians were intently writing notes in their pads. This pleased me because it would cut down on any bullshit questions asked later by them, especially if they were not paying attention.

The mood during this briefing was very professional but somber. Everyone was aware of the type of incident we were investigating and who our victim was. With this type of case, we had little time for lighthearted conversation. Everyone was very serene and professional. Our main purpose during this initial briefing was to provide the medical examiner with as much information as possible and to answer any of her questions. There would be ample time later to engage in our typical banter. Unfortunately, this was not one of those times.

Finally, I began the detailed briefing with Dr. Prince. Once she finished writing the basic information in her pad, this indicated that it was time for us to conduct our crime scene walk-through. Based on the initial information, Dr. Prince was first taken to Laudin's pick-up truck. While the doctor was jotting down additional notes, this allowed me the opportunity to communicate with Det. Gonzo. "Dude how long is it going to take for you to get here? I can't stall any longer and the walk-through has begun," I said with a stern voice.

Upon hearing the tone in my voice, he quickly replied, "Sorry dude, I'm almost there."

Once the doctor finished writing her notes near the pick-up truck, she removed her Nikon camera from its case and began to take photos. Usually, medical examiners will take their own photos to better assist them with their investigation. You see, in murder cases, the medical examiner's investigation is independent from the police investigation even though both are working to reach a conclusion. For medical examiners, they study the causation and mechanics of how the death occurred. On the other hand, investigators work on motive, victimology, and history to reach a conclusion. Inevitably, during any investigation both the medical examiner and investigator work closely to exchange vital intelligence that will assist in the case being solved.

As we walked from the pick-up truck to the front of apartment #3, I began discussing with Dr. Prince the type of field examination that would be conducted. She did not answer immediately as she was still busy taking additional photos of the apartment complex exterior. "Give me a minute Pepi, I just want to take a few more photos," she finally replied.

"No problem DOC, I'm on your schedule now," I responded. She knew what I meant since she was aware that a suspect was sitting in the homicide office waiting to be interviewed by me.

After several minutes passed, Dr. Prince said, "I'm ready to continue."

*Those words were music to my ears,* I thought, now we could begin the examination of apartment #3 interior.

For a few moments, we stood quietly at the entrance of apartment #3. Then, as if on cue I began describing the interior of the apartment and provided the doctor with a layout, how many people had been sleeping inside and the location where the victim was found. During this session, I could feel the uneasiness swirling within me. This was one of those cases where it did not matter how hard I tried to go about my usual routine, nothing could make this one bearable. The image of the victim was imbedded in my brain. That gruesome picture was not going away any time soon. Finally, Dr. Prince and I entered apartment #3, followed by the CSI technicians. Once we entered the apartment, the officer who was guarding the entrance was reminded of his responsibility, "Do not allow anyone inside without my permission." He nodded his head up and down in acknowledgment.

All of us, like sardines, stood cramped in the living-room for a few moments while Dr. Prince adjusted her vision to the extremely poor lighting conditions. "You weren't kidding when you said one could barely see!" she exclaimed.

"I told you, DOC," I replied. I then asked her if she wanted to take measurements of the inside of the apartment. She told me that would not be necessary, because she could use the measurements taken by the crime scene technicians. The inside of the apartment looked like a nightclub as the strobes from Dr. Prince's and CSI Bonny's cameras were flashing simultaneously. While they took photos, I continued writing my notes, depicting the time we made entry into the crime scene, our briefing, and my observations. Documentation for me is crucial; it allows me, or any investigator involved with the case to review them for accuracy.

Once all the photographs were taken, Bonny turned to me and asked if I could hold his flashlight. He wanted to begin taking measurements with the roller-tape and needed light to see. Holding the flashlight did not bother me, it allowed me to observe how he was performing his job. It also gave me an opportunity to correct anything that I felt was being done incorrectly. While moving the flashlight around, I slowly walked toward the kitchen area and stood in the hallway. There, I could observe the kitchen, living room and the bedroom where the tiny, lifeless body of the victim was laying. The doctor periodically would pause to take notes then proceed photographing different areas of the apartment, but not in any order. Her thoroughness, although warranted was driving crazy because I was pressed for time. Suddenly, without realizing, Dr. Prince was standing right next to me. "Are you ready?" she asked.

"As ready as I will ever be," I replied with a sigh of relief. We now stood in front of the shattered bedroom door that had been breached earlier by the officers. The faint odor of a body's fluids was obvious to those with experience.

The eerie glow of the lamp inside the room continued projecting uncomfortable shadows on the walls. Being so close, one could see the outline of the victim laying on the bed. Our silence was ever present, as we just stood there writing down notes as if nothing horrific had taken place. Suddenly, the silence was broken, "Was body removal notified?" I asked the doctor.

"Not yet, I'll do it now before we get started," she replied. Well, that was going to be another 30 minutes before their arrival, another unnecessary delay. Hopefully, if anything good came of this delay would be Det. Gonzo arriving before the body removal unit. *Wishful thinking*, I thought angrily.

# Chapter 9

It was a solemn task, but Dr. Prince and I slowly navigated our way through the bedroom. All parties were taking their own notes while I continued to document what everyone was doing. Dr. Prince began photographing the bedroom, this time with more precision and focus because she knew that this was the primary scene, and nothing could be left to chance. Every inch, nook and cranny needed to be photographed, measured, and documented. If any evidence were located, it would be numbered, documented, and photographed before being collected. Unlike crime dramas on television or in the movies, crime scenes are painstaking to work. Not like in shows where crime scenes are completed within moments. Unfortunately, there are those rare cases when the crime scenes can take days to process.

There was a big difference with this one, it was not your ordinary crime scene. its dynamics sent chills down the spine of veteran officers and all who witnessed the savagery. There are vicious and violent types of crimes, whose acts are unspeakable. Crime scenes that are emotionally draining, then, there was this one. The longer I remained inside the bedroom, the more my stomach churned. In the back of my head, a little voice whispered, "You should have done him."

*Shake that off*, I thought. This was no place and not the time to be thinking of what should have been done to that animal. I was here to serve justice, not to be an executioner. My responsibility was to perform my job to the highest standards, the way I was trained. Human emotions should not play a part, but they damn sure do!

While Dr. Prince was fumbling around with her equipment setting up the right angles, I was busy documenting everything into my Bible. I remember thinking, *this was one section of the case that I hoped never to read again once my supplemental report is finished.* The longer I stayed inside this room, its darkness was ever present. The negative energy was everywhere, and I could feel my emotions building. Thoughts of my young children kept creeping into my head. Thank God they were safe and sound sleeping, without a care in the world. You see, that is how all children should feel. Unfortunately, it does not always work out that way.

Impatiently, the words just blurted out of my mouth, "How much longer, Doc?"

"Not much longer Pepi," she replied. "Just a few more photographs." While she was about to finish photographing, I could see both CSI technicians directly behind her. They were documenting and cataloging each piece of evidence for processing. The collection of some evidentiary pieces would have to wait until the on-scene physical examination of the victim was concluded. I informed Dr. Prince that once she concluded with the photographs, she would have to give my CSI personnel a few minutes for them to accomplish their task. She understood and told me that while CSI was completing their work, she would call for the remains removal personnel. This was a good idea; we were probably going to need their assistance during the on-scene physical examination. This was the doctor's call since I had no authority over Sill.

Finally, Dr. Prince concluded by photographing the area around the victim. Just as I exited the room, I asked her to join me outside. She shook her head yes, flung the camera over her shoulder and followed me out of the bedroom. This minor break was probably more for me than anyone else. Once outside the apartment, we began discussing what type of on-scene physical examination would be performed. The veteran doctor was not committed to the usual on-scene examination, on the contrary, she vacillated whether to perform a cursory examination rather than an extensive one. This consideration was due to the victim's condition and location. I figured as much; it would be better if the complete examination were conducted in the sterile environment of the morgue. The thought of this was not natural for a victim so young.

In the morgue, one could observe the type of damage sustained during the brutal attack. Lighting and general conditions were better suited, one hundred times better than at the crime scene. Not just for this case, but for all death cases. The cold, sterile environment with that distinct odor of death never bothered me, but just the thought of attending this autopsy churned my insides.

"So, how are we going to handle this?" I asked Dr. Prince? Without allowing her to respond quickly, I continued speaking and explained how it would be better to have another detective present to be a scribe. There was no way for me to allow someone other than myself assist with moving the victim. This case was becoming too personal. It was as if, I was compelled to be the one handling this victim. Maybe this was God's way of allowing me to atone for past transgressions, who knows. I just knew that this was something I needed to do.

Suddenly, but not surprising I realized that Det. Gonzo had not arrived on the scene. *Where the fuck could he be*, I thought. He should have been at the scene by now. Time was a factor, there could be no more delays, there was a need to know exactly how this crime scene looked and if a weapon could be found. Finding the weapon would be a bonus before interviewing Laudin Matte. It was important to have as much information or evidence as possible before conducting the interview of that degenerate son-of-a-bitch. You see, investigators never know what the outcome will be of any interview or interrogation. Therefore, investigators must have enough information to perform effectively while interrogating a suspect or interviewing any witness. How else can an investigator clear a case?

If an investigator does not have good information or tangible evidence to bring forth on the case, then it all goes to shit. That was not going happen on this case. So, Dr. Prince and I continued our conversation while CSI Bonny and Jefferson finished documenting and photographing the crime scene. No evidence had been collected yet; I was hoping to teach Det. Gonzo a few things before I ordered CSI to begin collecting evidence. But for that, he needed to be present to learn. My blood began to boil when I watched the remains removal van pulling up to the front of the apartment building while my inexperienced trainee had yet to show-up. I recognized the driver, Sill, he was a heavy-set African American whose real name was Sylvester. We knew each other from other incidents in which his team came out to assist. As Sill stepped out of the driver's side, I heard him say, "What's up, Granado?"

I walked toward him, shook his hand, and replied, "It's all about you." Thinking about it, that was a lame response, but I needed to keep it lite. "This is not a good one, Sill," I said. As I turned my head, I could see the shadow of another person exiting the passenger side door of the removal van. "Who's the new meat?" I asked.

Sill just looked at me and said, "He just started this week, hopefully he can handle this one."

"I hope so, this one is not for the faint of heart," I replied.

With that, Sill handed me the removal report sheet and asked if I was going to fill it out. I let him know that my rookie investigator was going to do the honors, especially since he was late. He took it back and placed the blank sheet inside his metal clip board alongside a toe tag. I gave him and his partner a brief synopsis of what they were going to encounter. Both shook their heads in disbelief, giving me a blank stare as I was talking. The new guy's jaw just dropped. "Keep him in check dude," I stated.

"He'll be fine, I'll make sure of it," Sill replied.

Suddenly, my eyes opened from this daydream when I heard someone in the distance yell out, "Pep, Pep, wait up!" I raised my head and there I was, in front of courtroom 2– 3. *Man, I cannot get this case out of my head*, I thought. *Who the fuck is screaming in the hallway of the courthouse?*

I wondered. Just as I turned, I felt a hand on my shoulder. Standing next to me was Det. Gonzo with a shit eating grin on his face.

"Did I miss anything yet," he said.

"Nothing yet, let's go inside," I replied.

I coaxed him toward the opposite side of the gallery from where I was seated. I did not want anybody around me, for whatever reason, especially someone that was going to constantly talk. This was not the right day to have someone constantly giving a play by play. Once Det. Gonzo sat down, I returned to my spot in the last pew.

While sitting, I saw Lena turn her head and look at me. As our eyes met, I motioned to her with my hand to let her know that I would be sitting next to her when the time came. She cracked a nervous smile in acknowledgment and turned her head. Replaying this whole incident in my head was not doing me any good. Unsure if this was part of my healing process or a curse of things to come. Only time would tell. Hopefully, this was not going to be a reoccurring event on every case. Now I began understanding why officers are reluctant to become violent crimes investigators, especially if they are assigned to a homicide unit. Not everyone is cut out to deal with death up close and personal on a daily basis.

Who would want to live with such images? These images are the reasons for nightmares and why many homicide investigators find comfort behind a bottle as well as isolation from their personal drudgeries. Also, depression that can lead to suicide and let us not even talk about divorce. Contemplating all these variables, I was not seated for a few minutes when I looked up at the clock. What was taking so long, hopefully, this day would come to an end soon. I just needed to put this case behind me already, maybe then closure would come my way. The glamour and hype of being a homicide investigator, working big cases is bullshit when you break it down. Yes, being a homicide investigator is one of the biggest challenges for anyone that chooses to follow that path. What no-one prepares for is the constant pain that is felt because of all the violence and carnage one is exposed too. For instance, this case is a testament of what an investigator can feel emotionally. None the less, this was my case and I had to deal with it, now and forever. Whether I liked it or not, I owned it; it was all mine.

As I looked around the gallery, so much time had passed that the audiences in the gallery had changed several times. Every time a new person entered the courtroom, the same question kept coming up, when was the judge going to get started? Without saying a word, I would just look at them and shrug my shoulders. *Who knows*? I wondered. I just wanted this day to end. Hopefully in our favor. We worked too hard collectively to come up short. But juries are fickle, one never knows and that was the only thing that worried me.

Just as I leaned my head against the wall, the door leading to the judge's rear hallway opened and there stood the bailiff. He was holding the door open for the stenographer who was making her way toward her desk at the foot of the judge's bench. *Damn, still nothing*, I thought. Why would I think any different? I should know better; the jury will emerge from the deliberating room before the judge makes his grand entry. It is the pomp of the situation that calls for these protocols. Besides, the news media was not ready. They were all downstairs grabbing a quick bite.

For sure, this judge was not going to get this spectacle started before the cameras were ready. Now, this judge was not known for theatrics, but this trial was worthy. A trial such as this one was going to be all over the news, locally and possibly nationally. So, it was possible that a little kabuki theater would somehow emerge. I would not blame anyone for wanting their fifteen minutes of fame, I just wish it would be under other circumstances.

I was still fidgety and did not know why. Relax, I reminded myself, you have done everything possible to achieve a guilty verdict. Heck, you even went to a downtrodden town in Honduras to make sure that all I's were dotted, and T's crossed. All in the name of justice, not so much for the animal being accused but for the victim. It was my responsibility to make sure that nothing presented during the trial as evidence could be overturned on appeal because enough was not done to ensure a guilty verdict. Pondering if everything possible had been done brought me right back to the crime scene, reliving that night seems to be my obsession today. I did everything by the book, including taking the time to train Gonzo and Alvarez. Will they ever have the inner fortitude and dedication to become above average homicide investigators? Who is to say, only time will tell? They tried to assist me as best they could, but ultimately, it was my case.

But as chaotic as that dreadful night was, I can still remember my conversation with Dr. Prince before reentering the crime scene to perform the field examination of the victim. "Listen Doc, how are we going to approach this field examination?" I asked. Without allowing a response, I continued by telling her, "Since Det. Gonzo had not arrived and the remains removal unit was present, there was no reason to delay any further." Dr. Prince agreed; we began to hatch out a plan of how to best proceed with this case. If Det. Gonzo was not present within the next few minutes, I was going to use CSI Jefferson as my scribe while the field examination was conducted. Worst case scenario, I would get Sill to assist the Doc while I scribed. *Yeah, that is what I will do*, I thought.

We had just concluded our briefing and I finished writing my notes in the Bible, when suddenly, I saw Bonny's dark silhouette appear in the living room area of the apartment. Just as he approached the front door, there was Jefferson, right behind him. That living room was so dark, I had not noticed either technician until they got to the door. "What's next detective?" asked Jefferson.

"Give me a minute," I replied. Not having Gonzo present pissed me off, not that I hadn't worked a case solo before, but this would be a valuable learning lesson. Not too many investigators get cases such as this one. At this rate, he may not last long in homicide.

While we were discussing our options, the patrol officer standing at the door, securing the scene, was intently focused to what was going on inside the dark apartment. He was almost on-top of us every time we spoke. That was annoying, but I understood his curiosity. It reminded me of an earlier time in my career, so I made it a point not to be a total asshole toward the officer. I just looked at him and said, "If you give me a minute, I will answer your questions and maybe let you assist."

"Really," he replied. "For sure," I responded. Suddenly, that officer had a grin from ear to ear, stood up straight as an arrow and returned to his post. I could only imagine how he must have felt because I remember feeling pumped up when I was given the time of day by a homicide detective during formidable years.

Now that I got that issue out of the way, I began briefing both CSI technicians on what was expected to be done during the field examination of the victim. I informed them that it had not been decided who was going to assist me. Whoever it was, would be responsible for photographing and documenting any additional evidence that was discovered. Suddenly, Sill walked onto the porch where we were all standing, his assistant was behind him as if shying away from the inevitable. I could not help but wonder, "how is someone, who is working for the medical examiner's remains removal unit be so squeamish. Hopefully, that trainee gets his act together, if not, he will not last long on the job." Unfortunately, their task is crucial, but it is not meant for everybody.

Once Sill stepped on the porch, I knew exactly what role he was going to have regarding the field examination of the victim. He was going to assist me, his familiarity in dealing with dead children was a factor. Therefore, this incident would not affect him as much as it would others with less experience. Now that I decided on Sill, I felt better. Yeah, it would have been good to have Det. Gonzo with me, but time was of the essence. That is when I began barking out orders.

"Listen up guys," I said, just before passing out assignments. While assigning everyone their responsibilities, I told them the following: "I need all of you to understand the situation! This is not your typical case and I need for all of you to check your emotions at this door! I want no distractions when we begin! Is that understood?" while making direct eye contact with each person. Each of them looked at me and without saying a word they nodded, affirming that they understood the instructions that were just presented.

It was not my intent to come across as a hard ass, but they needed to understand how important their individual roles were going to be, and I did not want anyone's emotions to interfere with the task at hand. Looking directly at Sill he understood and immediately said, "I got it." Once he acknowledged, I looked at Bonny and said, "I need you to take the photographs, I am concerned that Jefferson won't have the stomach for the close-ups! So, it's better if she just documents the scene and bags the evidence!"

"No problem Pepi," he replied. Upon concluding with Bonny, he pulled his assistant aside to relay my instructions to her. I was certain he was letting her know how much of a stickler I was and did not want to have a new CIS person taking photos, especially of a crime scene of this magnitude.

This would make sense, having Bonny make me out to be the bad guy, since he had to work closer with Jefferson than I did. Realistically, I did not care. It was not my responsibility to worry about personal feelings. I was not about to have a new CSI technician have a trial-and-error session on this case. As I gathered the team who was going to assist me and Dr. Prince, I again reminded them of how sensitive this case was and for each to assert self-control. They were told what was going to be done during the on-scene examination of the victim. I purposefully did this to avoid any shock, after all, we are all human with feelings and emotions. There would be plenty of time to vent afterward. The entire team was given a final assessment to ensure they were prepared.

Before reentering the crime-scene, I remember commenting to those who were about to participate in this solemn act, "Are there any questions or concerns before we get started?" I wanted to make sure that everyone understood, myself included. For some strange reason, I knew this case would be one of those that was going to stick with all of us in one way or another for years to come. As we entered the apartment, an empty feeling came over me, a void of any love or humanity permeated from inside this place. Evil had its way on this night and instantly I found myself saying a prayer. Not just for my inner peace, but for what I was about to do and for those who were going to assist me. But most importantly, for the innocent child. Horrors such as these forces one to muster as much strength and internal fortitude as possible. So, these are the moments that test my faith in God, knowing that I am an instrument needed to bring comfort and assurance to a grieving mother. Performing my job keeps me grounded knowing that I will be the only one speaking for the dead. This was a responsibility, a task I took to heart.

# Chapter 10

As I was concluding my conversation with the almighty, out of the corner of my eye, I could see Jefferson just standing there staring at me. "Anything wrong?" I asked.

"No not really, I didn't think you were so spiritual," she replied. We kind of stared at each other for a few seconds and without saying another word we went about our business. I remember thinking, *what a weird comment to make.* Maybe that moment of silence caught her off guard or she was not expecting any such reverence during an investigation. Honestly, I have learned that investigators and police officers in general have their own way of coping with certain situations. Considering the amount of horror and carnage that we are exposed too every day; it does not hurt to be in touch with something or someone that centers you. For me, my strong belief in God has always sustained me during troubling times and horrendous cases. This was one of those incidents that shoots right to the top of unimaginable, I would not have wished it on any investigator.

While getting myself ready, and believe me, homicide investigators must go through a litany of self-imposed rituals before beginning any on-scene physical examination of the deceased. It is an unpleasant task and there are few within the law enforcement community that has what it takes. As I concluded writing my observations and thoughts in my Bible, there was Jefferson again, hovering around me. Hopefully, I did not offend her with my prayer, maybe she just wanted to ask a question. Closing my Bible, I asked her if she needed anything. Meekly, she looked at me and began to speak, but before completing her sentence, she suddenly stopped and walked toward the room where the victim was located.

Standing at the entrance to the bedroom, she began separating the evidence bags that were going to be used for securing any evidence that was collected. She made sure the biohazardous bags were available as well as latex gloves for those of us that were going to be in contact with the victim. Although she went about her business, not once did she look inside the room. *Why would she?* I thought. Soon enough she will come face to face with the unthinkable. Moments later, Bonny stepped around me and approached Jefferson. It seemed obvious to me; he was instructing her on what her responsibilities were going to be during the procedure. *Good*, I thought, the least person suspected was taking the time to teach. That was comforting to witness, maybe all those nights of me preaching how mentoring the next generation of investigators is so important was finally being employed.

Suddenly, Dr. Prince put her hand on my shoulder and said, "Are we ready?"

"Absolutely Doc, whenever you are," I responded. Without hesitation, she walked toward the dreaded bedroom with me directly behind her. Sill walked quietly behind me as Bonny began taking photos while Jefferson wrote down everything that we were doing. To assist her, I began dictating what seemed important and should be written. Dr. Prince began by photographing the bedroom from as many angles as possible. Although the bedroom was cluttered and dimly lit, she was able to maneuver herself around the room with no trouble, as if she had been there before.

While she was busy photographing, I was busy writing my notes. This was important because without another investigator, I would be depending on Jefferson's notes based on my dictations. Hopefully, she wrote everything I was dictating since it would be reviewed later for me to update my Bible. Investigators must think way ahead of the present moment if they are going to succeed. Notes that are missed on a scene cannot be captured later and written. There is nothing better than to write what is observed in the now, not rely on memory several hours or days later. It was for this reason that Det. Gonzo was required to be here, in the present. Not eating shit somewhere, which is typical of any apprentice investigator because they do not understand the urgency or consequences until it becomes their case.

The coolness inside the bedroom could be felt by all of us who were present. The air-conditioner had been left running at its coldest setting. The faint odor of exposed and drying blood was in the air, circulating amongst us, but at least working inside the bedroom would be manageable. The alternative would have been an enclosed, musty bedroom with minimal ventilation, which would have heightened all the odors. Such crime scenes are difficult because of the conditions.

Fortunately, we would not have to endure such conditions while working this crime scene. Other than the obvious, the conditions inside the bedroom were favorable. Once Dr. Prince and I entered the bedroom, we made our way toward the bed, its position made it difficult to take photos because it was wedged against the northwest corner walls. There was so much clothing strewn about the bedroom's floor that walking was made difficult for fear that evidence would be disturbed or overlooked. It was bad enough that the lighting conditions were limited but to have so many clothes and items thrown all over the room, it was like someone purposefully caused this mess. Something in the back of my mind suggested that Laudin did this. Or maybe this was how this family chose to live. For them, such conditions might be considered normal. Who was I to judge about this messy room, when on the bed right in front of me laid the lifeless body of a little girl?

Surely it could not have been Lena, she might have been working at that dive, but she certainly appeared to be a clean and well-ordered person. It was just a hunch on my part, considering I had seen my share of bar waitresses who could care less about themselves or others. On the other hand, she did not appear to fit that mold. I could have been wrong, but my gut said otherwise.

While looking at the mess, I told Bonny, "Let's use the portable lights that you have in the van, we need to make this room brighter." He agreed with the idea and stepped out of the bedroom. Immediately, I informed Dr. Prince of my decision; she was happy that additional lighting was going to be furnished. One could not blame her since it would make processing easier. Having to work in less than satisfactory conditions is a recipe for a mistake. While Bonny was getting the portable lights ready, I began drawing a diagram of the bedroom. This would certainly assist me later while preparing my supplemental report. Just as I was completing my rough sketch, Bonny came stumbling in with a spotlight and a tripod. "Do you think this is enough?" he asked.

"I don't see why not, it's more than what we have now," I responded.

While both CSI technicians were setting up the additional light, Sill was standing at the edge of the bed shaking his head. "Who could do such a thing," he commented out loud. There was no response from anyone, as we continued getting the lighting situation resolved. Finally, the extra lights were turned on, man, what a difference a few extra lights make. The room was totally lit-up. *Now that was better*, I thought. Now we could resume our work in a better illuminated environment. This would allow us to finish sooner, since nobody wanted to stay longer than they had too.

Bonny meticulously began photographing the crime scene and taking measurements of where evidence was located in relationship to the victim. These photos were for the criminal investigation report as opposed to Dr. Prince's photos that were for her medicolegal investigation, which is a totally separate and independent investigation, even though it is part of the same incident. This allows for the medical examiner assigned to the case to review their documentation in relevance to what they observed at the crime scene and during the postmortem examination. Based on these findings, Dr. Prince would be able to determine cause and manner of death more effectively.

During my assessment of the crime scene, cast off was observed. This particular pattern is caused when a sharp instrument penetrates the skin and as it is being violently withdrawn, the blood is sent flying through the air, causing a distinct pattern, "Cast Off." I continued to examine the area around the victim but only noticed the cast-off pattern on the wall, directly behind the victim's head. Upon closer scrutiny, a blood-soaked pillow was near the victim's arm and underneath the pillow a child's doll was lying still. Its glassy black eyes were opened, and it gave the impression of a startled object that was staring into the great abyss. Looking at the doll gave me a sinking feeling; I had not noticed it before because the room was so dark. While looking at the doll, it brought an image of my daughters. They too liked sleeping with their dolls. "Stop thinking like that Pepi, you have work to do," I counseled myself.

Minutes passed and Dr. Prince was still writing notes in her pad apart from taking additional photos. This gave me a chance to go over the notes in my Bible. Double checking my notes allowed me the opportunity to make sure everything was accurate. *Why so nervous*, I thought. It was important to make sure this scene was processed like any other crime scene, no exceptions. Putting aside the circumstance and the feelings it conjured, I still had a job to do.

While standing just outside the bedroom door, I reviewed my check list pertaining to the crime scene. It read something like this; The crime scene is located in the southwest bedroom of apartment #3. This apartment has one bedroom and one bathroom. A small bed was observed in the living room, near the entrance. Another bed was in the kitchen. It belonged to the victim's grandmother. The victim was observed lying supine on the bed located inside the bedroom, her head was in a northerly direction. The victim laid atop a yellow comforter; a large area stained with suspected blood was observed near or about the head and shoulder area.

Going over these notes was making me sick to my stomach, such a grotesque act. Now, I looked up from my Bible, slowly my eyes made their way toward the victim who was motionless. Several hours had passed since this innocent victim was laid down for what would be her final sleep, never imagining that her grandmothers kiss would be the last tender mercy of her life. Dr. Prince looked as if she were about to finish and I could see Sill motioning me to hurry the Doc. "Ready to start, Doc?" I asked.

"Let us get started," she replied, "it shouldn't take long, I want to do a cursory exam here and I'll finish the rest in the morgue." This was great news for me, it meant that we would be leaving this location in less than an hour. Hopefully, in time to interview my monster who was sitting in one of the interview rooms in the homicide office.

Now, my focus was again on the tiny frame of a once breathing, beautiful little girl. Concentrating on the wound, I wondered, *were we to slow in breaching the bedroom door?* If we only could have caught-up to the beast before he made his way inside the apartment. Maybe our chances of saving this little girl would have been greater. But 'IF', is the middle word in life, only that was not the case because her life was gone. For all I knew, Laudin could have committed this depraved act long before we entered the apartment. Now was not the time to be dwelling on 'what ifs', I would know soon enough when she was killed. The autopsy's result would let me know through scientific methods.

Finally, the on-scene physical examination of the victim was about to begin. Dr. Prince, Sill and I grabbed some latex gloves from Jefferson's bag and put them on. Just before getting started, I remember telling Bonny, who was photographing and documenting the crime scene, "Make sure you take close ups and good measurements, I don't want to leave any stones unturned." He gave me that funny look as if to say, "Really." I totally understood that look and continued with my observations.

Unable to write my notes, I began to dictate what I was observing to my scribe. "The victim is a two-year old girl. She is lying supine on her mother's and her mother's boyfriend's bed. She is wearing blue shorts, a diaper and a white T-shirt." This was how I presently observed the victim, but earlier, when we made entry into the bedroom she was lying on her stomach. That is when I turned her to check on her well-being before the paramedics entered the bedroom. The unspeakable horror was engraved in my eyes when I turned her little body. That moment will continue to haunt me forever.

Hoping we had made it in time, I reached across the bed to make sure she was still alive, but as I turned her diminutive frame, her body moved toward me as her little head with messy brown hair went in the opposite direction. In the dim light of the bedroom, I could see the dark stain of the pooling blood. This was a sight that no-one should ever witness, an act so grotesque. Who could commit such an atrocity? Refocusing on the task at hand, I continued dictating my observations to Jefferson, "the victim's throat had been slashed, a deep gash is observed." As I discussed the traumatic injury with Dr. Prince, it was her opinion at this time that a sharp instrument was used to inflict this type of wound. "Could it have been a knife?" I asked her.

"It certainly is a possibility," she replied.

I knew that the Doc would not be able to definitively say what caused the injury at this point, but it is always a question that needs to be asked. As we began to conclude our short examination, my eyes were focused on the amount of blood that had oozed from this little body. The extra lights that were brought inside the bedroom enhanced what only was imagined a few hours earlier. Now, the full effect and gore was there for all of us to see. There was no doubt that we were all mortified from the visual shock of what we had just witnessed, I know I was. Looking at Jefferson, I remember asking her how she was doing and if she had written everything I dictated. She responded that she was a little upset but had written as much as she could. Her instinct at that moment was to put down her pad and retrieve a biohazard bag. This act was as if to flip a switch, meant to disconnect by switching to another task. "Put all of the gloves inside the bag, I'll dispose of them with the other items," she said. Sill, who was the removal supervisor kept wearing his gloves.

As Dr. Prince and I removed our gloves, we discussed if this was going to be an early post-mortem examination or late. She was unable to give me a definitive answer or exact time but advised that as soon as she returned to the morgue, she would let me know. Now turning to Sill, my gaze let him know that it was time to remove the victim. He nodded his head and called for his assistant. As everyone was attempting to go about their business, I took a moment and placed my hand on this blameless little girl's forehead. I remember praying a Hail Mary hoping that her pain was minimal and that her journey to the Kingdom of the All Mighty was swift.

I felt the tears slowly running down my cheeks while uttering the final words, "Now and in the hour of our death, Amen." It was shameful how this beautiful little girl must have endured such a violent and unprovoked demise. Watching her motionless body was a reminder of why I became a homicide investigator. Not for the glory or notoriety but to bring comfort to grieving families by performing my job to the fullest and speaking for those who no longer can speak. For me, it was to bring justice for victims such as this one or maybe it was for my own cleansing.

Upon concluding my prayer, Sill tapped me on the shoulder. "We're ready," he said. I stepped aside and watched in somber silence as he placed the toe tag on the little victim's big toe. He delicately picked her up, making sure her head was cradled and placed her body on a white sheet, as if it were an ancient burial shroud. With utmost delicacy, he gently folded her arms, then snuggly wrapped her inside a green plastic body bag which is used to secure and transport victims to the morgue. Sill did not need his assistant to place the tiny victim on the stretcher, he just picked her up and gently placed her himself. Her little body was strapped down by the assistant to avoid her rolling off the stretcher. Once she was secured, the loud clank of the stretcher cracked the silence of the night. The sound of the metal echoed across the courtyard and peering eyes could be seen watching from behind closed curtains of the adjacent apartments.

Before long, the remains removal team were wheeling the stretcher out of the apartment, making their way to the transport van through the courtyard. They placed the stretcher alongside the van's rear compartment which had been opened and slid it inside.

While dealing with the victim's stretcher, a small crowd of curious neighbors emersed from their dwellings and were standing several feet around the van in silence and disbelief. The loud clank of the stretcher being locked in place inside the van startled the on lookers. Once it was secured, we stepped away as the van's doors closed. Like a statue, I stood motionless staring at the closed rear doors of the M/E's transport van. Then, I walked over to Sill and asked if he had received the M/E sheet. Looking down at his clipboard, he shook his head affirmatively and entered the van through the driver's side. Once the van drove off, I silently returned to apartment #3.

# Chapter 11

While slowly making my way back to apartment #3, it allowed me time to go over my mental checklist of everything that had been done up to this point. This included everything which was done at the crime scene. While second guessing myself, I opened my trusty Bible just to ease my thoughts. Reviewing my notes, nothing seemed to be out of sorts, each item of importance was accounted for, documented, and entered. The last and most important thing to be reviewed was the scene's diagram just in case anything was missed. After this review, I felt confident.

Upon approaching the front door of the apartment, I could see the officer standing directly at the entrance, staring out into the courtyard. Like a bolt of lightning, it hit me. "Damn dude, sorry, but I totally forgot about you," I said. "I understand, detective, I'm sort of glad 'cause I walked behind you and when I saw the little girl, I immediately returned to the front door. I don't know how you do it," he responded nervously. I gave him a nudge on the shoulder in acknowledgment and reentered the apartment. The distinct odor of blood and other body fluids were starting to become more pronounced. If not for the exposure to air circulating from the air-conditioner, the stench might have been worse.

Now that the victim had been removed, it would be easier to conduct a thorough search of the bedroom. So, I grabbed a pair of latex gloves from my pant pocket which were left over from examining the victim. With some difficulty, I managed to slip them on. Opening my Bible to the page where I made the last entry, I noticed an asterisk. Beside it I wrote, Det. Gonzo is not present. Immediately, without noticing, my blood started to boil. Angry and bewildered by his lack of urgency, I remember blurting, "What the fuck!" Anger should have been the least of my feelings. I was supposed to be working on this case with two brand spanking new investigators and the one that should have been with me, learning, was not present. Instead, he was taking his sweet ass time. Now, here I was, about to begin searching the bedroom and again I would be depending on the assistance of Jefferson or Bonny. Like previously, Jefferson became my scribe while Bonny photographed and documented items that were identified. Methodically, I began searching the bedroom, starting from the east wall while working my way around the room in a spiral technique bringing me toward the middle. I wanted to get these areas out of the way while intentionally leaving the area where the bed was located for last just in case valuable evidence had been tossed under or behind it.

After closer scrutiny, this room was a total mess, clothes, boxes, and suitcases were all over the place. An area near one of the corners inside the room was designated to toss what had already been searched. Each item of clothing was searched to make sure the weapon used was not folded and hidden inside. Once I finished with the clothing that were on the floor, I began searching the suitcases, Nothing. *Man, there is more shit than I originally figured*, I thought. Still, the search had to continue. While meticulously searching, all of us inside the room had to have been thinking that there was no way Laudin was able to get rid of whatever weapon he used to commit this brutal act. Hell, we were outside the door, unless he had killed the victim way before we arrived.

Once I concluded searching the suitcases, another cursory search around the room was conducted. Momentarily, I looked at the corner of the room and noticed a miniature mount Everest had been built, that is how much crap was in this room. Now, I was not done searching and in disbelief exclaimed, "Wow!" This might have been a mess to me, but for those who lived here, this might have been their only way.

Looking at Bonny, I told him to photograph everything to ensure this room was well documented, including the mound. Jefferson then asked if the dresser drawer was going to be searched, gee, that was a silly question. She had to have known we were not going to leave this apartment until every nook and cranny was searched. I was going to find the weapon if it was the last thing I did. Finding the weapon would be a solid piece of evidence to have during the interrogation. With the weapon in hand, there would be no speculation as to what instrument caused the terminal injury. Besides, in my experience, whenever a sharp object is used to commit a violent act, the offender usually has self-inflicted injuries consistent with the force used. On many occasions, the instrument used slips through the assailant's hands causing lacerations or cuts. Hopefully, the weapon is found and Laudin has injuries that are consistent to this vicious act.

I began by opening the top drawer of the dresser. There were only six drawers, so this should not take long. The first drawer was filled with miscellaneous papers, nothing of interest. The second drawer had polaroid photographs and documents. The documents were Laudin's that identified him as a Honduran national. In reviewing a few of these documents, it appeared that he was from a town outside of San Pedro Azula by the name of Olancho. I knew little of this Honduran town. Olancho, it seems is in a mountainous region of the country and probably was as rural as rural could get. I had every document photographed and collected, who knows, they might be of great use at some undetermined time.

The remaining drawers were full of women's under-garments, of all types and sizes. With such a variety, I figured this was the community drawers for those who resided in the apartment. All this searching and still no weapon. Then, I noticed the closet door. It was there, in front of me and closed. I could not believe how I had literally passed right by it and did not open it. Jefferson was standing next to the closet, so, I asked her to look around the knob for evidence of blood. She shined her flashlight around the doorknob and the edges, no trace evidence of blood was observed. Feeling comfortable with that report, I asked her to open the closet door. Once the door was open, a sigh of relief came over me. The closet was completely empty.

How crazy was this picture? The bedroom was a total mess, with clothes and various items thrown around and a perfectly good empty closet. The irony, but *One less thing to worry about*, I thought. Bonny was instructed to photograph the closet while I moved toward the area around the bed. "Let's photograph the bed without the victim," I instructed Bonny. "Make sure that once we are done, all the sheets, pillowcases and any items with blood are collected," I told him. "No problem," he responded. While standing at the foot of the bed, I slightly moved it away from the wall. Then, I grabbed the mattress, pulled it so that I could grab the blood soiled sheet that was tucked under the corner and remove it. Just as I began removing the sheet, a noise was heard from behind the bed. It sounded like if something solid had hit the wall. While I was removing the sheet, Bonny was collecting the pillowcases which also had blood on them. Each were placed inside separate evidence bags.

Then, a sick reminder, her lonely doll was just lying there, waiting for its companion who would never return. Its coarse blond hair was stained with blood of an innocent, so it was carefully removed from the bed and placed inside a red biohazardous bag. The last item was the sheet that I was holding tightly. Suddenly, Bonny was about to take it from my hands, but that was not happening. Instead, he opened a biohazard bag, and I placed the sheet carefully inside. Standing next to the bed, one could see the blood-soaked gray mattress. It was no longer red, instead, it appeared dark, almost like a deep burgundy. That poor little girl, it was as if every drop of blood from her little body was collected by the mattress. *How she must have agonized at the hands of Laudin*, I thought. Vicious and without remorse, that is what this crime scene painted.

This little girl had no chance. It was obvious that one of the pillows must have been used to cover her small head or entire body during the attack. The evidence seemed to indicate what had been theorized. Hopefully, Laudin speaks and confesses to this abomination. *But the longer I stay here, my chances of getting a confession diminishes*, I thought. Upon placing the paper bag with the sheet next to the other bags, I returned to the bed.

Standing on the side nearest to the bedroom's door which had been destroyed from the entry, I pulled the box spring and heard a thud. Peering around the edge of the box spring, I looked down toward the floor. Then, low and behold there it was, that bloody knife staring at me. It was a small, ten-inch Bowie type knife. Its handle was bone with a brown color tint. The blade was shiny about six inches with semi dried blood covering most of its blade. Strands of hair could be seen stuck to the caked blood along the edges of the blade. "Found it!" I exclaimed excitedly. I could hear both technicians saying, "Great." What a relief. Finally, after finding the possible murder weapon, I could leave the crime scene confidently now relieved that the weapon was located. I directed Bonny to document where the knife was located and to bring it immediately to the homicide office upon his arrival at the police station. I wanted Laudin to know we found it, maybe that would get him to react. Who can tell what will cause individuals to respond? It varies from person to person. While Bonny began documenting and photographing the knife, I stepped to the side and instinctively began writing notes in my Bible. Everything had to be properly documented, including my cursory diagram of where the knife was located. My heart felt heavy with sorrow.

I informed both technicians that once they finished, I wanted to brief with them outside before returning to the station. Just as I we exited the apartment, there was Det. Gonzo walking toward us with a shit eating grin on his face. When he reached the porch, I told him, "Dude, you're an idiot. You are never going to learn anything so long as you keep your head up your ass!"

"Sorry Pep," he replied. That was a piss poor excuse for a young investigator. There was too much work to be done, and little time to do it, for me to entertain his bullshit. Surprised with the response, he watched as I wrote in my Bible his arrival time. Forcefully, I told him that his times better be entered accurately without omitting his tardiness to the crime scene. With that, he began making his notations in his Bible.

I needed to bring him up to speed quickly because he had to stay with CSI on the scene until they finished processing and collecting all the evidence. So, without giving him a chance to come up with another lame excuse, I began going over what had been done and what was learned up to this point in the investigation. Det. Gonzo, without saying a word listened intently to my briefing while taking notes as fast as he could. He asked basic questions which is normal for someone with little or no experience. Still upset, I stayed professional and answered each question. Once he finished writing, I gave him a quick walk-through of the crime scene lecturing him on how he missed out by not being present during the initial stages of this investigation. An investigation such as this one was perfect for any investigator to gain valuable experience, especially one with limited knowledge. Det. Gonzo kept his head bowed, understanding what I was referring too.

Not many investigators get a chance to investigate a brutal killing of a child. I wish we never had too, unfortunately, I did. Still, as gruesome as this incident was, Det. Gonzo would have gained valuable experience from various perspectives. His most important lesson was how an incident such as this one is managed from an emotional to its technical aspects.

Once we concluded our briefing, he was told what Bonny and Jefferson were going to be doing. Additionally, he needed to make sure that once they concluded processing the crime scene and collected additional evidence, I was to be notified immediately. This crime scene could not be released without my authorization. Looking straight at this novice investigator, I asked him if he understood. He looked up and shook his head in acknowledgement. That was a relief, maybe he finally realized how serious I was about this case.

Immediately after finishing with Det. Gonzo, I stepped off the porch and on to the walkway. I began documenting my briefing in my Bible when both CSI technicians exited apartment #3. "Hey Pep, are you ready for us?" they harmoniously asked. Thank God they caught up with me, I had totally forgotten about briefing with them before returning to the homicide office.

"Yeah guys," I replied. The three of us stood outside, in front of apartment #2 where I began instructing them on what was needed from them before they cleared the crime scene. It was all about the details. I wanted them to go over and recanvass the crime scene again, this time with Det. Gonzo. Maybe, during this canvass he might be able to observe something that we could have missed earlier. Besides, I was going to hold on to this crime scene until my interview with Laudin finished and after briefing the state attorney, Ruby Sole, who had responded to the crime scene earlier.

Once our briefing concluded, both technicians hurriedly returned to the crime scene to finish their assignment. As they reached the porch of apartment #3, Det. Gonzo met with them. They stood on the porch for a few minutes, exchanged a few words and reentered apartment #3. While that was going on, I stayed a few minutes writing. There was so much information going through my head, it was about to explode. I wanted to make sure that every bit of information needed to brief Sgt. Martin, who like I figured, never bothered to come by the crime scene was at hand. Additionally, I was still formulating a plan on how best to approach the interview of Laudin. Well, that time was getting closer but first I had to leave this location. The longer I remained gave Laudin more time to reconsider any chance of speaking with the police.

Walking toward my vehicle, I grabbed my police radio and raised the communications operator and told her to contact Det. Alvarez. The communications operator notified Det. Alvarez and had him switch to the investigations tactical channel. This was a secured channel that allowed investigators to speak to each other without tying up valuable air space needed by other officers. Once we switched to the tactical channel, our conversation would be private. "Freddy, are you on?" I asked.

"Go ahead Pep," he replied.

"How's our boy doing," I asked.

"He's chilling, not really doing much," he answered.

"How are the witnesses doing," I asked.

"Everyone is fine, just waiting for you," he replied. That was great to hear. Now it was time to work fast because witnesses have a tendency of getting cold feet when too much time elapses. My steps quickened as I approached my vehicle, opened its driver side door, and entered. I took a moment prior to driving off, sadly glancing at the complex. Within my sorrow, I began thinking of my children.

# Chapter 12

Finally, while driving away, a sense of relief came over me. As much as I love my job, it was becoming difficult to spend another minute at the crime scene. Not that I was unable to handle it, but for the first time in my short career as a homicide investigator, the inhumanity of man was all too evident. For as many violent death investigations I have been associated with, nothing could have ever prepared me for an incident such as this one. Its magnitude was overpowering. The horrific image of my victim taken through the lens of my eyes will forever be engraved in my mind. There could never be a reasonable or rational way to thoughtfully describe such an incident to others.

Sure, everyone will certainly be curious to know and hear the ghastly details of an event that can only be produced on a movie set. Unfortunately, human nature will override one's humanity, which has become all too real. Getting closer to arriving at the police station amped me up. You see, by now, the entire department was aware of this case, and officers would be asking a million questions that will never be answered. My priority at this moment was to enter the station and turn on my most charming persona. Realistically, there would be no time for frivolous chit-chat with curiosity seekers upon arriving. Understand, one must totally get into a zone to avoid lapses.

During these moments, there is no time for unnecessary distractions by others, the investigation was the only thing that mattered. Just as I neared South-West 8th Street or as it is famously known, "Calle Ocho," the traffic light on 10th avenue turned red. The streets were deserted but for a few homeless people walking like zombies, no purpose, and no direction. A majority of these homeless were familiar to me from my days as a uniform officer working this sector. Ah yes, Little Havana my old stomping grounds was known as '50 Sector' for patrol officers and in the early eighties it went by the moniker of 'Little Vietnam'. Primarily due to the extreme violence associated with turf wars connected to gangs and drugs that were being sold on almost every street corner. Additionally, with street level dopers, hookers, wanna be gangbangers, seedy bars and Marielito Cubans running around, these streets were alive and kicking. Action occurred every night, shootings, stabbings, fights and yes, murder. Considering the amount of violence that officers were exposed to, I could not recall any case of such magnitude as this one.

The red light presented me with the perfect opportunity to get ready. So, I began to mentally prepare how to best approach Laudin while sitting in front of him in the interview room. Should I come across as some macho Latin, incensed by what had occurred or maybe play it down a notch, humble and understanding. All this preparation is great, but, in the end, Laudin's demeanor would dictate my direction. There was always a chance he could tell me to "Pound Sand." Either way, I needed to be ready for anything. Finally, the traffic light had turned green and I had not realized, *Damn, how long was I stopped at the light*? I wondered. However long, currently it did not matter. Besides, who was going to say anything? The walking zombies, other than them, the streets were empty from any vehicle traffic.

Slowly, I turned and drove toward the police station, located in the middle of downtown Miami, just off I-95. Driving toward the I-95 ramp, North, which was the quickest route to the station, I found myself driving past the ramp. *What the hell was I thinking?*

"Cafecito" was the answer. My impulse was to make a pit-stop at a little Cuban dive on 3$^{rd}$ Avenue NE 2$^{nd}$ Street. That spot was open 24/7, always full of miscreants and law enforcement. Everything under the sun wound up there at one time or another during a twenty-four-hour period.

The location was neutral ground, nothing ever seemed to happen there. Not that it was designated as such, but it was a great place to gather information and shoot the shit with seedy characters that one would normally not associate with in the open. The underworld unleashes a menagerie of individuals who will leak information unknowingly, so, for the astute officer who needs to know what is going on, why ruin this spot. Realistically, I am quite sure that one out of every five individuals that stopped by after 2:30 in the morning could be arrested for any number of infractions or open warrants, many of which were for minor misdemeanors. Was it worth drying up a location where information could be gathered or let it continue to thrive? Either way, those with open warrants would be apprehended eventually, maybe, even several blocks away from the spot. No one would ever be the wiser. Turning the corner on the street where the cafeteria was located, I could see the familiar glow of the multi-colored lights that lit up the entire intersection. Strangely enough, there were no taxi cabs parked as usual. *That's odd*, I thought.

As I approached, the spot was almost empty, just a few girls of the night standing at the far end of the open counter. One of the girls recognized me from a previous arrest and with a cheap smile, she asked if it was a busy night. Politely, I told her that it was a bad one while simultaneously ordering my Cafecito and Colada to go. Then, I overheard her say to the other girls how she had been arrested years prior by my old '50 Sector' crew. Suddenly, all those eyes stared in my direction before they began to devilishly laugh. I grabbed my order from the counter, smiled and politely told them to be careful. The way I figured it, this was all a game, and everyone has their part. I did not take what these girls did personally, surely, I was not going to judge their motives. Some needed the money to live and some to deal with their drug habits. But the more I looked at them and what they did to earn money, I began thinking of Lena Miranda. A mother who worked hard attempting to provide for her small child and avoiding the humiliation of having to sell her body. Still, here she was, having to come to grips with a situation that no parent wants, the heart wrenching deed of having to bury a child that was brutally murdered.

I finished drinking my Cafecito, left a few dollars on the counter and took the Colada. Police officers were never charged for café, but it was a habit to leave the equivalent of the cost and a little extra. Hell, we all know why they do not charge police officers; it is cheap security. As I walked toward my vehicle, the girl from the counter yelled out, "Stay safe detective, you're alright!" I smiled at her and entered my vehicle. Once inside, I reached for my Bible and entered a notation of having stopped at this spot for café.

Shifting my vehicle into gear, it began moving toward the station which was five blocks away. I grabbed my police radio from its charger and spoke with Det. Alvarez, letting him know I would be arriving within ten minutes. Now, these were crazy times in the City of Miami police department, filled with colorful characters. So, as I approached the rear gate to enter the main headquarters, the last thing I expected was to see an officer barbecuing. Dumbfounded, I came to a complete stop, shockingly realizing it was my old friend officer Celo.

Filled with curiosity, I rolled down my window, sheepishly asking, "What the hell are you doing, are you crazy?" Waiting for his response, all I could do was laugh.

As Ofc. Celo was flipping his burgers, he calmly replied, "I've been assigned to this back gate for two days, they never relieve me for dinner, so I decided to bring the grill. Do you want one?" he asked. This to him was like another day at the office and normal.

"Dude, if the Chief gets wind of this, they are going to send you to Dr. Axelrod!" We looked at each other waiting to see who would speak first. This moment was so bizarre that we began to laugh hysterically. With that, I rolled up my window, and drove off while he continued flipping burgers. This moment was the perfect antidote, I had not laughed with such enthusiasm in a long time. It could not have come at a more perfect moment. Driving my vehicle up the ramp, a parking spot was available in front of prisoner processing. *Perfect*, I thought. This was prime parking, right next to the elevator that will take me to the homicide office, located on the 5th floor. Before exiting my vehicle, I wrote some additional notes. Subconsciously, I believe I stayed writing just to gather my composure.

"Holly shit," I thought out loud. As I finished writing my notes, I suddenly realized, I had written more than ten pages of notes. This meant one thing, my initial 301 Report, which is a summary for Command Staff of an incident being investigated was going to be longer than most. Additionally, this was a good indicator that the final supplemental report was going to be long, probably 35 to 50 pages. Even though I was extremely confident that this investigation was going to be closed by arrest soon, barring any curveballs, much would depend on what the witnesses and offender had to say during their interviews. You see, there are times during an investigation when the follow-up investigation takes longer than initially intended.

Just as I was exiting my vehicle, some officers from the midnight shift were staggering up the ramp making their way into the station. Many were meeting with their supervisors to turn in reports while others were heading toward the property unit to pick-up evidence needed for court. Slowly, I walked toward the ramps retaining wall where several detectives from day shift were smoking and drinking café before going upstairs. We spoke for a few minutes but mainly about sports. Once our conversation concluded, we turned and watched as the sunrise slowly started to creep around the rear corner of the police station's walls. It created a soothing glow and a reminder that a new day had begun. Another night ended but evil committed its deed. "Shit," I cried out, running toward the elevator. I wanted to get to my desk and call my house before the girls went off to school. The need to hear their sweet voices was indescribable. After a night like this one, there would be no better medicine than the sound of my girls. They are the keepers of my sanity.

Perfect timing, upon reaching the elevator; the door opened, seeing that no one was inside, I pressed the button to the fifth floor. The doors closed without anyone else entering and I made the quiet trip to the fifth floor where all the violent crime units were located yawning. The elevator doors opened with difficulty, but those on the fifth floor did not notice, they were busy as usual. Several investigators were heading toward their respective units, Robbery, Burglary, Sexual Battery, and Homicide. While most of the units were on the east side of the 5th floor, Homicide stood all alone. The sensitive nature of Homicide was conducive to having an area totally separated from the other units. This was understandable due to the nature of the unit.

It was rare to see investigators from other units in the homicide section unless they were summoned. The stigma of homicide investigators being superior or better than other investigators is over-rated. We are not better than other investigators, we just have to be better prepared and trained. The skill sets of a homicide investigator is what defines us. The nature of a homicide investigation is rigorous, it has a way of taking its toll on those who cannot handle them mentally. It has always been said that homicide investigators are a breed apart, maybe because our expectations are higher and responsibilities greater. If one were to make an analogy, being part of a homicide unit is like being in the NFL or Big Leagues, except we do not make the big money. We accept our responsibility knowing that our good work goes unnoticed 99% of the time and the 1% that did not go well gets blasted on every network or media platform.

The secret is not to be a part of an elite unit, like Homicide, it is remaining, which can only happen if one produces. Investigators are responsible to work their cases diligently, arresting those who commit horrific acts and successfully assisting prosecutors prosecute the correct offenders. Homicide investigators are the only ones that can speak for their dead victims, all other investigators have the luxury of live victims. Homicide investigators are always under the microscope. They are scrutinized at every turn by many who have never worked on a Major investigation, given a deposition, or testified in open court.

Entering the waiting area of the Homicide Unit, I noticed several of the people who were sleeping inside apartment #3. Some were seated on the chairs and those seated on the couch were leaning on each other. These were the same people who really could not provide much information at the incident location, but I needed them away from the crime scene while it was being processed. Besides, I did not want them present when the body of our victim was removed. One of the transporting patrol officers was in the waiting room with them to avoid them from discussing the incident with each other. As an investigator, you never allow for unattended witnesses to sit or be together, they might exchange information about a case, and it creates a problem later in the investigation. I shook the officer's hand and told him not to let them speak about the case. He nodded his head as the swishing sound of my keycard was made, allowing me to enter the homicide office.

This section was off limits to all officers, including some chiefs and for good reason, there were too many sensitive documents on top of investigators desks that had limited access. Not that homicide units are secret squirrel societies, but information or data from the homicide board should not be known too just anyone. Sensitive information was disseminated on a need-to-know basis until the right time presented itself. Unfortunately, cases are so fluid that information constantly changes. Sometimes those changes cause people to believe one is hiding the truth.

Upon entering the office, I saw Det. Alvarez sitting at his desk which was directly across from the interview room where the offender, Laudin, was waiting. "Here, I brought some Cuban café for you," I said. Immediately, he jumped to his feet as if he had just won the lotto, "Awesome dude," he replied. Like everyone else, he knew the value of a good shot of Cuban café. While he was pouring and drinking his Cafecito, he briefed me on what he had learned thus far in the investigation. There was nothing earth shattering, just generalities directly from his Bible. This pleased me because at least he was writing down notes based on what he observed.

I asked him where he had placed Laudin, he advised me that he was inside interview room #1. Alvarez let me know that thus far, Laudin was calm and courteous. That was a good sign, maybe I will get lucky and this monster will not invoke his 5th Amendment. "Great!" I exclaimed. With that, I turned and walked toward interview room #1. It was important to introduce myself to Laudin and ask him if he wanted anything to drink or if he needed to use the bathroom. This introduction was critical, it would set the tone for the interview that was to follow. Furthermore, I wanted him to feel comfortable with me by providing him a simple consideration.

Upon approaching interview room #1, I placed my Bible on the table outside of the room, opened the door and observed Laudin sitting on the chair located along the far wall of the room. To put things in perspective, each interview room is eight feet by ten feet, a green carpet covers the walls and floor, with white acoustic panels covering the ceiling. The rooms are always cool with one table and three chairs. Laudin had his head on the table with his arms alongside of it. Observing how he was positioned, I thought it was a weird way to lay your head. Usually, one folds their arms and places their head on top, it is more comfortable. But, as I examined Laudin closer, I noticed what appeared to be dried blood on his hands. I surmised, that is why he did not rest his head on them. I took a mental note of that and began to introduce myself. He raised his head slowly at which time I told him my name in Spanish, further telling him that I was the lead investigator for this incident. He acknowledged me and with a soft voice said his name was Laudin Matte. I asked him if he wanted anything to drink or to use the bathroom. He informed me that he was fine and did not want anything.

Once we got the introductions out of the way, something caught my eye looking at his hands closer, I was now convinced it was blood on his hands. Not wanting to waste more time, I let Laudin know that I would return in a few minutes to speak with him. He looked at me and in

Spanish said, "Alright." Stepping out of the interview room, I closed the door behind me and motioned to Det. Alvarez who had returned to his desk to complete his 301 report regarding this incident. I told him to contact any CSI technician in the office and have them respond to our office immediately.

"What happened?" asked Det. Alvarez.

"You did not see the blood all over his hands," I asked.

"Not really, when I checked up on him, his head was on the table and I didn't want to bother him," he replied. Typical novice mistake, not paying close attention to details. These are things that can make or break a case.

While he rushed out of the office to find any available CSI technician in the building, I began to write down my observations in my Bible. I shook my head in amazement because of the number of notes which had been written. I cracked open the interview room's door and found Laudin in the same position as the first time I saw him. His head was on the table and his hands were alongside of it, as if nothing had happened. He was knocked out, probably drained from his deed.

I closed the door softly. As it shut, CSI Tech. Seinfeld entered the homicide office with Det. Alvarez. "What do you got, Pep?" he asked.

I apprised him of my observations regarding Laudin's hands and told him that he needed to be completely processed and there was no time to waste. Photographs had to be taken, especially of his hands, which also had to be swabbed. The swab was crucial in determining if the blood on his hands were from the victim or someone else. I told CSI Seinfeld, "Make sure you take measurements of his hands, I believe he might have self-inflicted offensive wounds caused by the knife we found at the crime scene." CSI Seinfeld informed me that CSI Bonny was about to clear the crime scene, so, upon hearing that information, I told him to hold off on processing Laudin. Not that I did not trust CSI Seinfeld, we had worked on other cases, but I wanted to maintain the integrity of this case and use individuals who were originally assigned to assist with the investigation.

After speaking with CSI Seinfeld and explaining my thought process for this request, I walked to my desk, picked up my police radio and had dispatch direct Det. Gonzo to switch to the Tac channel. Upon hearing dispatch's instructions, I switched to the Tac channel and waited for Det. Gonzo to acknowledge. "3161, are you on?" he asked.

Without any fluff, I asked him if CSI Bonny had cleared the crime scene.

"He's just pulling off," he responded. I instructed him to remain on the scene until I was finished with the interviews. I wanted to make sure that someone from my team was present in the event we got additional information that needed to be verified.

Surely, Bonny would be at the station within 15–20 minutes, which gave me enough time to get ready for the interview of Laudin. Det. Alvarez returned from wherever it was that he went, grabbed his Bible, and stood next to me. I immediately advised him of the situation and reasoning for me wanting to have Laudin processed. Something that should have been done sooner had Det. Alvarez observed the bloody hands. *It was an honest mistake so I won't bust his balls yet*, I thought, but it will happen at the appropriate time. He was now busy writing down everything I said, he even added notations as to why I requested Laudin's hands to be processed. That gave me hope for him, it showed initiative, something my other greenhorn had yet to demonstrate.

# Chapter 13

It is amazing how one can relive such a horrendous event so many times over knowing its collateral damage. From day one, I knew this incident was never going away. It did not matter how hard I tried to block out the horror. The Cause and Effects of this incident is what continued to flash inside my head. Shortly after leaving the scene, it was evident that my view of the world and of certain people had suddenly changed, impacting me deeply. Freely, I admit being a crusader once, wanting to save everyone and seek out justice for the dead. This cavalier approach was a nice attempt at making things right within my universe.

But in the end, I had to come to grips with the facts that my victims are still dead. And, has justice really been served? Sure, arrests are made, and trials are a way of moving the justice narrative forward but in reality, have we been able to satisfy the victims or their relatives? This incident for me has been a complete eye opener. There are times when I find myself intently gazing at my daughters, wondering what kind of life my victim would have lived.

Yes, an arrest was made, and I am waiting for the final verdict of an undeserving individual for a cruel act committed against an innocent child. My victim was dead and will remain dead still, her family will grieve her violent demise forever. Unfortunately, the final verdict will never erase the magnitude of the gruesome act itself. It can never heal the emotional scares it has left on those who worked this case, especially mine.

So, here I was, sitting inside courtroom 2–3 waiting in anticipation just like the rest of the gallery. Will justice truly be served today and if so, will it be enough? Has everything I have done during this investigation been sufficient to complete my task? Were my efforts adequate to satisfy a still grieving mother and a family desperate for justice? Would the results bring continued pride to myself and to my unit or would it bring disappointment because of unforced mistakes?

These were the thoughts lingering deep in the recesses of my mind. Failure was not an option for this case, there would be no excuse if that were the result. While time continued to pass, doubt kept creeping in my mind as I continued finding myself reliving bits and pieces of the investigation. In doing so, it reinforced my commitment to professionalism as well as the good work that was done by my team. This might have been my case, but I fully understand that every successful investigation has a supporting cast who in concert are lock step with the lead investigator's vision.

An unwanted anxiety fell over me, as if I were swimming in shark infested waters. Suddenly, a little voice inside me said, "What more could one expect, you're only human." This uneasy feeling was made worse by my constant fidgeting about the pew on which I was seated. Had a rag been glued to my ass, it would have brought out a perfect shine to the pew, that is how much I was squirming. A human buffer, that is what I must have looked like to those around me. Thank God for that little piece of wall on which I would rest my head, it kept me from moving as much. What it did not do was keep my mind from wondering about this incident. Its violence and gore were tattooed to my brain.

There are many variables that play a role while conducting a major investigation and one must be prepared for each. Investigators must be ready when changes present themselves and trust me, one will at some point during an investigation. It was no different during this investigation, like when Det. Alvarez overlooked the bloody hands of Laudin in the homicide office. That minor infraction could have meant changing my course of action if Laudin had somehow managed to wipe the blood from his hands. Fortunately, he did not, and I was able to observe the dried blood caked to his hands. Just like having various non-investigators assisting me at the crime scene because Det. Gonzo was not present. These were minor situations, setbacks, but they had to be dealt with in a manner that maintained this investigations integrity. These minor issues were replayed in my mind, unlike instant replay in sports, there are no do overs during an investigation, especially one like this one. Referees can overturn a bad call; investigators will lose a case on a wrong decision. From the moment I entered the investigative arena, I realized the stakes were higher, responsibilities greater and the results are life altering. This is real life, not a game.

The anticipation could be felt all over the courtroom, yet there was an eerie calm which filled this consecrate room.

Everyone was gearing up for what could happen, one way or another. Hopefully, this verdict would go my way. I would not be in the mood to answer questions posed by reporters if this case were lost. Why was I thinking this way? State Attorney, Randall Reid, had thus far managed to keep the defense attorney, Erin George, on the run with his constant attack and dissection of her claim that Laudin was insane when he committed this horrific act.

It is amazing how every coward reverts to being insane after they are caught, still, defense attorneys, like Erin, will use this lame defense as a fallback strategy. Defense attorneys do everything possible to find so called experts who will testify on a defendant's behalf. Undoubtedly, Erin will try to convince the jury that this monster suffered from being emasculated. Living in a male dominant society, he would exaggerate public displays to mask his personal inadequacy. Like all good defense attorneys, she will attempt to sway the jury that all of Laudin's problems stem from a traumatic childhood, one that cannot be verified. This strategy, being employed by Erin George was pathetic but it was her responsibility to make every effort on behalf of her client. Hell, Laudin is no more insane than I am Superman. Hopefully, the psychiatrist used to examine him will be able to speak today since he was on the list of those who were going to say a few words.

Insane, crazy, this defendant was none of that. He was a straight up piece of shit. Somebody who has always preyed on the weak and inflicted pain to those who would not fight back. Although he was treated above and beyond reasonable, this subhuman would never have survived in another day and age. Fortunately for him, this is the United

States and not Honduras. In this great country the rule of law still applies equally to all, whether you are an illegal or citizen. Here was a man who came to this country after fleeing from his for transgressions only known to him. Instead of turning the page and becoming productive, upon settling in Miami, he continued to be a parasite on society. And yet, he is being afforded the absolute best defense possible at no cost to him. He must have been content knowing that taxpayers were flipping the bill.

In my opinion, Laudin is no lunatic. The more I think about that night, when we first met, his demeanor was one of a timid man. That was my first memory of the monster. After my initial introduction, I remember reentering interview room #1 with Det. Alvarez. Having spent so much time at the crime scene, I wanted to interview Laudin first. I felt confident having all the pertinent information needed to conduct this interview. But before conducting the interview, I informed Det. Alvarez of my strategy. Like a bobblehead doll, his head swiveled up and down in agreement. What else was he going to do, he did not know any better.

Once I explained myself to my young detective, we entered interview room #1 and sat down across the table from Laudin. As before, he slowly lifted his head off the table and sat straight. In Spanish, I again introduced myself and Det. Alvarez. We informed him the reason for being brought to the homicide office. Upon carefully explaining to him the reason, he was read his Constitutional Rights in Spanish. As I read each right, he read it along with me. Once each right was read, he would place his initials on the designated location where it read yes or no. He initialed every yes, meaning that he understood each right. When I finished reading his Constitutional Rights as per the form, he was presented with the document and reviewed it calmly.

Once he concluded rereading it, he signed it at the bottom of the section which signified that he was willing to speak with Det. Alvarez and myself. Immediately following his agreement to speak with us, I showed him the Search by Consent form.

As he held and examined the document, I asked if he recalled giving detectives' verbal consent to search earlier in the morning. He shook his head yes. With the Search by Consent form in his hand, I also read it in Spanish along with him. He finished reading it, looked at me and told me that he had agreed earlier but still agreed to the search. Based on his response, I had him sign the Search by Consent form. Now that he signed both his Constitutional Rights and Search by Consent forms, I was ready. So far so good, Laudin was being more cooperative than I could have imagined.

It was hours later when I learned that Det. Gonzo had Laudin sign the Search by Consent form earlier, but he never told me. These small errors can come back to hinder an investigation, especially in one such as this one. For this reason, communication is vital throughout any investigation, especially a homicide case. Unfortunately, this young investigator failed in his duty to effectively communicate and being new in the unit was an unacceptable excuse.

Just as we finished with our administrative responsibilities, I heard a knock on the interview room's door, it was CSI Bonny. Apparently, CSI Seinfeld ran into him as he stepped out of the fifth-floor elevator and told him I was looking for him. I politely excused myself from Laudin and told him I would return shortly. Det. Alvarez and I stepped out of interview room #2 and walked toward our team's pod. All of us stood by my desk as I briefed Bonny on the offensive wounds that were observed on Laudin's hands. It was during this briefing that suggestions were made on how best to process his hands. CSI Bonny agreed with my strategy, then proceeded to tell me to wait while he retrieved his camera and a swab kit. The swab kit is a tool used to collect DNA samples for analysis by the crime lab.

While Bonny left the office to retrieve his equipment, I told Det. Alvarez to check on and ask our subject if he wanted any water or café. As Det. Alvarez walked toward Interview room #1, I continued writing notes in my Bible. Too many things were going on simultaneously and I needed to catch up quickly, if not, it was going to be hell when writing the supplemental report. Additionally, waiting these few minutes were a blessing for me. It gave me time to continue formulating my game plan while taking a quick breather. This moment of mental rest was desperately needed to conserve my energy.

Looking up from my desk, there was Det. Alvarez walking again toward interview room #1, this time holding a Coke can, which must be for Laudin since he did not drink soda. "Did you see Bonny?" I asked.

"Yeah, he was in the hallway," he responded.

I remember thinking, *great, the sooner Bonny gets here the better.* You see, I wanted to get on with the interview because too much time had passed, and now time was working against me. During a short pause from writing in my Bible, Bonny entered the homicide office. "Dude, are you ready?" I asked.

"Yes sir," he replied. That was awesome, now it should not take him long to photograph and complete the processing of Laudin. It was important to make sure that his hands were documented for their injuries and the blood stains swabbed. This procedure would be conducted quickly, thus allowing me to resume the interview.

The door to interview room #1 was opened, Bonny entered as I stood at the door to ensure that Laudin would not do anything stupid. Hell, it would not be the first or last time that a desperate offender lashes out at an unsuspecting member of law enforcement while in-custody. Playing it safe, I engaged him with idle chit chat while my technician proceeded with the processing. As Laudin stood near the rear wall of interview room #1, I noticed a reddish smudge on the white top of the table where he had been seated. "Make sure to document and process the table," I told Bonny. "Once I'm done with him, I'll get to it," he replied. It did not take Bonny long to finish processing our subject and the table. Today Bonny was on fire with his work; he was quick but thorough. Such diligence was not a Bonny trademark.

Upon concluding, Bonny placed his processing instruments inside his CSI bag and carefully secured his expensive Nikon camera in its housing. Once everything was secured, he picked up his bags and swab kit before exiting the interview room. Walking past me, he let me know that everything he had done would be entered in his report before leaving for the day. I thanked him and told him that a briefing with everyone involved case was going to be held after the interviews were completed. As he turned and walked away, he raised his hand while simultaneously nodding his head. Suddenly, I found myself thinking, *it has been a long night for everyone involved with this investigation, at least both CSI technicians are going home sooner than some of us. They will return tonight and catch up on their administrative duties, while I on the other hand, have no idea when going home would be possible. These interviews will give me an idea of how much longer this day was going to last, but for now, my team was going on pure adrenalin.*

Once Bonny left the interview room, I remember saying to myself, "It's time dude." I opened the interview room door and made my way toward the table where evil was seated. As I sat on the chair placed in front of this monster, Det. Alvarez quietly sat down next to me. He knew what his responsibilities were, write everything down, listen, stay quiet and follow my lead. This was not done to minimize him, quite the contrary, but done as a rite of passage. You see, one day, he was going to be a lead on a homicide investigation, and he needed to be properly mentored and prepared. While seated, we found ourselves starring at evil for about a minute, with an uneasy silence that engulfed the interview room. The silence was deafening, literally, I could hear the pen as its point rolled on the paper while Det. Alvarez wrote. It was at that precise moment, when the silence needed to be broken, if not, this interview was going to be over before it even began.

So, I immediately began speaking with Laudin in a diminutive voice, going over the initial information gathered in my bible. The most basic of conversations, his general information. How easy, what a concept to breaking the ice. I made it a point to maintain eye-contact with him throughout our conversation, without judgement or condemnation. I wanted him to feel comfortable, that we were treating him as a man and with respect. Having a rapport with him was crucial in getting him to spit out a confession, even then, it was not guaranteed. Although I felt comfortable with the case, a confession would be the icing on the cake but then again, I was dealing with an individual who just mutilated an innocent victim.

Maybe it was out of sheer anger or jealousy. In a moment of human weakness and cowards, he unleashed his frustration on a defenseless child. Deep inside, I wanted, no, I needed to know the reason why because I knew this case was going to haunt me forever. Only a confession would give us his reason and at the same time help me to better understand the reason for committing such an atrocious act. Selfishly, I wanted to obtain a confession to heal.

During our introductory conversation, I was able to obtain Laudin's basic information. He was cordial, receptive, and displayed a calm demeanor, as if nothing had happened. In a soft voice, he informed me that he was born in Honduras and entered the United States illegally. He further stated he was born in 1968 and was currently living where the incident occurred, 481 SW 9 St. Apt 3. After obtaining these basic details, I glanced at Det. Alvarez who diligently had been writing down every word. He looked back and nodded his head, this told me he was ready to continue writing. The interview continued, I explained to Laudin once again who I was and why he was brought to the police station. He looked at me and shook his head. He was told that it was important to hear his side of what happened to ensure that there were no misunderstandings.

Furthermore, I explained that there were always two sides to a story. How his side was just as important as anything and would help resolve certain concerns with this case. Taking a deep breath, Laudin's eyes welted with tears. He looked at both of us sorrowfully, appearing ready to unload the heavy burden from his chest, when suddenly he exhaled and said softly, "I want to tell you everything that happened and why." Feeling that a confession was forthcoming, I told him that I was proud of him as a man for the courage to do what was right. He softly shook his head in agreement, then, like a batter who is waiting for a fastball, out of the blue came the curve. Alvarez and I looked up in total disbelief when he uttered the words I did not want to hear, "I want an attorney." My heart sunk, Laudin was not stupid after all, he was calculating. He knew exactly what he did. Unfortunately, at this stage in the game he was not going to admit to anyone his transgression. So, there went the interview, dead in its tracks without a confession. Once he invoked his Constitutional Right to self-incrimination, all questionings had to stop. This phase was over.

Disappointed at this moment, I quietly stood up while Det. Alvarez, still in shock, began picking up the case file. Looking indignantly into Laudin eyes as if a bolt of lightning were shooting out, he was informed very professionally that based on the current evidence along with the witness's statements, I was charging him with First Degree Murder. He immediately replied, "I understand." While closing the interview room's door, I looked at Det.

Alvarez and told him, "A coward will always be a coward, now he's out for self-preservation." Totally disheartened by what had just occurred, I walked dejectedly to my desk. Deep inside I thought for sure he would confess but he did not. That goes to show that even with the best laid out plans, things can go south in a heartbeat. This was another dagger into Lena, his girlfriend's, spirit. Painfully, I questioned myself, "What happened, what went wrong?" But there was no time for such questions, for me to second guess myself was a moot point.

There was going to be plenty of time for analysis. Besides, now I needed to press forward in preparation for a trial that would come sooner than expected. Although this case was strong, it had to be solid. There could be no more slipups, that was not an option. Still, in the back of my mind I kept thinking, *maybe I should have left the crime scene sooner.* Although, taking a chance on a blind interrogation with minimal information was contrary to any sound strategy. It might have worked on this one. Well, it is too late now. Now, ASA Ruby Sole had to be informed and it was my responsibility to explain to her what happened. Besides, there were additional interviews that needed to be conducted. My confidence did not diminish from not getting the confession, certainly, once the rest of the interviews were finished, this case would be just as solid. So, I arrived at my desk and picked up my phone's receiver and began dialing Ruby's office.

With the receiver against my ear, I sunk down on my chair and grabbed a blank 301 report from my drawer. I remember holding it with my fingers, staring at it, trying to find a way to start writing my initial account of this incident.

Man, I was upset at myself for not obtaining Laudin's confession. *Was that just my pride? It better not be*, I thought, this case was not about me and far from being lost. I had to refocus, reengage, and redirect my energy toward the other facets of this investigation. In presenting the best case forward, it did not matter if Laudin confessed or not, the undisputed evidence and testimonies from key witnesses would send him straight to hell. *Just do your job*, I thought, it will all turn out fine in the end.

I placed the blank 301 form down on my desk, not wanting to write anything yet and listened to ASA Sole's phone ringing. I pushed the speaker button on my phone and continued listening to the ringing on the other end. While waiting on the line for an answer, I called out to Tania, our unit's Victim Advocate, who happened to have wondered into the office. "Can you bring me some coffee?"

"Do I look like a maid?" she replied.

"Oh come on, be a sweetheart!" I exclaimed. As I continued working at my desk while waiting for ASA Sole to answer, I saw a hand holding a cup filled with coffee.

Tania placed the cup on my desk and said, "Here you go, only because you've been working all night."

"Thank you," I replied. She smiled and walked away. I could still hear ASA Soles's phone ringing, when suddenly it stopped and a voice on the line answered, "hello." Finally, Ruby picked up her receiver.

# Chapter 14

Now it was my turn, "Hi Ruby, sorry for the bother so early," I responded. Hell, I knew she had been waiting for my call, I just wanted to be as polite as possible, considering the news I was about to drop on her. News that she was not expecting. "No problem Pepi, I was getting ready to head to the office. What's up?" she asked.

There was no way around the obvious and I was sure that Ruby could sense it in my voice. "It didn't go how I planned it!" I exclaimed, "I had it set up, went over Miranda with him and the Consent to Search, he was receptive, speaking with me but once we got to the part of hearing his side of the facts, he stated that he wanted to say everything but invoked his rights." Dejected and pissed, I took a moment before continuing.

"So, I immediately stopped my interview and informed him he was being charged with 1st Degree Murder." There was a slight pause before Ruby's response, then, she asked if I felt comfortable with the arrest. That was a crazy question, but I guess she just wanted to hear the tone in my voice as well as my conviction. "Absolutely, there is no doubt this is a righteous arrest and should be a perfect Death Penalty case," I replied.

Ruby agreed with my assessment but suggested that there was much more to be done. Pleasantly, I agreed with her and provided my game plan. Having worked with me in the past, she knew my reputation and was comfortable knowing that I was not going to leave any stone left unturned. Before hanging up, I let her know that I had additional interviews lined-up and would keep her informed if there were any developments. She thanked me for briefing her then told me that if I needed anything that would help expedite the investigation to contact her immediately.

No sooner had I placed the receiver on the phone's holder, Det. Alvarez planted his ass on my desk. "Well, what did she say?" he asked. "Was she pissed?" I looked up at him and with a stern voice told him to find another seat. He got the message and returned to his desk but not before asking me if there was anything else that needed to be done.

"Yeah," I responded, "there are additional interviews that must be conducted." Excitedly, he nodded his head and stated he was going to call his wife to let her know that he would not be going home anytime soon. *Welcome to Homicide*, I thought, this was just the first of many times when you will not be going home at the time you thought.

While gathering my thoughts, I could hear the day-shift crew entering the homicide office, they were joking and shooting the shit. Sure, they were fresh and had just returned from having breakfast. "Must be nice," I shouted, "the least you guys could have done was bring some Cuban Café." All of them began to laugh, you see, working days was not as hectic as working midnights. They mostly handled the routine Natural or Accidental deaths. Sure, they worked homicide cases but as overflows when the afternoon or midnight squads got swamped. It was uncommon for a homicide to occur during the day shift hours, unless it happened prior to their shift beginning. Traditionally, senior investigators worked day shift to avoid the non-stop action. Very few senior investigators, like me, enjoyed midnights. That is when all the action took place, I could not work the day shift schedule, it was too mind-numbing. Little action and too many bosses walking around.

Well, once this moment of levity past, I called out to my shadow. His head popped up from behind his desk, "ready whenever you are Pep," he replied. "Good, let's get started, there's a lot of work to do," I told him. I got up from my chair and grabbed the case file that was laying on my desk. All I needed to continue working was contained inside. Right now, my primary mission was to conduct as many interviews as possible before going home. The most important one for me was that of Lena, the victim's mother. I knew some of the witnesses had been interviewed earlier, at least preliminary interviews, by my team. Now, I had to listen to each witness to ensure they did not change what they said earlier or had additional information that was pertinent to this case.

Satisfied that there were no changes, their statements would be immortalized and used during preparation for trial. It was important to make sure that all statements were recorded. Investigators, like witnesses do not always remember every single detail years later. Sometimes, stories change if one tries to just rely on memory but if the interview is recorded, it makes it easier to remember or clarify any discrepancies found.

Besides, defense attorneys love to have cases drag on, they figure the longer it takes to go to trial, the easier it is for witnesses to disappear or just forget what their original statements were. Maybe, they simply or expediently forget important details. These are specific points that jurors listen to during trial and sometimes the bad guy wins. How convenient.

Upon reviewing all the witness statements, I was focused on one, given by Mr. Claro Hipolito. He was truly clear and seemed to remember specific details about the incident and the offender's demeanor. Det. Alvarez and I reviewed Mr. Claro Hipolito's statement since it was Det. Alvarez that initially interviewed him. Once I felt comfortable with how the initial interview was conducted, I asked Det. Alvarez to introduce me to the witness. As we walked toward the interview room, I took a minute and requested our dispatcher to send an officer to the homicide office for a prisoner transport. This was a typical request, one that was welcomed by patrol officers since they got credit for an arrest. Investigators enjoy the glory of capturing offenders and clearing cases, but we allowed patrol officers to take the arrest statistic, especially the officers that are always helping us out when we need them. This request was confirmed, and the dispatcher advised me that a patrol unit would be responding soon to the homicide office.

Now that I got that out of the way, we continued walking toward the interview room. We entered the room and seated on the chair was Mr. Claro Hipolito, he looked nervous but calm while sipping on a cup of coffee. One look at him and I could tell he had been worn out during his thirty some years. His features were more of a man in his early fifties, not thirties. His looks really did not matter at this point, but it told another story. Still, I needed his cooperation and testimony. My mission now was to solidify this investigation, nothing could be left to chance.

While Det. Alvarez was setting up, I extended my arm, introduced myself to Mr. Claro Hipolito and shook his hand. He did not speak English so the interview would be conducted in Spanish. Having the ability to speak multiple languages fluently is a great asset. Miami is a vibrant city with a vast colorful ensemble of cultures, from Central and South America to those from the Caribbean in addition to tourists from all over the globe. Det. Alvarez spoke Spanish but not fluently, especially when it came down to certain slangs used by those from other Latin American countries. So, with this in mind, I again had him scribe our interview before the sworn statement was taken.

I briefly informed Mr. Hipolito what my purpose was and why his cooperation would be so vital. His nervousness was visible, and he informed me that he wanted to cooperate as much as possible because the victim did not deserve to die in such a manner. I thanked him for his civic duty and for standing up to injustice. He looked at us with a pouty face, then took a deep breath. Upon regaining his composure, he said he was ready to do what was right. Thanking him again, we immediately began our conversation with respect to what he knew about this murder. The longer he spoke while recounting what he remembered, it seemed that his nerves settled. He was very articulate and detailed with regards to what he observed and heard. It became obvious that his nervousness was caused by what had been witnessed and nothing else.

Upon concluding my review of the preliminary interview with Mr. Hipolito, I provided him the opportunity to make any corrections he felt were necessary to effectively depict what he wanted to express. I specifically wanted to ensure that nothing was lost in translation between him and Det. Alvarez during the earlier interview. He understood everything I was explaining, and he appeared willing and eager to assist us with the investigation. Like any normal person being questioned by police investigators, he had been nervous but deliberate, not hesitant to answer questions. It could have been different had my approach been aggressive. Understand, he was in this country illegally, he could have shut down and decide that his testimony was not worth his deportation. Throughout the initial stages of our interview, I continued to assure this man that my concern was to solve this case, not his immigration status. This was not a lie; I could have cared less about his status. My main concern and focus were for him to speak with me without fear of retribution for his cooperation. Besides, unless he committed a crime, no one in law enforcement was going to just stop him and ask his immigration status.

As the interview intensified, he seemed more at ease with me and opened up. He came to the United States from his country, Honduras, to find work and help support his family who were still living there. He has been living in Miami for the past two years, wherever he could until meeting Laudin who proposed an option. Because of his circumstances, he accepted Laudin's offer to move in with him, his girlfriend Lena and others from Honduras. They were all living in the cramped Little Havana apartment for the past year and a half. This was not what he wanted but beggars cannot be choosers.

Besides, Laudin and the others were fellow countrymen trying to help each other in a foreign country. The victim was the daughter of Laudin's girlfriend from another man. She was an incredibly happy little girl, everyone in the house helped take care of her while her mother worked. Momentarily, he became visibly emotional while speaking of the victim and could only say, "how could something like this happen." I consoled him and told him to continue his observations from earlier.

He resumed by telling me that he worked odd jobs every day and would stand on the corner of 10 Ave SW 8 Street every morning starting at 6 am for a chance at finding work. Desperation forced him to work with any of the various job pools that preyed on those needing work. His specialty was construction or landscaping. He tried to work as much as possible because he did not earn much. He felt exploited but knew that he had to work multiple jobs if was to bring his family from Honduras. But still bore the burden of responsibility to send as much money to his family in Honduras. After sending what he could, whatever amount was left over went to pay his share of the expenses. This seemed a small price to pay, considering his options.

For that reason, he did not mind living with other people because it afforded him the ability to have extra money for himself, plus the meals were shared among those living in the apartment. But he conceded that living like this was not ideal. He would have enjoyed a simple efficiency, but even that was more expensive. Our interview was filled with many different topics to ease his anguish, but it mainly focused on the incident.

Once we concluded with the basic information, he advised that he got home from work late and was very tired. After waiting to take a shower, he ate a small meal consisting of leftovers and decided to go to bed around 9 pm. He was unable to get much sleep because throughout the night, he kept getting woken up by Laudin who was making noises while pacing around the apartment, going outside then coming inside continuously. He would enter the bedroom where the victim had been sleeping, three or four times.

The last time he saw him enter the bedroom, he heard him say, "You're going to regret this, you're going to Cry Tears of Blood!" As soon as he shut the bedroom door, the police entered the apartment. They went directly to the bedroom and tried to enter, calling out his name. While this was happening, other police officers began waking up the others in the apartment and escorting them outside. Mr. Hipolito could hear the police officers at the bedroom door pleading with Laudin to open it, but he refused to do so. The police officers asked another resident to assist them, that resident called out to Laudin and asked him to open the bedroom door. This went on for about two or three minutes, but it seemed like an eternity. Just as he began to exit the apartment, he saw the police kick down the bedroom door and bring out the offender, Laudin. The police officers stayed inside the apartment not letting anyone enter the bedroom and some stayed outside with the residents. At a distance, he could see Lena, the victim's mother. She was screaming and crying. The police officers allowed some of the residents to enter the apartment to gather some clothes. While he was getting his belongings, he curiously looked inside the bedroom and saw blood on the bed sheets. It happened so fast; he did not realize whose it was.

He continued by saying that he has known the offender for some time and noticed that Laudin had been having arguments with Lena daily for several months. Sometimes, it would get physical. He would punch her for no reason, but never did anything to the baby. Mr. Hipolito began to cry and stated that he had never seen anything like this in his life and could not believe it happened. He raved about how sweet the victim was, always laughing and playing. After calming him down, I asked if everything he had said was the truth, he replied that there was nothing to lie about. We concluded going over the preliminary interview and the sworn statement was recorded.

The sworn statement went just as smooth with no surprises. Mr. Hipolito remained composed. I thanked him for his assistance and how his cooperation was crucial in bringing justice to an innocent child. Det. Alvarez escorted him to the waiting room to be transported back to the apartment. The distinct look of horror was still on his face as he walked out of the interview room. Surely, he did not expect to be involved with such an incident when he decided to come to this country. I could only imagine what was going through his mind, seeing something so horrific and knowing everyone involved. These types of incidents are the ones that give birth to nightmares.

My adrenaline was on full throttle, there was no time to relax thinking of the next important interview coming up.

Det. Alvarez was now beginning to slow down. "Dude take a shot of coffee and don't sit down," I told him. I knew that if he got into a comfortable position or found a spot to chill, he would be worthless to me and I needed him to be sharp, at least for the next hour. He wanted to be in homicide, well, welcome to the big leagues. One had to be committed in this unit. There were going to be days like this, and he needed to get used to it or find another unit.

Just as a precaution, I had him go to the waiting room and ask Mr. Hipolito if he wanted anything to drink. I sent him on this errand to allow me to gather my thoughts and to keep him alert and busy. Det. Alvarez returned from the waiting room and told me that Mr. Hipolito felt better and was being transported to the apartment by one of the day shift detectives who was heading toward that area. *Awesome*, I thought, *one less thing to worry about*. Besides, I would be following up with the witnesses later tonight or early tomorrow. Then, I grabbed the coffee mug sitting on Det. Alvarez's desk, gave it to him and told him to fill it before we started interviewing Lena. "Do you want any?" he asked.

"No dude, my cup is filled to the brim," I replied. "Hurry up so that we can get started, we've wasted too much time already!" I exclaimed.

Just as I was opening the interview room's door, he grabbed the handle and held it open. There was Lena, shriveled, seated on the chair; she had leaned it back against the rear wall that was covered in that green hideous carpet panel. She looked pale and weak. Her eyes were swollen from the countless hours of crying. Still, what a trooper, enduring all these hours knowing that her daughter's lifeless body was now lying on a cold slab in the morgue. Lena understood her daughter was killed, she just did not know how or the extent of the injuries that were inflicted. My instincts were telling me that at some point during the interview, she was going to ask how it happened. It always puzzled me why people were so interested in the gory details of how a loved one was killed, not that those details would bring closure. The impressions of how the act was committed and the results will never be forgotten; besides, she was going to eventually see the crime scene photos as well as the autopsy photos during the trial.

After entering the interview room, I made myself comfortable sitting in one of the chairs and looked at my watch, it read 8:05 am. Damn, it was five minutes past 8 o'clock already, and barely halfway through with what I needed to complete before heading home. The most pressing matter on my mind was to complete this interview. My focus had to be spot-on, there was no time to feel tired. That is when I stood from the chair and walked toward this frail looking young woman and reintroduced myself.

Gently, I took her hand in mine and offered her my condolences for her loss. In a low tone, she told me her name was Lena Miranda. Holding back the tears, she looked at me and trembling asked "why" in Spanish. The words she expected were not forthcoming. There was nothing I could come up with to adequately answer her question. Delicately, I avoided giving her an answer, but quickly followed up by asking for her assistance to better understand why this incident occurred. She was informed that the next several hours would be exceedingly difficult and her cooperation would allow me to bring about a better case and justice for her daughter. Lena, displaying faith in me said, "I will do whatever needs to be done but no matter what, my daughter will not have justice because she's dead." Her words, like a dagger, pierced right through me; I never expected a response such as the one just heard. Her pain and anguish were sentiments only a mother in her position could feel. Sadly, there was no way of consoling her now and selfishly, I needed her to answer my questions. This was the cruel reality of my job.

During our initial conversation, Lena was informed that I was the lead investigator assigned to her daughter's case and Det. Alvarez was one of the assisting investigators. I continued by letting her know how we were going to discuss the incident and review the information she provided earlier to him. She lowered her head solemnly, then told me she was willing to assist in any way possible for her daughter. Whatever it took, she was prepared to help. Taking a deep breath, she collected herself for what was about to transpire, it was as if a bolt of energy and courage entered her body. My initial evaluation of her disappeared, no longer was she fragile, this was a mother fighting to get justice for her dead daughter. Many of the questions I would be asking her were going to be tough, sometimes personal but to obtain the truth, layers of the onion had to be peeled back and removed. It had been my experience that no matter how cooperative people want to be, human nature stops them from saying too much to avoid embarrassing situations or events.

Wanting to make her feel comfortable, I told her that if at any point she wanted to take a break, use the restroom, or wanted anything to drink, all she had to do was ask. Lena's resilience was admirable while stating that she was ready and wanted to get this interview over. Understanding how she must have been feeling, I could not help but pray that she finds the courage to continue. Only a mother can muster the nerves to face this moment.

As the interview commenced, she again told me her name was Lena Miranda, she was 21 years old and born in Honduras. Her daughter was Lena M. Miranda, two years old and was born in Laredo, Texas. According to her, the biological father abandoned her before their daughter was born and has never been heard from again. She entered the United States illegally through Mexico to make a better living for herself and her baby. Not having any skills, she worked odd jobs in Texas and eventually made her way to Miami. Once in Miami, she met Laudin at a local bar called 'Cafeteria Honduras'. The bar was frequented by unsavory characters but Laudin seemed different, less threatening. Soon after meeting they began a romantic relationship. They have been living together for approximately one year. Unfortunately for her, she did not have a work visa, so her only option was to work under the table. That is when she found a job waitressing at the 'Del Rey Cafeteria' located on Northwest 27th avenue, near the Miami River.

According to her, the current location where she works is rougher than 'Cafeteria Honduras'. At this establishment, unlike the other, there was a mixture of Central and South Americans as well as Cubans. The patrons were low life's, drunks, small time dopers and plenty of hustlers. Every night, fights would break out over some of the waitresses, cheating at the pool tables or monies owed to the drug dealers. Even though it was a risky place for a woman to work, she felt safe. Her demure look was not threatening to the other girls, so they treated her nicely and protected her.

During her shift, which was late at night, guys would try to pick her up. Always making passes at her, or touching her, something that she did not care for but overlooked because she needed to earn money, so she would act as if it were okay. Those were the moments when some of the other girls would help. There were many nights when shootings and stabbings occurred, but the police were never called. This frightened her, thinking that one night it might be her getting stabbed or worse, shot. Still, she went to work every night thinking about her daughter and wanting to provide for her. It was for that reason she put up with so much of the unwanted advancements by some of the rougher patrons. The work was mentally and physically exhausting, but she had no other recourse.

Lena explained, the first several months were not so bad, she would go home and let Laudin know everything that happened during her shift and he would patiently listen. In her mind and out of respect, she did not want him to think anything bad about her. But recently, his demeanor toward her began to change, he was distant and constantly angry. He increasingly disrespected her verbally in front of her family and strangers, especially when he had been drinking. Her family never saw him hit her, but they suspected.

She explained how in the past six months Laudin found it difficult to get steady work. This occurred mainly because he drank too much and slept in most mornings instead of looking for work. His weakness put a heavy strain on their relationship, one that was shaky at best. With each passing day, his anger increased, along with his physical abuse. He would beat her for no reason and was always threatening her. He became increasingly jealous because of where she worked and all the men that would patronize the establishment. Even with all the physical abuse Laudin inflicted on her, she never called the police for fear he would kill her. Although he was violent toward her, he never displayed anger toward her daughter. Instead, he treated her daughter very well, taking care of her as if she were his own.

After obtaining the background information on her relationship with Laudin, it was time to find out what happened last night. What went wrong that it ended with this nightmare? Instinctively, I reached across the interview table, took her hand, looked at her and softly pleaded for an answer. One which would tell me what occurred that could have led to her daughter being killed.

As if a faucet had been turned on, tears began to stream down Lena's cheeks. With a soft whimper in-between her breaths, she began to purge herself of this ungodly horror being experienced. This was for her daughter and nothing else. Regaining her composure, she continued speaking. Her shift began last night at 9 pm, it was remarkably busy and Laudin had been trying to call her on several occasions, but she could not speak with him. Suddenly, around 2:30 am he unexpectedly arrived at the cafeteria. She told him angrily that he could not stay for fear that her job would be in jeopardy. Upset that she was disrespecting him, he angrily told her he was going to play pool and ordered a drink. While he was playing pool, he paid for a beer which she brought to him. But before she realized, he gulped it down in front of her and slammed the bottle on the edge of the pool table. Upset, she turned to attend to the other customers. This infuriated Laudin who then grabbed her arm forcefully and ordered another beer.

Afraid of what would happen, she walked to the bar and returned with another beer. He took the beer, drank some and grabbed her arm again and demanded she leave with him. Removing his hand from her arm, she told him that could not happen because she would be fired immediately. This response infuriated Laudin more than expected and he grabbed her thin arm tighter than before. Pleading for him to let go, she continued trying to free herself from his grip and almost fell. Watching the spectacle, some of the patrons intervened and pulled him away from her. The men that helped roughly escorted Laudin out of the cafeteria, but he remained on the sidewalk. While outside, he began yelling at her and asked if she was leaving with him or staying. She told him that she was going to stay and finish her shift.

After hearing her response, he became enraged beyond anything she had ever seen. It was then when he told her, "Suffer the consequences, and you better not call the police. If you do, you're going to cry tears of blood!" After he left the area, she immediately called the police out of fear something was going to happen. It was a feeling like she had never experienced. The police arrived within minutes, and she even commented that I had been present. She explained to the officers what had transpired and let them know that she feared for her daughter's well-being because her boyfriend was mad at her for not leaving with him. The fear was instinctive, not due to any direct threat made by Laudin toward her daughter.

Within minutes, the officers placed her in one of the police cars and drove her home. Once they arrived at the apartment, she saw Laudin on the steps outside of her apartment. As soon as he saw her exit the police vehicle, he ran inside the apartment, locking himself inside the bedroom where her daughter was sleeping. While the police officers were inside the apartment, they pleaded with him to open the bedroom door. That is when he yelled out, "Why did you do it!" He continued yelling but she did not understand him, that is when she told the officers to break down the bedroom door. After several minutes, the officers were finally able to kick the door open. Once they gained entry, they took Laudin out of the bedroom. He remained silent while being escorted out of the apartment.

According to Lena, her daughter slept in the same room with her and Laudin. She last saw her daughter alive before going to work, leaving her with her mother who babysat. Overwhelmed with emotions, exhausted, and anguished, Lena began to cry uncontrollably. Between each sob, she kept repeating how she needed to work because Laudin was not working or earning sufficient money. Desperation led her to do whatever it took to provide for her daughter. Then, she stated that nobody else was inside the bedroom when Laudin was taken out, everyone else was sleeping in the living room or kitchen. I provided Lena with a tissue for her tears. As she wiped them away, she looked at me and stated, "All this was my fault for calling the police!" Upon hearing those words, I thought to myself, *None of this was her fault, circumstances dictated the events from last night.* I slowly stepped out of the room, giving her some privacy and a break. Returning moments later, I brought her a cup of water and informed her that a sworn statement was going to be needed. She understood why and agreed. As difficult as this moment was, her courage is a testament of a mother fighting till the very end for her daughter.

Several minutes later, Det. Alvarez and I recorded the sworn statement of Lena Miranda, mother of the victim. Once the statement was concluded, I explained to her the complete process going forward. Feeling that she was overwhelmed, I put her in contact with my Victim Advocate, Tania, who began assisting her with funeral and burial arrangements as well as other benefits. Once I left her in the hands of Tania, I immediately returned to my desk to complete my administrative duties before calling ASA Sole. Sitting in my chair, I found myself starring at the ceiling in disbelief, wondering, *what goes through the mind of a young mother as she prepares to bury her only child.* This goes against everything that is natural.

Like this case, I was certain that there are many more just as cruel. Unfortunately for me, it did not make this case any easier. The guilt that Lena must be feeling is something that I wish on no one. What will this do to her? What will her future hold? I just hope that she can move beyond this nightmare and stay strong. She is going to need all the strength she can muster because this stage was only the beginning. Once we get closer to the pre-trial phase and during the trial, her wound will be ripped open a thousand times. She will be forced to relive this incident and exposed to its brutality. An incident that was a direct consequence of desperation from a single mother in a foreign country who attached herself to a man without knowing his past just to survive. Eventually, she paid a heavy price. Then again, so did everyone who was involved. How much will she punish herself for this mistake? Hopefully, she will find solace knowing that justice for her daughter was served. Truth be told, I need justice to be served because a piece of my humanity was left on that scene after observing what no one should ever see.

Just as my thoughts could not get any darker, I heard Det. Alvarez's voice in the distance. Looking up, I could see his lips moving but had no idea what he was saying, that is when I realized my headphones were covering my ears. That must have happened inadvertently to drown out the noise in the office. I waived at my sidekick while removing my headphones and said, "What's up?"

"Just wanted to know if we were returning to the crime scene," he replied.

"Probably, just give me a few minutes, I still have to speak with the ASA," I responded. With that, he went back to catching up with his paperwork as I reached for the phone. I picked up the receiver and began to dial ASA Sole's number, hopefully she would be in her office. Looking at the clock on the office wall, it showed 9:15 am, it felt much later. Having just pushed 30 hours straight; I wonder how much more is left in my tank. That is when I realized that the medical examiner had to be contacted to find out at what time the autopsy of 'Little Lena Miranda', my victim, was going to be performed.

Suddenly, I heard ASA Sole's voice on the other end saying, "ASA Sole, how can I help you?"

"Hey Ruby," I replied. "Let me brief you on what I've got so far."

"Awesome, go ahead Pepi, let me write this down!" she exclaimed. Once she got her things in order, ready to write down what I told her, I began speaking. She was a great listener and did not interrupt me much while I was speaking. She allowed me to finish before asking follow-up questions if I had not covered a specific point. Once I finished going over everything that was learned to this point, we reviewed the Arrest Affidavit for errors. Thank goodness the errors were minimal.

Once the minor corrections were made, she was in total agreement as to the narrative on the A-Form and the charges. Ruby gave me the green light to proceed and ended the conversation by reminding me to conduct another canvass of the area around the crime scene. I acknowledged politely, knowing full well that it was the next thing to be done. Once we hung up, I thought, *who does she think she's working with, she knows better*. I chuckled to myself and began writing my notes. While I was finishing making the entry, Officer Rolly Herbert entered the homicide office. Ofc. Herbert was a super nice guy, short in stature at 5'5" had a thick frame and wore his uniform two sizes smaller making him look as if he were about to pop. As if on cue, he entered an area that demonstrated little mercy for ordinary folk, let alone an officer barely taller than a munchkin. The investigators in the Homicide Unit historically were unforgiving.

This was part of the unit's charm. Suddenly, every detective began busting his balls because they knew he would get pissed and begin to curse in Spanish. He did not disappoint, spewing a Ricky Ricardo tone of curse words in Spanish. All of us stood there for what seemed like an eternity laughing, including Ofc. Herbert. Taking it in stride, he knew that investigators in the homicide unit had a reputation of busting peoples chops whenever an opportunity arose. It was all in good fun and never personal, raunchy humor has always been the cornerstone of homicide investigators for as long as I could remember. How else could we perform our job without some sort of humor. Plus, today it was the perfect antidote.

Up to now, there had really been nothing to smile about, since my night had been crappy from the moment, I responded to the cafeteria with the patrol units. Rolly was now casually walking toward my desk and sat down next to me. He started off by asking, "Are you going to play in the softball tournament this weekend?"

"You know I'll be there unless something comes up," I replied. We were members of the Miami Police Departments' softball team and this was the time of year when tournaments would prepare us for the Florida Law Enforcement Games. These games were a big deal in Florida, every major police agency competed to claim their prize of being number one, something very prestigious. This minor conversation was Rolly's way of breaking the ice, he knew exactly who he would be transporting to the Dade County jail. I appreciated it because every officer that has shown up wanted to hear the grisly details.

After reviewing the arrest affidavit again for any grammatical or technical errors, it was now ready as it had been the previous times. This must have been the tenth time and still no errors found. It was silly of me but better safe than sorry. Now, feeling comfortable with the document I read it to Rolly. While reading it, I could see him shaking his head and in a soft somber voice he said, "What an animal." He got no disagreement from me. I handed him the arrest affidavit which he gladly took. We both stood up and walked to the room where Laudin was seated. As we walked, I made sure to let him know that Laudin was to be treated with kid gloves, no bullshit comments, or conversations. He was to be transported to the County Jail without issues. The only additional instructions I gave to Rolly were, if Laudin began speaking about the incident or make any spontaneous statements, he was to write them down and let me know immediately. I again reemphasized that under no circumstances was he to engage Laudin in conversation.

While Rolly was placing the handcuffs on the monster, I took the opportunity to contact CSI Jefferson and told her that the knife which was seized at the crime scene needed to be sent immediately to the County's Crime Lab for processing. Additionally, everything collected of evidentiary value needed to be processed urgently. She let me know that it would be taken care of directly.

While concluding my conversation with Jefferson, Rolly exited the room with Laudin, hands behind his back, securely handcuffed. As they walked past me, he looked up and in Spanish said thank you. It was as close to remorse as was expected. I just nodded and without saying a word walked away. As they exited the homicide office, Rolly turned, and said he would call me once Laudin was booked. "Thanks, I'll be here for a while," I replied. Exhausted from sleep deprivation, I now leaned against the coffee counter, poured me another cup of coffee, and returned to my desk. Finally, evil had left the office, and out of my sight for now.

With him gone, I began catching up on my administrative
work and there was plenty to catch up on.

# Chapter 15

Now that Laudin was out of the homicide office, heading to the Dade County Jail, I continued preparing for the uneasy task of calling the medical examiner. You see, this call was necessary to find out when the autopsy was going to be performed. While gazing at the phone, I slowly began extending my arm to pick up the receiver when suddenly, I pulled it back. Not ready yet, entered my mind, while disregarding the receiver and picking up my pen to enter some more notes in my Bible. Eventually I had to make this call, delaying the obvious was not going to change anything other than me showing up late to the autopsy. The thought of attending that autopsy was difficult and heartbreaking. Unfortunately, this was part of a homicide investigators responsibility.

While trying to compose myself from thinking about the autopsy, I noticed Randall Reid's assistant entering the courtroom, she had enlarged photographs of the crime scene and autopsy tucked under her arm. To the lay person, these large 18 X 36 photographs were like any other poster boards. Fortunately for the gallery, these poster boards were covered to hide their content. I knew from watching Randall's assistant, bring in the photographs, he was going for the jugular. He wanted to make sure and impress upon the jury of the heinous act which caused undue suffering to this little girl. *The cherry on the cake*, I thought. This was a brilliant strategy, allow these jurors to again see for the last time what a heartless monster had done. Allow these images to sink deep into their psyche before returning with the verdict.

While Randall's assistant was setting up the photographs on the easel, I turned my head and saw Dr. Anastasia Castillo enter the courtroom. I had not seen her in over a year. Dr. Castillo was the psychiatrist that spent countless hours examining Laudin weeks after the murder. Well, now we will hear directly from the psychiatrist if he was really insane. The doctor will eviscerate the defense's claim and put it to rest once and for all.

Being your typical Latin male, the one good thing about Dr. Castillo, she was a knockout, a gorgeous woman with an awesome personality and highly intelligent. Hopefully, her statement to the jury will reinforce our case. Now that I finished eyeing the doctor, I went back to relaxing in my corner. Like any caring investigator who obsesses with their cases, I continued to relive that dreadful early morning call while sitting here reevaluating my performance. Not even the sight of Dr. Castillo could stop me from thinking about June 3, 1994. Still, there were subtle distractions throughout the courtroom.

The low murmur of whispers in the courtroom were ever present, like an idling diesel engine. Everyone was anticipating this final act. Once completed, there will not be another show unless something comes up during the appeal process. Today was in God's hands. My prayer is for everything to work out so that Lena can find peace knowing justice was served for her daughter. Closure is the term we use, but does a mother really find closure? I often wonder if any mother can find such peace. As a mother, she will undoubtedly live with a guilt that will eventually consume her.

Now, there I was staring at the easel which stood in the center of the courtroom and Dr. Castillo who had walked in earlier. This was totally crazy, knowing those photographs were horrific but watching Dr. Castillo who was gorgeous. So, my internal fantasy conversation occupied a few minutes. "Could this be a psychological mind fuck? What meaning could these thoughts have? Maybe I will ask Dr. Castillo to join me for Cafecito after all of this is over. We can probably discuss my inner most feelings regarding this case. Wishful thinking, Pepi," I said to myself. After this nice little fantasy, I again leaned against the wall comfortably. Soon, this final episode must begin, I said to myself. Sitting here, I felt like a school kid who was just told by a teacher not to move. Deep inside, I just wanted for this case to be over. Scares were going to be left for everyone directly involved and there was no escaping that reality.

Just as I was about move to the front pew, to sit next to Lena, the bailiff discreetly opened the courtroom's rear door. That is the door which leads to the back hallway, connecting to the judge's chambers. While slowly making my way to the open space next to Lena, the judge began his grand entrance into the courtroom. He quickly walked toward his bench, climbed the two steps, and immediately sat down on a plush, red leather executive chair. As he adjusted his chair and organized some papers, Judge Banks had total command of his courtroom without saying a single word. The judge entered and sat on the bench so fast that his bailiff had little time to sound out, "All rise!" Fortunately, we were all use to courtroom etiquette, so by the time the bailiff opened his mouth, everyone in attendance was standing.

Several minutes passed while Judge Banks apologized for the unexpected matters that caused delays and inconveniences to the jury, Randall Reid, Erin George, defendant Laudin Matte but especially Lena Miranda. Judge Bank's words were eloquent while presenting a synopsis of this case and trial to those in attendance today, which was a packed courtroom. He made it a point to acknowledge Lena Miranda for enduring undue stress and anxiety during such difficult times. He thanked her for her patients in allowing the judicial process to play out.

Judge Bank's recognized her courage as well as her mother's in open court. Once he concluded with his remarks, he immediately addressed the prosecuting and defense attorneys. He reminded them of their responsibilities, thanked them for their professionalism and implored that they maintain their decorum. Randall Reid and Erin George were adversary's during this trial, but they respected each other's abilities. They momentarily looked at each other from across their tables as Judge Bank ended his speech, then, simultaneously turned their heads toward the judge and stated, "Yes your honor."

While I was explicating to Lena what Judge Bank's referenced seconds prior, I could hear him speaking to the jury. But I so wanted Lena to understand that I barely could make out what he was saying. It really did not matter so long as Lena comprehended what he expressed. I was certain that his words to the jury meant nothing to Lena. Upon finishing my explanation, Judge Bank was turning his chair to face the entire courtroom. The silence was deafening. One could have heard a feather drop, that is how quiet it felt in the courtroom. Even so, the only exception was that of the wheels on the judge's chair. One could make out a faint sound as they rolled on the bench's floor.

His gaze toward both sets of attorneys was stern and direct. It reminded me of an eagle sitting high on a perch, intently watching over the landscape in search of prey. Suddenly, he motioned to defense attorney, Erin George, and stated, "Are you ready Ms. George?" She looked up at the judge and replied, "Ready, your honor." This was followed by the judge who stated, "You may proceed." Suddenly, a lump appeared in my throat as she began to speak.

"Thank you, your honor," were the first words uttered by Erin as she stood up from her chair while making her way to the lectern positioned in the middle of the courtroom. Erin removed some notes from a folder, placed them on the lectern and proceeded to take a sip of water. She cleared her throat while rolling the lectern closer to where the jurors were situated. Once she positioned herself, she stepped to the side of the lectern. Her left hand remained on the flat surface as security, not wanting to stray too far. Watching her, I could tell that her nerves were firing like spark plugs. Although she was a seasoned attorney, how would she approach her final closing to this jury? What could she possibly come up with to convince them that Laudin should be given the benefit of the doubt? My curiosity to hear her was overwhelming, so I leaned back in my pew and intently listened.

"Good afternoon, ladies and gentlemen of the jury, my name is Erin George and I represent Mr. Laudin Matte." Listening to her, a distinct crack was noticed in her voice. There was no way for her to pull this off. While she began explaining to the jury the statutes and what constituted each degree of murder, I understood where she was going. Hit the jury with enough fluff and legal verbiage and maybe they would be unable to decipher each meaning. Surely, if she confused them enough, she might have a chance of getting a favorable verdict. Certainly, Not Guilty, was out of the question. Possibly, she was banking on the jury rendering a verdict of Manslaughter by Reason of Insanity but even that was a stretch.

The more she spoke, the more confident I felt that Laudin Matte would be found guilty of 1$^{st}$ Degree Murder. My feeling was purely personal knowing that she would be unable to convince this jury otherwise. Erin's strategy was simple, try to gain sympathy for a monster by creating a fog of convoluted theories and reasons. Layer them so thick that the jury would be unable to see the truth. Having heard her on previous cases left me with little expectation, her uncanny ability of persuasion was truly an art. But what I was hearing today was desperation, like a Hail Mary pass to try and win a football game. For some reason, her argument was not resonating to those listening. She was throwing everything at the jury except the kitchen sink, hoping that doubt would set in.

Hearing her voice in a low tone, cracking and with little confidence gave me room to pause. Suddenly, my nerves began to subside and that queasy feeling I have had throughout this trial disappeared. Regardless of what theories or sob stories Erin was going to inject into the jury, I knew Reid and Dr. Castillo would have a good response. In my experience, a jury usually sees through bullshit if they have been paying attention throughout the trial. And thus far, this jury had been all over this case.

Still, Erin was giving it that old college try and setting the table for what I expected, making her client seem like a victim, which caused him to snap. "Put yourself in Laudin's place!" she exclaimed to the jury as she inched closer to where they were seated. Her hand was now completely removed from the lectern, leaving her untethered. She paced from one side of the jury box to the other, making eye contact with as many jurors as possible. She had to be convincing and say anything that could give her client a fighting chance. Watching and listening to her made me feel good. It felt as if we had her on the ropes. Not that I was overconfident, but I knew that once Dr. Castillo presented her retort and Randall Reid concluded his closing remarks, victory would be ours. Hopefully, this was not a premature wish since Erin was still engaged with the jury.

While Erin was attending to her business, I could see Randall writing down some notes every so often. Surely, these notes were taken based on comments or statements being made by her. Points that Reid was sure to debunk. Scanning the courtroom, all eyes were focused on Erin and everyone was hanging on every word she was uttering, except Laudin. He sat there, motionless, with a blank unwavering stare. As the Spanish interpreter whispered everything Erin was saying into a microphone, Laudin would adjust his headset. That was the only emotion being displayed by him to this point.

While momentarily distracted, looking around the courtroom, I had not realized that Erin was about to pour her foundation of doubt. Her approach with the jury was methodical to this point. She was laying the groundwork for her final push. As I refocused on her closing statement, I caught it as she was speaking about the victim's mother, Lena. Lena, who was seated next to me was caught off guard when she heard her name mentioned. Immediately, she turned to me and asked if I could tell her what Erin was saying. I shook my head and proceeded to translate.

Erin spoke in a quasi-disparaging manner, painting a picture of how Lena worked at a bar or seedy cafeteria as a waitress. Working a shift that commenced at seven o'clock in the evening until three or four o'clock in the morning. She told the jury that while Lena was working, her daughter would be taken care of by the grandmother, Floria or by Laudin Matte. She depicted Laudin as always being gentle and affectionate with the victim, as if she were his own daughter. *Man, Erin was really laying it thick*, I thought. As I continued explaining to Lena what was being said about her, tears began to stream down her cheeks without making a sound. Devastated by the negative comments just seemed to reenforce her fragile emotions.

The jury heard Erin detail how the relationship between Lena and Laudin was not going well and how he wanted to leave her but decided against it. Well, that was a crock of shit because it was Lena who had been trying to end the relationship because of his abusive treatment, verbally and physically. Erin was painting a picture of Laudin as this great partner, one who would clean, do laundry, cook, and take care of the victim. In hearing her, one could imagine a Norman Rockwell painting coming to mind. Even if this was not the case, it is what she wanted to portray.

After making Laudin seem like this meek, simple, decent man, she began her final descent. Erin now wanted to hook the jury into feeling pity for this animal. I wondered what she could possibly come up with to convince this jury. What was her angle? Whatever it was, we would soon find out. Pausing, she turned away from the jurors. As she regained her composure, I observed her taking small steps.

This skillful attorney was now walking away from the jurors and returned to the lectern. Upon arriving, she took a deep breath, grabbed her notes, making believe she was organizing them. She reached for her cup which had been placed on the lectern by her assistant, filled it with water and brought it to her lips. This small display of theatrics was annoying. But, at that moment, I said to myself, "Man she must be getting ready for a massive ending, or, delaying the inevitable." There was only one route to take in trying to convince this jury of Laudin's shortcomings which caused him to snap. The foundation had been laid out earlier in the trial when she attempted to establish insanity as a cause. Trying to put myself in her position, I could see why she was continuing down this path. If the jury conceded to a theory of abuse and mental anguish suffered at a young age, they could possibly take Laudin's side. Suddenly, reality set in. There are no guarantees on how a jury will decide a case.

Once again, Erin stepped away from the lectern. This time, she stood between the jury box and the table where her client was seated. As she began to speak, Laudin raised his head, not fully erect but his eyes were still looking down. Her first words to the jury during this phase were striking, "Look at this man, he barely stands 5'2", is out of shape and physically unimposing." Damn, she just cut him up big time, emasculating him in front of the whole world. These words were meant to set up a bigger picture for the jurors.

She continued by explaining how Laudin lived in a male dominant society, where he needed to fit in to establish himself as a real man, a provider. If he was unable to bring out that persona, he felt vulnerable and inferior around other men in his culture. Remembering that earlier she painted a picture of him cleaning, cooking, and performing other household chores. Now, she had to convince the jury that these tasks somehow diminished him as a man.

She impressed upon the jury that Laudin going to Lena Miranda's place of employment was normal. He would go to play pool and socialize with the other men, mostly to watch out for Lena. There were times when he was overheard telling other male patrons how he was the boss in their relationship and could make Lena leave early if he wanted. Much of these comments were dismissed as jealousy and his need to dominate but Erin spined it differently.

She was emphatic when telling the jury that these demonstrations of male posturing and exaggerated public displays reflected his damaged sense of masculinity. Finally, her expected revelation, Laudin suffered from a sense of personal inadequacy whose origin stemmed from a traumatic childhood experience. *Wow, what a shocking surprise*, I thought. This was a joke, something I knew was going to happen. Sooner or later, she had to bring up some type of traumatic issue. An issue that could not be verified, even after meeting with people from his neighborhood in Honduras.

Erin eloquently detailed how Laudin at a tender age of nine years old, along with other family members witnessed his sister, who had been his care giver, being shot to death. Ironically, none of these family members were present, in court, to substantiate or demystify this story. So, she continued with additional tales. One such account explained that when Laudin was eleven years old, he was brutally raped by a circus clown. Was this something made up by him and replayed for the jury by his skillful attorney. Hell, it is a tall tale but plausible, except this also could not be verified. Listening to her detail these incidents allow for a recipe of horror and nightmares, if true. Unfortunately, these stories were from him and nothing to corroborate such fables.

Proceeding with such heartbreaking stories stirred my stomach. How many more horrific events was Erin going to conjure up to persuade this jury. At this pace, Laudin should not be convicted of brutally killing a child, he should be canonized for enduring such abuse. Fortunately, I was certain this jury saw beyond each story. Surely, they recognized the attempt by a desperate defense attorney performing a most difficult job. Unexpectedly, I began feeling sorry for her, but like a true defense attorney, she marched on by explaining how her client was the youngest of eleven brothers and sisters. How he lived with his family in various migrant camps, traveling from one to another based on the harvest season. She impressed upon the jury that his mother was too tired to care for him, so his sisters took on this responsibility. That while growing up, he lived in a wooden shack without electricity or running water and sold food prepared by his mother. Such difficult conditions for a young child, certainly, *but why become a brutal murderer?* I wondered. There are many who endure these challenges without becoming murderers.

Finally, Erin was now nearing the end of her closing. She lectured the jury on how childhood traumas effect personality and development. That long term consequences could hinder the growth of a young boy, leaving him with an overwhelming sense of helplessness, terror and a fear which leads him to question his competency and to doubt his masculinity. As compelling an argument, I felt that nothing she said would convince a lay person of Laudin's innocence, let alone this jury. In conclusion, she implored the jury to think of how difficult growing up in these conditions would be to a child, how such trauma could cause someone to snap. She instructed the jury to pay close attention to the judge's instructions and to understand how prosecutor, Randall Reid, was going to portray Laudin as a callous individual. Upon concluding, Erin thanked the jurors for their service, saying she trusted and was sure they would make the right decision.

Upon concluding her sentence, she turned to judge Banks, saying, "thank you, your honor." Silently, she began to clear the lectern of all her material while the judge acknowledged her good work throughout this trial. With her notepad in hand, she rolled the lectern to the center of the courtroom and returned to her table. She sat down, gave her notes to her assistant then leaned toward Laudin. The court interpreter listened to what Erin whispered while simultaneously translating for him He shook his head and Erin gently patted him on the back in reassurance. Looking at that picture, I could only imagine what she must have told him, possibly letting him know that everything she could have done was done.

While the courtroom was settling down from Erin's closing argument, I informed Lena how this was part of the judicial process. Feeling extremely confident, I assured her we had enough evidence introduced, plus the testimonies heard were sufficient for a conviction. She squeezed my hand tightly and semi-smiled. Suddenly, I realized the error that was committed. "How could I let myself say such things to her," I thought? We were still in the process and the jury had not listened to Dr. Castillo or Reid. What if their arguments and opinions were not compelling enough and the jury finds Laudin, not guilty? These negative thoughts needed to be purged from my head and refocus on the positive side. Looking down at my watch nervously, I determined that Erin's closing took approximately 55 minutes. For sure, a short recess was going to be ordered by the judge. He wants to keep these closings going but wants to make sure that the jurors were fresh and alert.

Just as I expected, Judge Banks struck his gavel and silence fell on the courtroom. The judge looked at Randall Reid and asked him if he was ready. Reid responded that he was but let the judge know that Dr. Castillo was going to address the court before his closing remarks. Upon hearing this, Erin interjected by saying, "sidebar your honor." Judge

Banks then motioned for Reid and Erin to approach the bench. Both attorneys with their assistants walked to the side of the judge's bench, followed by the court stenographer. You see, everything being said had to be permanently immortalized so that no misunderstandings could be brought up at a later date.

The sidebar lasted five minutes as both sides went back and forth arguing their points. Both attorneys returned to their tables and remained standing. Judge Banks addressed the jurors, then turned to the courtroom and stated, "let's take a fifteen-minute recess." He struck the gavel and as he stood from his chair to exit the courtroom, the bailiff yelled out, "all rise." By the time everyone in the courtroom stood, his honor was halfway out the rear door, entering the hallway to his chambers. I started to exit the courtroom when someone began tugging at my arm. I turned and it was Idalma, the victims advocate. She had a puzzled look on her face which I determined was from her overhearing my comments to Lena. Sure enough, it was, followed by, "Are you crazy?" she said in Spanish. "Do you know what will happen if the verdict is not how you expect it to be?" she asked. I knew her concern was for Lena and Floria. Idalma caught me a little off guard but she had a point. We had worked together on enough cases where she felt comfortable approaching me in such a manner, something I appreciated.

So, I paused for a moment and replied, "Believe me, that came to my mind, but I wanted to reassure her, besides, we're not losing this one."

I had just doubled down on a cardinal sin, do not guarantee anything. With that, I looked at Idalma after glancing at Dr. Castillo and said, "let's get some Cafecito, it's on me." She smiled at me and said, "Pepi, you're crazy." We walked pass everyone, exited the courtroom and walked toward the escalators. The main hallway in front of the courtrooms was packed. People were walking around, attorneys were talking to clients and attempting to work out last-minute plea deals with prosecutors. Every courtroom has a story but today, the main event was in courtroom 2–3.

As we walked toward the escalators, the news outlets were setting up in the hallway and the reporters were trying to look pretty, standing in front of their cameras reporting on this trial. "What a shit show," I said to myself. Amazing how news outlets gravitate to such tragic events. All at the expense of a victim's family, only to get ratings. Even under the guise of human interest, unfortunately, this case was being followed by many in Miami from the very beginning. Mainly, this incident became a blazing inferno of attention because the victim was so young and so brutally murdered. Idalma and I arrived at the cafeteria. "Let me have a colada of café and a bottled water," I said. The waitress who had been waiting on me throughout the day replied, "you're going to go through the roof if you keep drinking that stuff." I laughed and told her that the café was not for me, but the water was, she laughed and said, "I hope so." She rung up the total but by then I had left a five-dollar bill on top of the counter and began walking away.

Upon exiting the cafeteria, the waitress yelled out, "gracias." While we continued walking, I told Idalma to give some café to Lena before anyone else. She shook her head and asked if I was going to return with her. At that moment, we split up indicating that she was returning without me. Not that I did not want to but out of the corner of my eye I spotted Cecy. I made a detour toward her direction. I wanted to thank her for the help she had provided earlier, something she was not required to do but did it anyway because of our friendship. She was near the elevators when I caught up to her. We spoke for a few minutes, before I thanked her.

Unexpectedly and in her own nutty way, she replied, "Just bring me a diet Coke." We started laughing as I walked away saying, "you got it." There are so many good people who work at the State Attorney's Office, that they become an extension of an investigator. One usually gets more things accomplished by going directly to an attorney's assistant than the attorneys themselves. Some attorneys were great but there were those that thought their shit did not stink. Such arrogance had a way of exasperating me beyond belief. So, I always made it a point to be nice to those that assisted me the most.

As I stepped off the escalators, it felt strange because the hallway was not as full. *Oh shit, I'm late*, I thought to myself. Sprinting toward courtroom 2–3, I saw Randall Reid approaching from the opposite direction. He smiled at me and remarked, "Are you okay?"

"I thought I was late," I replied. He told me that people had just started to make their way into the courtroom to find better seating. *This was definitely the center ring*, I thought. Then, Reid let me know that my seat had been saved. I opened the door for him as we both entered the courtroom. While making my way toward the first pew, Judge Banks entered the courtroom. He briskly walked toward the bench. Suddenly, the bailiff roared the all too familiar, "all rise."

While everyone began to stand, I took this opportunity to inch my way toward my spot on the first pew. By the time the bailiff yelled out, "be seated," I was already in my spot, sitting down without missing a beat. Lena turned to me and thanked me for the café. I smiled and began paying attention as the judge spoke. This was important, because now it was our turn to bring this case to a close. Not wanting to miss a thing, I noticed when Reid turned his chair and motion to Dr. Castillo. The doctor inched closer to the railing and leaned forward. Reid got closer, and I could barely make out what he told her, but I did hear him say, "are you ready." Dr. Castillo nodded and immediately sat back on the pew. He then rolled his chair back to the prosecutors table and told his assistant to have his notes ready.

Immediately, his assistant began fumbling through the slew of paperwork that laid on the table. Watching his assistant gave me pause to silently laugh, it was as if she had lost a wedding ring. The notes were nowhere. Suddenly, Reid reached over and grabbed his notes. They had been on top of the other papers the whole time. *Well, this definitely was a moment of levity,* I thought. His assistant had to be shitting bricks as he grabbed the notes. She turned away, slightly embarrassed, saying, "Sorry about that." He did not respond, for there was no time for an answer. He was laser focused and intently reviewing his notes.

While he was buried in his notes, Judge Banks took a moment to speak with the court stenographer. Surely, it must have been a lighthearted exchange, since I had not seen the judge speak to the stenographer during the trial. I was positive that these extra minutes allowed for Reid to soak in as much of his notes as possible before starting his closing argument. Just then, Judge Banks head rose, looking at Reid he asked, "Are you ready to proceed?"

Reid stood from his chair and replied, "yes your honor, but before I continue, I believe Dr. Castillo would like to address the court."

# Chapter 16

Immediately, Erin sprang from her chair like a Jack-in-the-box to address Judge Banks. "Your honor, this is unnecessary since Dr. Castillo has already given testimony." No sooner had Erin finished her sentence, Reid chimed in, "Judge, Ms. George made some points during her closing regarding the defendants state of mind that must be reexamined, therefore, I believe Dr. Castillo, who is present can shed some light for the jury." With that, Erin instantly asked for a sidebar. Judge Banks replied, "Counsellors please approach the bench." Both attorneys approached the side of the judge's bench, along with their assistants and court reporter. Their conference lasted but a few minutes, then they scurried back to their tables.

Both attorneys remained standing while the judge made his remarks. Speaking to the packed courtroom but looking straight at the jurors, Judge Banks announced the following. "Based on the defense counsel's remarks regarding Mr. Matte's mental condition during closing, I will allow for Dr. Castillo to provide an explanation. It will be limited in scope, strictly referring to Ms. George's allegation of Mr. Matte's mental health."

Erin then replied, "Thank you, your honor."

Judge Banks turned and addressed Reid, "Mr. Reid, you may proceed." Immediately, almost interrupting, he replied, "Thank you, your honor, if the court allows, I would like to introduce Dr. Castillo for some remarks before my closing."

"You may proceed," the judge responded. With that, Dr. Castillo made her way toward the witness stand, looking great. Her tan and toned athletic body were to envy, along with her firm legs that were accentuated by her high heels. I believe that all eyes in the courtroom were examining her from top to bottom. Why wouldn't they, hell, who would not want to look so fit. But prior to sitting down, she was reminded that she was still under oath. Dr. Castillo acknowledged and sat down in the witness box.

Reid walked toward the lectern. He did not carry his note pad with him, unlike Erin who did earlier. You see, he did not need too; he was already mentally prepared to present the closing. It was unnecessary to have his notes for review; his closing had been played repeatedly in his head for the past week. Knowing how well-prepared he was provided me great comfort. My confidence grew as I watched him prance around, without a care in the world. He was engaged in pleasantries with the jurors as he reintroduced himself to them. I imagined he was allowing Dr. Castillo to compose herself. She needed to be on point if the theory of Laudin's mental condition was going to be brought into question in his closing.

Finally, the moment of reckoning arrived when Reid began speaking. The courtroom was suddenly deathly silent as his voice echoed off the courtroom walls. "Members of the jury, I bid you a good afternoon and thank you for your patience and diligence throughout this most difficult trial."

All the jurors had their eyes fixed on every word he spoke, their intensity was evident, more so than when Erin gave her closing, less than an hour ago. He proceeded to explain the complexity of this case and how their final decision was going to affect its outcome. One way or another, they had a solemn responsibility to demonstrate that justice would prevail in this case.

The way he was speaking, was as if I were listening to a football coach motivating his team before kick-off or a preacher on a Sunday morning bellowing a sermon. I had never heard Reid so emotional and animated. For a moment, I thought I was about to stand up and shout, "Oh yeah!" It was fun watching him take such command of the courtroom, even the judge appeared to be totally into this closing. Then, he tempered his tone, stared intently at the jurors, and said, "Before I go on, let me bring your attention to a claim made by the defense. Ms. George will have you believe that Mr. Matte suffered from a mental condition caused by incidents during his youth, well, we will visit those issues with Dr. Castillo who has been patiently waiting on the stand." Reid, who was near the jury box slowly turned and began walking toward the witness stand where the doctor was seated. He walked past the easel where the graphic photos, that were covered, had been placed earlier by his assistant. I could not help but wonder how he was going to effectively use those photos without causing Lena further pain. I knew it would be necessary to show the jurors as a final and ever lasting impression. For sure, those photos were going to affect everyone who saw them. Now, my focus was back on Reid who was near the witness stand. I could hear him greet the doctor, "Good afternoon, Dr. Castillo, thank you for your patience." There was a sense of comfort and confidence in his tone.

Dr. Castillo politely replied, "Good afternoon, I'm happy to be of service." With the pleasantries out of the way, Reid commenced by illustrating several points that Erin discussed during her closing argument with respect to Laudin's mental condition. He was quick to bring out how Erin described Laudin's masculinity as damaged because he suffered from a traumatic childhood experience. He further commented how these allegations were just that, allegations. There came a time when he abruptly stepped away from the witness stand, looked straight at the jurors and exclaimed, "It's always great to come up with an allegation when it can't be independently proven, how convenient!" Erin, in defense stood up from her chair like a missile being launched and stated, "Your honor, I object to Mr. Reid's assertion."

Listening to her pleas, Judge Banks responded, "Ms. George, these are closing arguments, you had your turn. Mr. Reid, stay within the guidelines that were discussed."

Simultaneously both attorneys answered, Erin, "Thank you, your honor,"

and Reid, "Yes, judge."

Once this small squabble and posturing was quelled, Reid continued. Obviously, Erin had to put up some type of fight for her client, at least make it seem as if her case was better. But it was not. While this back and forth was going on, I could see the jurors had inched up on their chairs. They were hooked, line and sinker. During this moment, I gazed at Lena and let her know everything was going well so far. Her head was bowed and without looking up, she just smiled. By now, Reid returned to the side of the bench where Dr. Castillo was seated, as he approached the doctor, he looked out toward the crowded courtroom.

Slowly, he turned and focused on his expert, asking, "Dr. Castillo, you examined Mr. Matte prior to this trial commencing, so based on your professional experience, can you enlighten the jurors and those present in this courtroom of what you learned during your examination of the defendant?"

"I would be delighted too," she replied. Everyone in the courtroom was riveted.

Taking a moment to gather her thoughts, Dr. Castillo turned her seated body to face the jurors directly. She began by letting the jurors know what her profession entailed and her educational background, which was quite impressive. She was not just an elegant woman, who could have graced the cover of a fashion magazine. You see, Dr. Castillo earned her medical degrees from Harvard University and the University of Miami. While speaking of her academic accomplishments, she informed all in attendance how she was head of Jackson Memorial Hospital's Department of Psychiatry. She went on to explain the importance of mental health and her commitment to treating those with such illnesses.

Upon completing her initial statement regarding her qualifications, her gaze moved from the jurors and onto Reid. During this brief pause, he asked the following question. "Dr. Castillo, in your professional opinion, based on your examination of Mr. Matte, was he insane on the night he murdered two-year-old Lena Miranda?" The doctor grabbed the cup of water, which was placed in front of her, brought it to her lips, then took a sip. She placed the cup down, pressed her lips and took a deep breath. Gathering her thoughts, she began by telling all in attendance that the defendant had been interviewed on several occasions before the trial. While explaining to the jurors what she learned during each interview, I could see how they were intently listening and clinging to each word.

Dr. Castillo informed the jurors that during one such session, Mr. Matte informed her that as a child, he saw his sister murdered. He also told her that he had been raped by a clown several years later. She concluded that such events seem horrible in and of themselves, but she did not see any diagnosable mental illness and no direct link between those events and the victim's murder. She further determined that Mr. Matte used the psychological defense mechanism of denial. This, in his mind would minimize his symptoms. Additionally, the doctor explained to the jurors that based on her extensive examination of the defendant, he was not under the influence of an extreme emotional disturbance on the night of the murder. Also, he was able to conform his conduct to the law, although he was jealous, enraged and possibly under the influence of alcohol.

While everyone in the courtroom remained captivated, listening closely to what Dr. Castillo was saying, I could see Laudin slouching with his head bowed as the interpreter was translating for him. He showed no emotion, probably the same as the night he murdered 'Little Lena'. I wondered if he ever cared or felt remorse for his actions, maybe his goal of watching Lena suffer was enough. As I refocused on Dr. Castillo, her testimony was concluding with her saying, "Although Mr. Matte claims he is mentally ill and

201

periodically suffers from memory loss, he appears to be acting mostly in what he feels is in his best interest and certainly did not show any signs or symptoms of suffering from an active mental illness."

"Thank you, Dr. Castillo!" Reid exclaimed.

Judge Banks then said, "You may step down."

"Thank you, your honor," she replied. The doctor slowly stood up, then stepped down from the witness stand. As she walked past Reid, I could see her smiling at him, not in a sensual way but one of satisfaction. The kind of smile one gets when accomplishing a goal.

She continued walking until she reached the courtroom's door, as she exited the courtroom, the creaking of the door opening, and closing could be heard but no one paid attention. That is when I leaned toward Lena and explained everything that Dr. Castillo expressed to the jurors. Soon, the doctor was a distant memory as Reid proceeded with his closing argument. Now, all the focus would be on him. He had to bring this case to a successful close, especially after Dr. Castillo's brilliant explanations. As everything was playing out, I could not help but think of anything better than a baseball analogy. This was the bottom of the ninth, with two outs and runners on second and third. The winning run is on second base, the opposing team's best hitter is at the plate and the closer steps on the mound. Well, Reid was the closer in this game.

He confidently returned to his table, slowly picked up his cup and took a sip of water. He placed the cup back where he got it and picked up a retractable metal pointer. With pointer in hand, he turned and deliberately walked toward the easel that stood in the center of the room. He bypassed the easel and approached the jurors. Just as he was about to speak, I observed Erin. She grabbed her note pad, scribbled something on it and leaned behind Laudin, showing what she wrote to her assistant, who was seated on the other side of the defendant. The assistant read what was on the note pad and shook her head. Maybe she had come up with something of interest or maybe she just wanted to cause a minor distraction. Either way, it did not work. The jurors were totally focused on Reid, "The Closer."

He was now leaning on the railing which separated the jurors from the center of the room. He again thanked the jurors for their patience and for how attentive they had been throughout these proceedings. In explaining the difficulties related to a trial, he emphasized how crucial it was to understand everything, even if some points seemed miniscule in scope. His delivery was smooth and on point, like a Bob Gibson fastball.

Reid then, looking straight at the jurors said, "It is your responsibility and yours only to ensure that justice for 'Little Lena' is served. All of the evidence before you will lead you to determine if the defendant, Laudin Matte, is guilty or innocent. Maybe there is something that needs clarification or maybe it's all too clear. Either way, your decision will be final and should be fair and without prejudice."

He paced slowly in front of the jurors with a somber face, running his right hand along the railing. Just as he reached the far edge of the jury box, he lifted his right hand and slightly struck its palm with the pointer being held in his left hand. "Such difficult decisions, but decisions that must be made," these words were stated out loud but in a soft pensive manner by Reid. "What theatrics," I mused. He was getting ready to inflict the final blow and it was not going to be pretty. My gut was telling me that those photos, hiding their horrific sense of cruelty would be unleashed again, for the final time. As Reid approached the easel, he extended the pointer and turned to face the jurors and exclaimed, "We are never going to understand what goes through the mind of an individual who is intent on inflicting pain! But I want you to look closely at what such an individual will do!" The loud, anguishing gasp of most inside the courtroom could be heard outside, into the hallway.

Purposefully, Reid had removed the blank cardboard that shrouded the first photo. The 18 x 36-inch glossy color photo showed the victim, lying supine on top of a mattress soaked with her congealed blood. The diminutive frame was dressed like any child would be when going to sleep. This beautiful little child, even in death looked innocent and helpless. With a doll by her side, as if a companion to comfort her, one no more lifeless than the other. The courtroom suddenly fell silent after their sudden gasp that was let out by many in attendance, including some of the jurors. Lena, who had been composed up to this point grabbed my arm and began squeezing it as if she were attempting to stop a bleeding artery. Her eyes were fixated on the photo of her little girl's final day and ultimate demise. She wept softly, never looking away, still gripping my arm, in a manner envious of a vice.

This closer glanced at the jurors but looked straight at Laudin while stating, "I want you to see this photo along with the others, seer them into your memories, because this was the work of a sadistic, selfish monster." He went on to remind the jurors of what Erin had told them earlier during her final closing. How Laudin had been mistreated as a child, watched his sister's murder and finally his rape at the hands of a circus clown. Was it a Honduras version of *Pennywise* from the Stephen King novel? These were events, if true, that occurred many years earlier and now everyone was supposed to believe that some manifestation drove him to murder. "What a convenient excuse, wouldn't you say?" Reid rhetorically asked the jurors.

Now, he paced toward the jury box. He was working the room like any good closer and making it a point to cover as much ground as possible. There was no doubt in my mind, he wanted everyone in the courtroom to feel his urgency, not just the jurors. Reid was now the puppet master, twirling the strings of truth in a manner that kept all in attendance wanting to hear his conclusion. Hell, I knew everything about this case, including the truth, having worked it from the beginning and I wanted to hear the conclusion.

Suddenly, he slowed his cadence but in a monotone voice continued addressing the jurors. While speaking, he made sure to inch closer, ever so slightly, to the easel which held the gruesome photos of a little girl, lying on a blood-soaked bed. Watching him do this, I was amazed, he was using the easel and its content as an immensely powerful visual effect. The genius of this strategy must have surprised Erin and everyone else who was sitting in the courtroom. Who could have imagined such a maneuver? My jaw nearly dropped as I observed him stimulate the juror's senses, using his words to bring the photos to life. By doing this, Little Lena was now real, not a photograph.

With his audience totally captivated, he continued presenting his argument behind Little Lena's murder. He articulated to the jurors, in graphic detail, how painful her injuries must have been. Reid used examples to demonstrate pain, maybe not at the level Little Lena must have felt but pain none the less. During one of these moments, he asked if anyone in the jury had ever needed stitches. Some of the jurors rose their hands, immediately, he suggested that such pain must have been felt at some level depending on the severity of the injury.

No sooner was he concluding his statement that one could see many of the jurors shaking their heads in agreement with his assertion. Based on this, he concluded that pain would be felt regardless of the wound, whether it was minor or like one depicted in the photos being shown. Many of the jurors grimaced at the ghastly sight. As Reid continued with his closing, he made sure each juror was part of his theatrics. He did not stay near the lectern, he made it a point to spend several moments in front of each juror as he brought his point across. Involving everyone was a perfect strategy since they had been a part of this trial from its inception. Keeping them at a distance now would be a grave mistake for this case.

Fortunately, this was not going to happen as some jurors could be seen reaching for tissues as their eyes welted and tears could be seen rolling down their cheeks. Truth be told, my eyes were misty as well, listening to Reid and observing those photographs. What normal human being would not be filled with such emotion. I hesitated to look at Lena fearing she would lose her composure if she witnessed my moment of weakness. Now, his voice began to crescendo to grab each juror's attention when he stated, "How much fear do you think Lena M. Miranda felt in her final 10–20 seconds of life? Her last moments were terrifying while in the clutches of a man she trusted, as he inserted the dull blade of the knife into her throat!" This was the unhittable fastball.

His description was powerful and heart wrenching, painting a picture of Little Lena's last moments alive. Here was this little girl that looked to Mr. Matte as a father figure, as someone that would protect her. Instead, this monster placed one hand on her small frame, keeping her from moving, and with the knife in the other hand, he began to insert its sharp tip slowly and deliberately into her throat. Without any regard for this little, helpless child, he slowly opened a wound so deep that it nearly severed her head, just leaving enough tissue at the base of her neck that prevented her head from detaching from her body.

Reid's forceful tone resonated off the courtroom's walls. Each word echoing with resounding energy, creating a dramatic effect as if spoken by some unknown deific entity. He continued his influential closing argument by posing to each juror what a normal person would believe to be true. "It's true that Little Lena had gone to sleep earlier that night, way before Laudin stepped into the bedroom on that fateful morning. And yes, no one can say for certain if she was awake or not, but even if asleep, wouldn't a normal person be wakened if forcefully being held down, let alone a knife blade piercing the flesh. Such an act, inflicted on any normal person would be cause for them to wake-up in shear horror and panic!" Following each spoken sentence, Reid would remove a photograph from the easel.

He held each photo with both hands, paced in-front of the jurors for them to see what a barbaric act looked like. "These photos are to remind you of what an innocent little girl was made to suffer through," he said to the jurors. As each juror was fixated on the photo, he purposefully would point to the abrasions on Little Lena's right shoulder and the two superficial cuts around her chin. These minor injuries were evidence that a struggle, ever so slightly, took place. Meaning that Little Lena was indeed awake during her final moments. Thus, the act committed by Mr. Matte was Heinous, Atrocious and Cruel (HAC) and must not be considered anything less. To do so would be a travesty. One could have filled a pool with the number of tears being shed.

# Chapter 17

Reid continued doing a masterful job explaining to each juror why Laudin should be found guilty. As he hammered his points across, while continuing to show each graphic photograph, I began drifting back to the day the autopsy of Little Lena was performed. Again, there I was in a self-induced trance. Reid's voice was slowly becoming faint in the distance, even though he was less than ten feet away from where I was seated. *God please*, I thought. I did not want to relive the dreaded autopsy. An event that was a continuous reminder of the worst acts of man.

Suddenly, my ears no longer heard Reid's voice explaining HAC or paying attention to the jurors. Once again, I was in another place and time, seated at my desk in the homicide office, staring at the phone. As it had happened throughout this trial, I was reliving this investigation and its darkness. Mentally being transported right back, like a Steven King novel, into the horrific murder of this little girl. My head was lowered, I closed my eyes, then the gruesome images of this incident became vivid. God, how I wanted those images to stop. I did not want to continue reliving this case or any other for that matter. Then again, maybe this was a divine indicator.

Maybe it was my responsibility to absorb this pain, indirectly, to better understand what family members must endure to do my job better. I wondered, *could this be one of the many burdens Luis Alburne would talk about*? carrying the pain of each death investigation.

Currently, Reid's voice continued being a distant murmur, fading to nothing, Suddenly, I found myself about to pick-up the receiver of my desk phone to call Dr. Prince. Officer Herbert had just left the homicide office with Laudin, who was being transported to the Dade-County jail. Finally, I grabbed the receiver, placing it to my ear while scribbling some notes in my Bible, such as the time Officer Herbert departed the homicide office with the offender. It was important to make sure that every detail was noted, nothing was to be left out. Upon concluding, I closed my Bible, placed my pen on the desk and began dialing the medical examiner's office. Surely by now, since it was 10:00 am, the time for Little Lena's autopsy should have been scheduled.

The noise in the homicide office was getting louder as Sandy, the secretary for Dr. Prince answered my call. "Medical Examiner's office," she announced with a pleasant voice. "Hi Sandy, this is Det. Granado!" I exclaimed.

"Hey, Pepi, I'd know your voice anywhere. What can I help you with?" she asked. Sandy was great to work with; always willing to assist investigators as much as possible. She had an incredibly good understanding of what investigators went through while working death cases. Her agreeable disposition acted as a calming effect, not just for investigators but for desperate and sometimes irate family members that have a loved one in the morgue. How can anyone get upset at a person with such a pleasant disposition? Very few, years of experience allowed her to permeate a soothing feeling to those she helped.

After exchanging pleasantries, we discussed several pending cases before I worked up the courage to ask the inevitable. Instinctively, she knew exactly why I was calling. Suddenly, as if on cue, Sandy provided me with the answer to a question that had yet to be asked. "By the way Pepi, Lena Miranda's post (short for post-mortem) is scheduled for 1:30 pm today. Dr. Prince was unable to schedule it sooner."

"Thanks Sandy, I might be able to grab a bite to eat before attending," I replied. With that, she responded, "See you then." After the uttering of the last word, I heard the click of her receiver hanging up.

Leaning back on my chair, I looked up, staring at the ceiling. *Man, another three hours before the dreaded post-mortem was to begin*, I thought. At this rate, I was on pace to be working 48 hours straight. There was no way to avoid it. Well, right about now another shot of Cafecito would come in handy. Standing up from my chair, I began to organize my desk, when Lt. Weeks called me into his office. "What can you tell me about your case Pepi? Chief Books wants an update!" he asked.

For a moment, I thought to myself, *Are you kidding me?* But like everything else, this was part of the job. Chief Books could give a rat's ass if I had been up all night, without sleep or if there were additional follow-ups that needed to be performed. So, now I found myself in an unenviable position, wasting valuable time briefing Lt.

Weeks. It was not the lieutenant's fault, he himself was a seasoned homicide investigator. He was aware of what I was doing but like any bureaucrat, he had to pass on information to those that are clueless at their whim. Therefore, it fell upon him to brief the Chief, so he wanted to have all the facts straight.

Normally, this task would have fallen on my supervisor, Sgt. Martin. Unfortunately for me, he had been pretty much MIA throughout this whole investigation, so he could not have briefed the lieutenant even if he wanted too. Besides, who better than me to give the briefing. I did not want anything said to be lost in translation. My briefing lasted 20 minutes. While exiting Lt. Weeks' office, he said, "Make sure to get some rest and show up whenever you wake up. I'm sure your team can hold down the fort until you return." Looking back, I could see his big smiling face. Those pearly whites against his dark skin were like a lighthouse light shining in the dead of night. "Thanks lieutenant," I replied. He was a great team supervisor and an incredibly good homicide lieutenant. We had worked on several cases in the past, although I was not on his squad, which lent its elf for us to have an incredibly good rapport. Plus, I knew he trusted me and that was most important. Trust within the homicide unit was paramount if an investigator wanted to survive.

Walking out of his office, I passed by my desk and picked up my Bible. Placed some reports that were left on my desk in my in-box and headed straight for the door. Upon arriving at the elevator, I pressed the button to go down. While waiting for the elevator, CSI Platt walked up, and we began to shoot the shit until the elevator arrived. "Are you going down?" I asked.

"No, I have to meet with Lt. Weeks," he replied. With that, the elevator arrived, and the doors opened. I entered and pressed the button that would let the elevator know to stop on level 2. Leaning against the elevator wall, I began going over in my mind everything that still had to be completed before going home. It always struck me how the follow-up work was more taxing than the initial investigation. That is why I laugh when patrol officers and civilians say that our jobs are easy once an arrest is made, if they only knew. Unlike them, investigators press on way after their shift has ended. Investigators do not have the luxury of just working a 10-hour shift. Our responsibilities are much greater than most but that is the Profession we have chosen, even with all its challenges.

Exiting the elevator on the floor leading to the ramp, I reached into my pocket and grab the keys to my vehicle. Once I stepped onto the ramp, I looked toward the area where my vehicle had been parked earlier and hoped that one of those nasty, No Parking, stickers had not been plastered on my windshield. You see, there was a particular sergeant that had nothing better to do, other than gig individuals who parked on the ramp for an extended period. That was such bullshit, he was retiring soon, so he was given this final assignment. Truth be told, I believe he enjoyed busting officers' chops with those stupid stickers.

The brightness and heat of the sun was just killing me, like a bug under a magnifying glass. I walked around my vehicle to make sure that no stupid sticker was observed. Great, there was no surprise left on my windshield. Upon getting past that small issue, I proceeded to place my key in the lock and opened the driver's side door. Just as I was about to enter my vehicle, I was spotted by several officers who were walking up the ramp escorting a prisoner. One of them, being a smart ass stated, "Damn Pep, you took my parking space." We began laughing as I entered my vehicle. Closing the door behind me, I placed the key in the ignition. Once the engine turned on, the air conditioner was cranked up to its coldest setting. With the cold air, now hitting me, full blizzard mode, I Instantly began to feel fresh and rejuvenated.

As the car got colder, the better I felt. Personally, if it were winter year-round, I would be in heaven. This was on my mind, knowing that to most Miamians it would be sacrilegious hoping for year-round cold weather. Shifting the gear into Drive, my vehicle began to move slowly down the ramp, while I maneuvered carefully making every effort to avoid the other parked vehicles. The last thing I needed was to be involved in a crash on the ramp. While navigating my way through the parking lot, there was Det. Alvarez's vehicle. Its driver's seat was totally reclined which was odd, this could only mean one thing. Det. Alvarez was taking a quick power nap. Even though he was new to investigations, he was picking up on the minor nuances which was to take naps when possible. Something that is common amongst investigators, especially, during prolonged investigations.

Parking my vehicle behind his, I exited and approached the side where he was sleeping. Tapping on his window, he slowly woke up, raised his seat, and lowered his window. "Did I wake you?" I asked sarcastically with a smile.

"Just getting a little shut-eye," he responded. "Are we going to do the canvass now or later?" he asked.

"I thought about grabbing a bite to eat, but I think we should return to the scene and see if we can come up with anything else, who knows, we might find additional evidence or even a witness," I commented. Just looking at him, it was obvious, he had to be feeling like having just been run over by a Mac truck. I did not blame him; he was not used to this pace. Seeing him took me back to my beginnings as an investigator. This was part of being a big city homicide investigator and we all must go through drudgeries of the job.

Ensuring he was alert, I told him to meet me at the incident location in 30 minutes. He responded by lazily nodding his head. As I began walking away, returning to my vehicle, he opened his driver's door and exited. "Just stretching Pep," he stated. "No problem, dude see you in 30," I replied. With that, I entered my vehicle, put on my Ray-Ban's, and began driving toward the rear exit of the police station. My stomach began to growl, why wouldn't it, I had not eaten since Wolfie's. Thinking about it, the meeting with Lt. Weeks killed me, now there was no time to stop and grab a quick bite to eat. Instead, I was heading straight to the crime scene to conduct my follow-up canvass. Sometimes investigators get lucky and can develop additional leads based on their follow-up canvass's. Unfortunately, not every canvass yields' pay dirt. As for this one, anything I uncover now, whether it is a witness or physical evidence would be a bonus. I was certain I had recovered everything which was needed to put Laudin away for good, hopefully, he would get the 'Chair'. It would not bother me in the least to have this monster fry.

Driving underneath the I-95 overpass, which was directly in front of the rear gate, I could see my sidekick's vehicle through the rear-view mirror. It was approaching the rear gate. *Good,* I thought, *we would get to the crime scene together and cover more ground.* This was especially important for me because I needed to make it to the autopsy on time. This task, truth be told, was not something I looked forward to. Attending an autopsy is not pleasant, but it was a part of my responsibility that could not be unheeded.

We made our way through the mid-morning traffic and over the Flagler Street bridge that crossed the Miami River. Heading west, I turned on Southwest 6th avenue and drove south through the rundown Little Havana neighborhood. Det. Alvarez was right on my tail as we navigated through this old section of Miami's Little Havana. This section was filled with dilapidated apartment buildings, abandoned vehicles and local small-time dopers riding their bicycles, hoping to pedal their Crack or Weed to junkies that came from everywhere. Driving past these miscreants, it dawned on me, there was no way they would make any sales today, it was still too early, and the sun was already blazing. Anyway, they were not my problem right now. Just to make it interesting, I radioed the dispatcher, informed her of what I observed and requested one of the area's patrol officers to investigate. This was and has always been a rough, violent neighborhood, affectionately known as 'Little Vietnam', a name given by the locals.

Still, as officers we have a responsibility to those innocent citizens that have no choice but to live amongst the evil despots who run this area. Once I radioed dispatch and heard the operator put out the call, I did a quick drive by to check for additional dopers. Det. Alvarez knew exactly what I was doing since he heard my transmission, so, as I made an unscheduled right turn, he made a left turn. We each drove around the blocks and met up again on 6th avenue and continued driving toward our destination. Hell, thinking about it, this area looks less menacing during the day then it does at night when all the ghouls are out. Chuckling to myself, I cranked up my car's radio as the song *Even Flow* by Pearl Jam was playing. That is exactly what was needed right now, some good grunge music to get the juices flowing.

Singing along with the song, I suddenly realize that I arrived and parked my vehicle right where it had been parked several hours earlier. Placing the car's gear in park, I stayed inside the vehicle long enough to conclude the ending of the song as if I were Eddie Vedder himself, "Oh, whispering hands, gently lead him away, him away, him away!" The song concluded and just as I was about to exit my vehicle, there was my shadow. I wonder how long he had been standing there or if he even saw my rendition, hopefully he did not hear me. If he did, I would never live it down.

While exiting the vehicle, I told Det. Alvarez to meet me at the trunk area of my vehicle. It was easier there, to come up with a game plan and write our notes. He knew the drill, we always meet at the trunk of a designated vehicle to brief and write our notes, this was a habit picked up from seasoned investigators who trained me early in my career. Standing near the trunk, we discussed what had been learned up to this point of the investigation. Then, I instructed him to canvass up and down the block to try and locate any possible witnesses or neighbors that new Lena Miranda or Laudin Matte. Most importantly, if he found anyone, he was to notify me immediately.

Finally, my exhausted partner was told that once we concluded our canvass, he could go home to rest. That was crucial since I still had to attend the autopsy and he would be on-call tonight. There was no need in having everyone tired. Det. Alvarez looked at me and said, "Dude are you crazy, how much longer are you going to be awake?"

Raising my head, I returned the look and replied, "No one is going to do your job for you, and we have a responsibility. What did you think, this was like television where everything is resolved in an hour?" What other type of response did he expect of me? No sooner had my lips stopped moving, he slowly looked up, apparently getting the message.

The expression on his face changed as he realized, being an investigator was harder than most people thought, especially working in homicide. "No problem, Pep," he said, "I'll meet you back here when I'm done," he continued speaking as he walked away. Good, now that I got that out of the way, maybe I can continue with my part of the canvass, looking for additional physical evidence. During my canvass of the complex's courtyard, I wondered if I had been too harsh on my young apprentice, we have been working a lot of hours and emotions were running a little high. It was no fault of his, he was still learning and did not know any better. Hopefully, one day, this lesson will assist him when he becomes a lead investigator.

While looking for additional clues, I glanced at my watch, *Shit*, I thought. It was 12:30 pm, the Post-Mortem was in one hour. We had to hurry if we were going to finish here in time for me to drive to the medical examiner's office. That alone was going to take 25 minutes with traffic during this time of day. Grabbing my police radio, which was hanging on my waist band, I radioed Det. Alvarez and asked if he had concluded his assignment. He informed me that he was returning to my vehicle and would arrive in ten minutes. Acknowledging his transmission, I let him know I would be waiting for him near my vehicle.

The sun was having its way with me as I was standing in the middle of the courtyard. Wiping my brow, I examined closely the exterior of apartment # 3, wanting to make sure nothing was missed. The yellow crime scene tape was still strung up in front of the apartment's door and a patrol officer was standing watch. I deliberately began my walk toward the apartment in a slow and methodical manner for the final time. Approaching the apartment, I informed the patrol officer that it would not be much longer before the apartment was released back to the family. The officer thanked me and said he would wait for my call. With that, I turned and began heading toward my vehicle feeling miserable. Upon arriving at my parked vehicle, I observed Det. Alvarez crossing the street to meet me. He was visibly dragging his ass, obviously worn out from having worked almost 20 hours straight.

We convened at the trunk of my vehicle, the sun was blazing, and several curious neighbors began to walk around us, wanting to be nosy and ask questions but they did not. I was glad too, there was no time to entertain nosy neighbors who would have received a very curt response from me had they started asking bullshit questions. They were like sharks swimming around a possible meal. Besides, surely this incident would be the neighborhoods story for the next few days. Suddenly, I looked up, called out to a roaming middle-aged woman, and asked if she wanted to help.

The response, in Spanish, was great. "Hell no, that's not my business what happened, that goes to show you how bad this neighborhood is that not even a little girl in her own bed is safe." After her response, she high tailed it out of our area and went around the corner. There, she sat down on a milk crate under a mango tree and began talking with a group of men and women who had gathered. I could only imagine what she was telling them. While watching the woman turn the corner, I turned, looked at Det. Alvarez and said, "See, that's what you will get at most crime scenes, especially when you are on your second and third canvass. People floating around wanting to know what is going on. In some cases, they might have information but refuse to speak with you at that moment, so make sure to pass out as many business cards as possible. You just might get the magic phone call that solves your case." He shook his head and began to brief me on what he learned during his canvass. There was nothing new and very few people were willing to speak with him. After informing him on what I had done, we wrote down our notes in our Bibles. While we were writing, he was told to go home after we concluded. I needed him to be fresh for tonight. Without looking up, he responded, "Okay." That really was not the reply I was expecting.

Being new and learning, I hoped he would have resisted a little and asked to attend the autopsy, but not everyone is cut from the same cloth. Had that been my response to my mentor, heaven knows what his response would have been. While walking toward my driver's side door, I told Det. Alvarez that if anything of interest was learned during the autopsy, I would inform him. He thanked me and began his half step walk toward his vehicle. Upon entering my vehicle, I turned on the engine and moved the A/C vents directly toward me. With the cold air hitting me, I paused one last time and surveilled the entire exterior of the apartment complex. *Man, it looked so much different last night*, I thought.

I shifted the gears into Drive and speed off toward the medical examiner's office. Driving like a mad man, my stomach was growling something fierce but there was no time to stop and grab a bite. I wanted to be inside the morgue by the time Little Lena was wheeled out of the freezer. For some odd reason, I felt an obligation to stand beside this little girl, as if to comfort her. At this point in time, that was the least I could do. It sounds crazy, but in my heart, there was a type of holistic connection or maybe in some weird way my small children were seen in her. Deep inside of me, I did not want her to feel abandoned again. It sounded crazy, but in some way comforting.

Weaving in and out of traffic toward SW 8th avenue was becoming a trying task with street construction and clueless drivers on the road. But during this period, the least of my worries was the traffic or crazy drivers since I was too busy questioning if my thoughts were normal. Maybe I was getting to emotionally vested in this case. Surely there must be a good explanation for these sentiments. Finally, I reached SW 8$^{th}$ avenue and began driving through the back streets that would take me toward the 12$^{th}$ avenue bridge, located in the NW section near the Miami River. Once I crossed the bridge, the medical examiner's office was just a few blocks away.

During my drive, I was so immersed in what needed to be done on this case that I was not paying attention to the radio. It was just background noise of rock music, unfortunately for me, considering how much I loved it. Another thing that kept me preoccupied; was how in the world could anyone work during the day. Angrily, I thought to myself, *What would have taken me five minutes of travel time during my shift has now turned into a road-trip where packing a lunch was a requirement.* Finally, the 12$^{th}$ avenue bridge was in sight and no cars were in front of mine, so I pressed on the gas pedal and five minutes later I was turning into the rear parking lot of the medical examiner's office. This area was reserved for the body removal vans who were transporting the victims and unloading them inside the receiving bay. I pulled up next to the gate and rung the buzzer. This part of my trip to the medical examiner's office was always amusing.

A voice came crackling over the intercom and said, "How may I help you?" So, me being funny and figuring that my voice on the other end was crackling too, replied, "Land shark." This was a reference to a skit from SNL, but much to my surprise, the gate opened allowing me to drive in. All the bay doors were open, each one was occupied by a transport van, so, I found a parking spot near one of the dumpsters and backed in. I grabbed my Bible and wrote down the time of arrival; it was 1:27 pm by my watch. It really was 1:17 pm since my watch was 10 minutes fast.

This was my habit to ensure I was never late to any appointment, especially with the reputation that Cubans have for never being on time. Because of that, the saying 'Cuban Time' was coined. It was funny to many but not to me. Besides, it was a sign of disrespect to be late. As I finished jotting down my thoughts in the Bible, I took a deep breath while catching the tail end of *Welcome to the Jungle* by Guns-n-Roses and air drummed the final verse. *Great song,* I thought. While exiting my vehicle, I continued humming the song as I walked toward the receiving bays. Once inside the bay, I spotted some of the remains removal technicians standing around the body trays, which were being washed to remove any biohazardous fluids left over from some of the victims they transported earlier. None of them were paying attention to me until I got closer and belted out, "Welcome to the Jungle" as if I were Axle Rose.

Suddenly, they all turned and began laughing once they recognized me. Some of them even made the comment, "What the hell are you doing here at this time, shouldn't you be sleeping?" *Such a true statement,* I thought.

In the wake of a loud laugh, I yelled back, "Some of us have to work for a living!" These guys, which I have known and worked with for some time mumbled some inaudible words as they returned to their duties of making sure each tray they washed became as sanitized as possible. Hell, one cannot be too careful. Exposure to disease can occur from being careless, therefore, extra precautions are important and taken seriously.

Leaving the guys to continue with their duties, I made my way to the receiving window. Sitting behind the double pane glass was the on-duty security guard. We knew each other from my many adventures to the morgue. We exchanged pleasantries while I signed the log-in book. I checked off all the right boxes before getting to the one denoting Victim. My heart sunk. I began writing the victim's information, when out of nowhere a hand crawled out from under the glass window holding an ID badge. Grabbing the badge, I clipped it to my shirt, finished entering the victim's information and began to enter the morgue. Upon approaching the entry area, the outside heat mixed with the cold from inside felt unpleasant.

As I entered the morgue through the secured sliding glass doors, its distinct, unimaginable odor of death was permeating the air. It was not pungent, it was just those subtle mixtures of cleaning products, biohazardous aromas along with the combination of decomposed body smells emitting from the multiple corpses that were stored inside assigned preservation coolers (freezer). Now, add the smell of sanitizing products to the mix. The byproduct is one hell of an unpleasant, pungent smell. Such smells can irritate the untrained person, except for those like me, where time has allowed me to become numb to such odors.

Obviously, these smells are a permanent feature within the morgue's walls and oblivious to those of us who are constantly visiting the morgue or for employees of the facility. Now, I stood in front of the double doors waiting for the buzzer to unlock the doors that would allow my access into the morgue's hallway. This was the only way since access was limited to authorized personnel.

# Chapter 18

Finally, a loud buzzing sound emitted from the morgue's doors and the entry light above them changed from red to green. Once the light came on, I heard the programmed clank of the doors unlocking. As if by magic, the doors opened automatically toward me. Suddenly, a quick burst of cold air hit me as I stepped through the double doors, having just entered the morgue's long, main hallway. Alone, I stood still, looked around and took a deep breath while staring down the long corridor. Where the porcelain tile floor ended, I could see another set of double doors. Those were used to enter the administration section of the medical examiner's office from the morgue.

Authorization to enter the administration section was not afforded to everyone, special clearance was needed. It was an eerie feeling looking down the hallway, with its sterilized, freshly polished floors that met the glossy off-white-colored walls. Some of the ceiling lights flickered, adding to the drama. Could such an event be caused by the ghosts of the thousands of victims who have been examined here, *Damn Pepi, this is not some Stephen King movie*, I thought. Chuckling awkwardly to ease the nerves, I began walking slowly down the hallway toward the morgue's examination entrance. This should have been routine considering how many times it had done previously, but this time I felt different.

It took me several seconds to make my way to the morgue's examination room entry door. Upon arrival, I looked up and noticed an illuminated sign that read, "Autopsy in Progress." The sign was to intentionally prepare those, unsuspecting, who were about to enter an unnatural world. Even for homicide veterans with years of death investigation experience, this area never feels comfortable and today, I was in that unenviable position. Pushing through the metal door, I spotted Karen, a heavy set African American, who was the morgue's senior assistant. She had a smile and an infectious laugh that eased the tension of those who entered the morgue. I have known Karen for years and with time, we became good friends. "Hey beautiful!" I exclaimed.

"Hey Pep," she replied as she approached. We gave each other a hug and friendly peck on the cheek. As we separated, I suddenly felt her hand grabbing mine. She gently squeezed it and brought it closer to her. Then, in a low whisper, she said, "I read your name on the M/E sheet. Will you be staying for the post or are you just here to speak with the doctor?"

Realizing what she was trying to do, I looked at her and said, "There is no avoiding this one, sweetie."

After so many years working together, she knew my intention was to be present during the autopsy, no matter how difficult. "I know Pep, it's not going to be pleasant," she replied. With that, I stepped up to the counter where all the copies of human diagrams were neatly stacked. These diagrams are used by the Forensic Pathologist to denote each wound where they are located, along with each corresponding measurement. They are not welcomed but needed.

These diagrams are such a grim reminder of what the end entails. It is important for each wound or injury to be properly documented. Knowing the importance of such documentation, I took it upon myself, early in my career, to immortalize what the doctors were describing on my own diagram sheets. Today, this task was made harder.

Diagrams, that although were not to scale or legally admissible, assisted me during my investigations and when writing my supplemental reports. On any other day, I would have gathered the diagrams pertaining to an adult victim – but not today. Today, I was looking for a different set. One that I wished never had to exist, but unfortunately, they do. Fumbling through the stacks of diagrams, I finally came across the ones pertaining to children. I paused for a moment and began collecting the copies needed, full body (front and posterior) view, side (left and right) view as well as one for the above the shoulders which had a larger outline of a child's head. What an unpleasant task preparing each sheet by placing Little Lena's name in each corresponding box along with the police case number.

While preparing each diagram, I could feel Karen pacing behind me as she prepped the area where the autopsy was going to be performed. Without looking, I asked her if the doctor was coming down from her office. She let me know that it would be another few minutes before the doctor's arrival. This was good because it would give me extra time to complete my unenviable task and update my trusty leather-bound notebook or Bible.

Finally, I completed the entry into the Bible, zipped up the binder and slowly turned around to lean against the counter. Taking a moment to soak it all in before continuing to my next task, the dry chill of the morgue began penetrating my skin deeper and deeper. It was slightly uncomfortable but tolerable. Still, my eyes became fixated on the area directly in front of me. While staring at an anchored, stainless-steel slab several feet in-front of me, I noticed a dull shine being immitted from the empty examination table. This was caused by the dimmed surgical lamp located directly above the slab which had been left on. My eyes scanned the area closely, observing malevolent looking tools laid out perfectly for their next use. These medieval tools looked like something out of a horror movie but essential for those who must wield them. This section was one of fourteen such stations in this part of the morgue but not the one being used for Little Lena's examination. Still, standing alone the smell of body fluids and disinfectants hovered over the area from earlier examinations performed on other unfortunate souls.

Just then, my eyes disengaged from the empty slab and focused on the attendant wheeling away the final victim of an earlier autopsy. The bumpy sound of the wheels from the stretcher echoed throughout the almost empty morgue. I watched silently as the attendant made his way toward the freezer, parading the shrouded corpse before me. The attendant stopped in front of the big stainless-steel door that secured the victims who were inside, he moved around the gurney to the front, grabbed the doors' latch and with a forceful tug, slid it open. He returned to the back of the gurney and began pushing it to enter the foggy freezer. As he disappeared, the heavy stainless-steel door closed behind him. A loud eerie thud was heard from the door closing and locking in place. Now, the morgue was empty again, just waiting for my case.

Soon, Little Lena's autopsy was going to take place. Having purposefully scheduled this case to be the final autopsy of the day, Dr. Prince decided to use the morgue's rear examination room. It was in an isolated location, mainly used for teaching and special cases. Very few people ever ventured into that area because of its limited use for routine autopsies.

This particular station was desolate, compared to the others. However, it was equipped with an audio set-up for recording as well as video to capture everything the doctor was seeing and doing during the autopsy. Principally, it was my contention, since this was a teaching facility that this station would be used to properly record this autopsy for future presentations to students and interns who were training or during medicolegal lectures. You see, it was not uncommon for doctors to document specific and unique cases for presentations.

Well, at least now I understood why such a long delay. This was all well and good, but I was beat, sleep deprived and needing to eat something soon. Still, leaning against the counter, my eyes were now closed while trying to get a quick five-minute cat nap. Then, off in the distance, the sound of Karen's voice calling out my name surprised me. Her voice was getting louder. As my eyes opened and readjusted to the environment, I could see her out of the corner of my left eye as she was coming around the corner of the counter. "Pep, I figured you'd still be here, Dr. Prince wants to start in fifteen-minutes," she stated.

"That's fine," I replied, "what other choice do I have?" I continued. "Do I have time to grab a coffee from the break-room?" I asked.

Her big smile lit up while continuing to walk past me, "Absolutely, I can wait for you," Karen replied.

I knew exactly what "Wait for you" meant. She was about to wheel out the body of Little Lena from the preservation room (freezer) and wanted me to be present. *Wow, that was very nice of her*, I thought. I stepped out of the morgue and found myself right back in the main corridor. I hurried my steps, making my way toward the double glass doors that led to the administration building. Pushing through the doors, I continued down some steps that led to another corridor which would take me directly to the break room. Five minutes later, I was returning to the morgue with a nice cup of hot coffee, extra cream, and extra sugar. The warmth of the coffee was soothing to combat the morgue's chill. It was not a meal, but it would have to do for now.

Though it was frowned upon to bring any food or drink into the morgue, for obvious reasons, today an exception was made. Upon reentering the morgue with coffee in hand, I hurried to the counter, where minutes earlier I had been leaning against. Placing my coffee on the countertop, I walked to the cupboard where the latex gloves were kept. A box that read 'Large' could be seen through the clear glass doors of the cupboard. I opened one of the doors; reached inside and grabbed several tan, latex gloves. Quickly, I put on the pair of gloves, then placed the remaining ones in my pant pocket. Now ready and prepared, I called out to Karen who was inside one of the offices located in the morgue. These offices were used primarily by the doctors for privacy when writing their case notes or dictating specific case findings into their recorders.

As Karen was walking out of her office, she could be heard saying, "Ready Pep?" Shaking my head, she began walking toward me. "Are you going to wait out here or going in with me?" she asked.

Somberly I replied, "I'll be going in with you."

"You're one of the few, Pep; not every detective would do this!" she exclaimed. How could I not, this was my case and an obligation that came with the territory. True, not all detectives would have gone this far, but how disrespectful to those who trained me had their teachings gone abandoned? Besides, I figured Luis would be disappointed in me if I did not follow through.

Both of us were now walking toward the preservation room's stainless-steel door without saying a word. The morgue was unnervingly silent as we stood before the door that guarded the dead. Karen took hold of the stainless-steel handle, turned it until the loud sound of its latch unlocking was heard. With great force, she slid the door open. Once open, a gush of cold air immitted from the freezer, with a foggy mist swirling inside. Nervously, while standing outside of the dimly lit freezer, I could faintly see through the cold fog a lone gurney placed against the wall. The outline of a small body could be distinguished. Since the plastic body removal bag used earlier had long been removed, a white shroud was now covering this once live form.

Little Lena's body laid under that veil, her back laid flat against the cold stainless-steel gurney. Motionless, to be sure, but the wind from the air ducts and swirling fog inside the freezer gave one the impression that something was moving underneath the cold sheet. *Damn Pepi, now your eyes are playing tricks on you*, I thought. Such things happen when one is sleep deprived and hungry. Suddenly, I felt Karen's hand gently take hold of my right elbow as we entered the freezer. The gurney was no more than twenty feet away from us, but it could have been a mile, that is how long it felt for us to reach it. We took our places on either side of the gurney, closest to where my victim's head laid. While Karen was unlocking the wheels, to roll the gurney out, I placed my hand on Little Lena's forehead. I dared not withdraw the shroud to reveal her face, that would come soon enough. But with my hand on her forehead, for some reason, unbeknownst to me, my lips began reciting the 'Hail Mary'. Karen, hearing me pray under my breath stopped what she was doing and stood still. Upon concluding, I could see her wiping her eyes. "That was beautiful Pep, I have never seen anyone do that," she said.

I shrugged my shoulders, and without looking at her I answered, "That was the least I could do."

This gesture was my way of somehow connecting with God, to muster the strength needed to continue my mission, no matter how uncomfortable. Then again, it might have been my way of giving this child the veneration, a tender mercy, she so deserved. Honoring her by reciting a simple prayer was my pleasure. Those words brought a sense of peace over me, a cleansing of my soul if you will. Such peace just reaffirmed my belief in God and his greater purpose. Removing my hand from her small forehead, I slid it to the side of the gurney. Silently, like a choreographed dance, Karen and I began rolling the gurney toward the door. I was intently focused on making sure Little Lena's body did not move more than necessary. Strange as that might seem, she had gone through enough.

As the gurney slowly rolled, my heart felt heavy knowing what was to come. Once we reached the freezer's door, Karen let go of her side and hurried to open it. I was still pushing the gurney but at a snail's pace, allowing time for her to open the door and return to her place. Karen managed to regain control of her side of the gurney while it was half-way out of the freezer. Seconds later, the freezer's door slammed shut, causing an involuntary flinch.

We began steering the gurney toward the designated area where the autopsy was going to be performed. While guiding the gurney down a dimly lit corridor, every time we neared one of the overhead lamps, they would brighten automatically, providing us with a clear vision of the area in-front of us. Then, once we passed through, each lamp would dim again, returning the area to its original gloomy state.

Finally, we arrived at the designated section where the autopsy would be performed. Karen took over, navigating the gurney, since she knew exactly where it was to be positioned. This area was isolated from the other autopsy bays, slightly smaller but very private. While she was adjusting the gurney, I could not help but notice a diagram of the human body framed on the wall. Because this was a teaching facility, it was there as a guide for students or other visitors. As usual, Karen had this area prepared to a 'T' Being a perfectionist, that is what set her apart from the other technicians. Not that the others were not good, because they were, she was just well ahead of the curve.

Glancing at the instrument table adjacent to the gurney, I noticed all the shiny implements that would be used during this procedure, arranged in perfect order. While Karen was doing her thing, it gave me time to set-up an area where I could take notes to describe each injury onto a diagram. I had to be close enough to observe what was being done yet leave enough room for the forensic photographer and the platform which was going to be used. I knew Karen would be assisting Dr. Prince, but I was not sure if anyone else was going to be attending this postmortem. The doctor was not in the morgue, so, this meant I had enough time to scamper and retrieve my coffee that was left on the counter. No sooner had I reached my coffee, when Dr. Prince came walking through the morgue's entrance, "Hey Pep, good to see you," she said.

"Hi Doc, just grabbing my java," I replied. She continued walking past me without saying another word, especially about the coffee.

While Dr. Prince was walking toward the section where the autopsy would be performed, I grabbed my coffee and high tailed it back through the same dim corridor that was used earlier. I arrived at the bay where Little Lena was lying motionless moments before Dr. Prince. She apparently made a pit stop in one of the offices, located on the opposite side of the morgue to grab a cassette tape filled with a medley of music by The Beatles. Standing by my makeshift counter, I opened my Bible, noted the doctor's arrival time, then grabbed one of the diagram sheets I had prepared earlier. Suddenly, Karen had removed the shroud that covered Little Lena, whose innocence was now exposed. My eyes were now fixed on her diminutive body. She looked like a large doll, still wearing the same pajamas from earlier. Pale now, with glassy eyes that were half open and lips that were somewhat wrinkled. The dried blood stains on her shirt were dark, brownish red with additional blood detected around her tiny chin and shoulder.

While the photographer was perched on her stand taking photos from an elevated position, I approached the examination table. For the first time, I clearly witnessed the savagery committed by Laudin. Although unable to fully appreciate the extent of each injury, I returned to my counter and described my observations on the side of the diagram sheet. Meanwhile, Karen began removing each article of clothing attached to this little angel with reverence. As each article was removed, one could hear the shutter of the camera going off.

This was particularly important because everything had to be properly documented. Then, out of nowhere, "Norwegian Woods" by the Beatles was heard through the speakers of a small boom box. That is when Dr. Prince returned, prepared to begin the daunting task of dissecting this small child. Now, Little Lena, laying on the cold slab had her head tilted back. This was done using a wooden block which was placed under her neck. She was now uncovered, naked for all to see, like the first moments when she entered this world. Her lifeless, bare body was cold to the touch with an ashen tone. Upon closer examination, she looked familiar.

I must have mentally been in another place and time because I had not noticed that Karen finished removing Little Lena's clothing. Now, the entire morgue was dim, except for the brightness of the operating lamp above the slab. That is when Dr. Prince said, "Hope you like the Beatles." Her words were muffled by the surgical mask she was wearing. The doctor stood on the right side of the slab while I took my position on the left side, behind Karen.

Carefully, I watched the doctor begin to take measurements of every defect and injury associated with this incident. As each measurement was taken, Karen would write them down while Dr. Prince dictated into the microphone which was hanging above the slab. Every word regarding each defect or injury was documented on my diagram sheet. Obviously, nothing written was to scale but I was able to make notations where needed to have a better understanding of how and what was used to kill Little Lena.

As I shadowed Karen, it afforded me the opportunity to do my job without necessarily looking directly at this tiny victim. Unconsciously, I did this by making sure to stand behind my friend. While pacing behind her, I would write in my Bible the location of each injury on the diagram sheet. Periodically, I would catch a glimpse of Little Lena's wavy hair as it dangled over the edge of the slab, still, I could not find the courage to look at her directly. It was not the fear of death or certainly the site of a dead body that had me at a loss. My biggest anxiety was seeing this innocent child, lifeless, then substituting her face with one of my children's. As a father, I already carry the guilt of not spending enough time with my children, let alone a child's death and she was not mine. *How could anyone in this day and age commit such an act of cruelty?* I wondered, as I continued entering information. Faintly, I could hear Dr. Prince giving instructions to the photographer and Karen. Suddenly, without warning, Karen moved quickly away from the slab. Surprised, Little Lena was now on full display. The photographer began to take photos from various angles. I guess that is what the doctor was instructing when I heard her muffled voice.

Now, there I was alone, standing in-front of Little Lena trying to answer the reason for such savagery. Dr. Prince and Karen had stepped away from the slab and were conferring near the examination counter. Since I was not in the way of the photographer, who remained on the scaffold, there was no reason for me to move. Pure silence fell over the morgue except for the camera's shutter. Not a word was heard from the doctor or Karen who were now inside one of the offices. It was like watching a silent movie. I could see their lips moving but no sound. My throat was becoming dry, so I grabbed my coffee from the makeshift counter. Placing the cup to my lips, I took a sip. *Not too bad,* I thought, even cold it still tasted rather good. I finished drinking what was left and placed the cup inside the trash can. Setting my Bible on the counter, I returned to Little Lena like a dedicated sentinel watching over her.

While standing next to the slab, I removed a pair of the latex gloves from my pocket and slipped my hands inside. With gloves on, I placed my hands on the edge of the stainless-steel slab. It was chilling, so cold, almost unbearable. Little Lena was supine, fully exposed, with her head tilted back from the wood block underneath her neck. Her wavy hair, it looked adorably messy and undone, like any small child who had been sleeping. Now panning the entirety of the slab, a clear garden hose was observed attached to a sink located at the foot of the slab. The open end of the hose was laid on the dry slab. It would not be turned on until the autopsy commenced. Once the water began running, it would assist in cleaning and washing away any biohazardous fluids that trickled onto the slab.

Standing near the middle section of the slab, it placed me adjacent to Little Lena's feet. Her small frame was not enough to extend beyond the mid-point of the slab. I began inching toward the top of the slab with my hands gliding on its edge, when suddenly my hand felt the tiny cold fingers of her left hand. Upon feeling those icy little fingers, I found myself placing my hand on-top of hers. Not that the warmth of my being would make a difference, but once again, a small measure of kindness for a little girl so undeserving of her fate. Just then, I closed my eyes and it felt as if the little hand was that of my daughter's. An uncanny warmth fell over me, as if blanketed by some unknown power, not allowing the bitter cold slab or ambient temperature affect me. The warmth was soothing, and now I could faintly hear a child's laughter off in the distance. Suddenly, the laughter of the child faded away, and my eyes opened. How could I explain what just happened? For me, this was yet another example of God's greatness and an affirmation of the importance of my work. Such a divine mystery was meant to be embraced, not examined.

Slowly, I opened my eyes and clearly observed the extent of damage caused by Laudin. Dried blood was detected on her little shoulders, right forearm, and some edges of her wavy hair. But as my eyes panned toward her head, they became fixed on the section where her neck had been prop-up by the wooden block. The horrific injury was now more pronounced, especially with the brightness emitting from the surgical lamp. Her throat had been unimaginably slit, to such a degree that her head was barely attached, if not for the neck muscle and fibers. Upon closer examination, I could see torn, serrated skin tissue, a severed larynx and damage to her carotid artery. "She was never going to survive such mutilation," I imagined.

Now, I am not a doctor or pathologist but upon observing these gruesome injuries as well as some minor defects around her chin, there was no doubt in my mind that Little Lena suffered and felt excruciating pain while she was slowly being murdered. *Undeniably, she had to have suffered*, I thought. While closely examining her injuries, the more I thought about the knife that was recovered at the crime scene. It was dull looking, not appearing to be able to cut through human flesh, tissue, or muscle with ease. Still, it was a type of hunting knife which could possibly account for these injuries. Then, recalling the spatter at the crime scene, it was conceivable that it was caused from the initial thrust to her throat.

Surely, at this moment, had anyone walked in on me, they would have thought of me as some sort of ghoul. You see, there are very few people outside of the medicolegal field that would be so immersed in viewing such injuries so closely, especially when inflicted on a child. Even in my profession, very few investigators go this far. Yes, they would have attended the postmortem but not to this extent.

In the end, they would rely on the medical examiner's report.

As for me, I could hear the voice of Luis Alburne singing in my ear, "Dude, you must be thorough during each investigation, even if it's uncomfortable." Now normally, viewing victim's that have suffered extensive trauma would not bother me, especially, having studied Mortuary Science. But today was different, Little Lena was different. The way she was murdered was horrible. An act so unimaginable that even seasoned officers were shaken.

While panning away from the small child, her injuries were committed to my memory as well as the stale smell of dried blood that now enveloped my nostrils. Suddenly, a voice from the heavens, "Are you done, detective?"

Startled, I slowly looked up. It was the photographer. I had been so focused on Little Lena that I totally forgot about her. "Oh, yeah – sorry about that!" I exclaimed.

"No problem, you weren't bothering me, I just have to notify Dr. Prince," she replied.

As she climbed down from atop the scaffold, I slowly returned to my counter and continued making entries into my Bible while fresh in my memory. Standing stoically as I gathered my thoughts, "Strawberry Fields" could be heard in the distance. Not bothering to turn around, footsteps could be heard, it was Karen. "Pep, I am about to start cutting, are you staying?" she asked.

Without turning around, I replied, "I'll be here for a few more minutes, I need to catch up before I forget anything." There was no reply from Karen. Upon finishing my entry, I turned and noticed Dr. Prince reviewing some notes that were written by the photographer. Waiting for her to finish reading, I saw Karen fumbling with some instruments that were on the examination table. She then moved to the sink and turned on the water. Now, that once dry hose began to trickle water out of the front nozzle like a fountain.

Dr. Prince began walking toward me as Karen returned to her original position. We met at the head of the slab, just inches from Little Lena's hair. We discussed the case and went over all the visible wounds. Gradually, Dr. Prince moved to one side of the slab and I moved to the other. While standing adjacent to each other, with the victim lying between us, she began describing in detail each visible injury regardless of its size. Silently, I watched and listened.

This is what made working with Dr. Prince so enjoyable, her teaching style made it easy for any investigator to fully understand. Plus, she was always prepared to answer questions, no matter how trivial or elementary. Before long, I heard all that needed to be heard. But instead of leaving, it became difficult to pry my eyes away from Dr. Prince who had widened Little Lena's neck further to examine the wound closer. The gash was now wide enough for me to fit my fist inside. My heart sank, like no other time as an investigator. I had never felt such sorrow.

I took a step back and began removing my gloves, tossing them inside a biohazard bag for proper disposal. Now returning to my make-shift counter, I opened my Bible and made a few additional entries before departing the morgue. As I was about to close the Bible, I looked up and asked the doctor if this was going to be classified as a Homicide. She nodded her head, then said, "The cause of death will be Incised wound to the neck and the manner will

241

be Homicide." I thanked Dr. Prince while closing and zipping up my note pad. Just then, there was Karen, standing at the head of the slab. A small circular saw in her hand which is used to remove the skull. Except, before using it, she must first peel Little Lena's skin (mask) from her forehead, bringing it down below her small nose. Then, her scalp is peeled back to expose the skull before sawing around it. I watched as this little angel's last bit of innocence was about to end, and I wanted no part of it today.

Hurriedly, I grabbed all my belongings from the counter, placed them under my armpit and began walking toward the exit. That is when Karen yelled out, "Be careful Pep, see you next time." My steps quickened while heading through the dim corridor. I had been inside this place long enough; it was time for me to get out of this morbid reminder of death. Upon reaching the morgue's exit door, a sudden warm sensation fell upon my forearm while pushing open the door. It was as if someone had gently caressed my arm, but no one was around. Entering the main hallway, an eerie shiver went up and down my spine. Slowing my pace, I walked toward the double doors that would lead me out to the receiving bay area. Once there, I came to a stop and pressed the button that would open them. For some strange reason, the doors were taking longer to open.

While waiting for them to open, off in the distance, I heard the faint sound of a child's laughter coming from the area of the doors which lead to the morgue. Suddenly, the automatic doors began to open; I turned my head in the direction of the laughter but all I saw was the long empty, dimly lit hallway. Quickly, I walked through the doors and headed straight for the reception window. *Man, what the hell was that? I wondered.*

# Chapter 19

After exiting the remains receiving area, I went directly to the reception window, needing to return my morgue pass and retrieve my police identification. While waiting, I could not help but think of that ghostly child's laughter. My mind must have been playing tricks on me, hell, fatigue must have definitely been the cause, I deduced. Disregarding this Alfred Hitchcock moment, I reached under the opening in the window to retrieve my ID from the security guard. With ID in hand, I turned and noticed the receiving bay, that once was full of transportation vans and technicians was now empty. Most likely, every technician was on pick-up runs, after all, this is Miami. Walking through the receiving bay, one could begin to feel the excruciating Miami heat as it penetrated through the bay doors, which had been left open. Exiting the bay area, my feet immediately stepped onto the asphalt, which felt like a George Foreman grill. Once outside, it was so bright, without a cloud in the sky, I had to squint my eyes just to find my vehicle. A quick glance at my watch told me it was 3:45 pm, *Damn, I was in there much longer than anticipated*, I thought.

For me, these conditions were unbearable, being so hot and humid. *How I hated working during day light hours*, I thought, arriving at my vehicle. Reaching into my pocket, I hurried to take out my car keys. With keys in hand, I immediately inserted the one key into the door lock. The door could not open fast enough. Finally, within seconds I was seated behind the steering wheel, instantly turning on the engine. Now that the engine was running, I reached toward the A/C knob, turning it to the coldest setting. I closed every vent except for the two directly in front of me. Instantaneously the cold rush of air was hitting me. Wow, that felt great. Even though I had just exited a very cold facility, it was not the same. The air in my vehicle smelled fresh of pine, not of death and cleaning fluids.

Taking a few minutes to relax in my seat, gave me time to properly process what had just been observed in the morgue. Instinctively, I reached for the radio, changed the band from FM to AM and adjusted it to channel 560, a local sports station. While listening to the sportscaster, I closed my eyes. Several minutes passed. With my eyes now wide open, I reached for my Bible to review the notes. Opening the notebook to the last entry, the diagram sheet of a child's shoulders and head fell out. Picking it up from the floorboard, I held it in my hand and gazed at it for several minutes.

While intently reviewing my notes to ensure that nothing was missed, I found myself focusing on the area of Little Lena's neck. My description and drawing on this diagram sheet seemed extremely graphic for being so cursory. Such detailed depiction was necessary, if only for my attention. Still, my primary focus was on the massive neck wound. The closer this gaping injury was studied, the more I thought of how much that innocent little girl laying on a cold slab had suffered. While her little body was right now being cut open, all in the name of science and justice, my heart sank knowing she would never again enjoy a sunny day such as this one.

For her, such days were long gone. Now, her pain from the sharp medieval instruments was no longer existent, but pain was real several hours earlier. What horror? *How could any human-being commit such an act*? I thought. My heart continued aching for Little Lena and her family. Finally, I mustered enough energy to make some notations in my Bible before leaving the Medical Examiner's parking lot. Once I finished writing, I folded the diagram sheet and placed it inside my Bible but not before taking another long hard look at the wound. That dreadful image and remembering how Dr. Prince opened the wound further was extraordinarily vivid. With that vision, my eyes began to moisten from the sadness I was feeling, an emotional pain wished on no other person. This case was going to test my resolve, one way or another. Then, during this solemn moment, I felt tears as they gently rolled down my cheeks.

Suddenly, I could hear Reid's voice emphasizing a point he must have made to the jury. A point I did not hear, but forceful enough to return me to this place and time. Clearing my eyes, I felt them moist as if I had been crying. *Gee, that's weird*, I thought. Anyway, Lena and Floria were listening to Idalma while I was trying to gauge the jury's reactions. For now, there was no reason to pay attention to him for I knew where he was going with his homily. The jurors were now on the edge of their seats, listening intently to the final moments of his closing argument. One would have thought that Billy Graham was speaking. Reid's skillful and eloquent sermon was now reaching its crescendo while he pranced up and down, directly in front of the jurors, like a flirtatious peacock.

Finally, his exclamation of "Ladies and Gentlemen of the jury," could be heard by everyone inside and possibly outside the courtroom. He was deliberate while emphasizing this phrase for effect. As well he should have since he was about to land the final blow of this trial. Now, throughout the courtroom, there was an eerie crypt like silence, with all eyes focused on the prosecutor. Laudin Matte was about to receive a taste of true justice. There would be no knife used to slice his throat like he did to Little Lena. The scales of 'Lady Justice' would be tipping against him on this day, not while he slept, as Little Lena did but with full awareness of the legal process. Reid was now on a full out offensive attack. His steps were faster as he paced before the jurors. One look at him and you would think he was in the middle of a workout. He continued speaking about the diminutive victim to the jurors and every so often stop near Laudin Matte. He wanted for the jurors to observe how little remorse was exuding from this vile individual. Prior to continuing, he glanced at the defendant intently, as a punctuation of his determination.

Now, he was standing close to the easel. Everyone in the courtroom could feel him about to bring everything he was pontificating to its conclusion. Just then, Reid's words began to reverberate within me like a steady beat of a percussionist against a timpani drum. "So, as we reach the final stages of this trial, let me leave you with these words!" he exclaimed. He then proceeded with what I can only describe as the best closing ever, at least the best one that I have heard.

"The ghastly and grotesque crime committed two years ago, should send chills down your spines while you reflect and deliberate. I have just summarized and discussed a weeks' worth of evidence in a fraction of the time. So, I want to thank you for your patience. Let me be very clear, that fair inference submitted was undeniably supported by physical and verbal evidence. The defense skillfully presented their version of the event to exonerate, Laudin Matte, but all they did was make the State's foundation stronger. Ms. George stood before you and painted a picture of a feeble man that had a rough childhood, a sad story at best – one to soften your hearts, so as to look past his brutal, unjustifiable act as an adult. You heard from eyewitnesses recounting what took place on that early morning of June 3, 1994. You heard from a grieving mother, who told you that her biggest fear came true when she heard the words, 'You're going to cry tears of blood' being uttered by the defendant. Let us not forget, the emotional testimony of the responding officers as well as the lead detective, who were the first officers on the scene."

While Reid was just bringing out every point, my heart was racing. I anxiously needed for him to finalize his speech. So, as I continued listening intently, this was how he concluded. "But when you drown out their testimony's and open your eyes, how can you not be swayed by these photos, the last moments, of two-year old Lena Miranda as she laid on her bed – instead of sleeping – she was brutally and cold-heartedly butchered. When you say, 'I want to tell you everything,' like the defendant told detective Granado and you do not – I submit to you, that is a sign of guilt – when your hands are covered in blood, that is not yours – that is a sign of guilt. So, as you evaluate all of this physical evidence and sworn testimony – think of Lena Miranda."

"In conclusion, Laudin Matte had a long-standing grievance with his girlfriend, the mother of Lena Miranda. He was jealous, manipulative and physically abusive toward her but on June 3, 1994, he decided to resolve his grievance in a manner that was emotionally terrifying, and so violent that it eventually ended with murder."

"For the prosecuting team and I, it has been a pleasure, all bit difficult, to represent the victim, two-year-old Lena Marcela Miranda and her family. We have done so through a system of due process; but now, due process is over. It is now your job as jurors, your privilege, your duty as well as your responsibility to bring about justice. On behalf of the State of Florida and the Miami Dade State Attorney's Office, I ask that you return a verdict of guilty as charged against Laudin Matte – Thank You!"

This had been an emotional battle of biblical proportion. Reid, visibly moved and worn from his closing argument, took a deep breath, thanked the judge then walked slowly toward the prosecution's table. Once there, he pulled out his chair and sat, not gently but with a slight flop. Sitting directly behind him, I could tell he was mentally exhausted. He had to be, hell, I did not present the closing and I was mentally drained. Reliving this case repeatedly was not helpful. Reid could be seen running his fingers through his medium wavy auburn hair. Finally, he lowered his head, resting it on both hands, that were perfectly cupped as if they were holding a delicate sphere.

While he rested somberly, his assistant began organizing all his trial notes along with the additional documents that were on the table. Each document was placed meticulously and neatly, inside folders. These folders were inside a huge banker's box, located underneath the table. This banker's box was used to store every important document pertaining to this case. It was equivalent to an investigator's case file, like mine, filled with everything case related.

During this brief period, Judge Banks called for his bailiff, who immediately moved from his post, near the witness stand and scurried toward the side of the judge's bench. They spoke for a few minutes, then the bailiff shook his head and repositioned himself on the opposite side of the judge's bench. Some jurors looked tired, leaning back against their chair's backrest, while others were reviewing whatever notes they managed to write during both closing arguments. What struck me was how they appeared to be extremely interested and vested. These jurors wanted to perform their civic duty well and that was visible to all who were inside the courtroom.

Suddenly, Judge Banks cleared his throat softly, then struck his gavel. The bailiff, once the sound of the gavel resonated throughout the courtroom shouted, "Silence in the courtroom!" No one uttered another word. Not that there had been much talking prior to this moment, just enough of a low murmur amongst the gallery which could be annoying.

With all eyes fixed on the judge, he cleared his throat again, then looked at the jurors and stated, "You've had a long morning, we will take a five-minute break before we continue."

Upon finishing the sentence, his bailiff sounded off with, "All rise," as the judge stood up, he moved his chair to one side. Then, without saying a word he hurriedly stepped down from the bench, heading straight for the courtroom's rear exit door that granted his quick departure toward his chambers.

Soon after, the low murmurs became an all-out conversation inside the courtroom. The jurors were escorted to the deliberating room, where they could grab a snack or something to drink. For sure, a bathroom break was going to be needed. Once the jurors cleared the courtroom, I turned to Idalma and asked her to stay with Lena while I stepped outside. Idalma, with a smile shook her head as I stood to exit. Exiting the courtroom through the double doors, I entered the hallway, it was uncomfortably packed with people. It seemed like everyone and their mother was waiting outside, this was almost like an intermission during a Broadway play. Reporters from various media outlets were setting up their equipment near the courtroom in the hopes that a verdict would be announced soon. Looking at them scurry about, I wondered, *If they only knew that the deliberation had not started*. Amused by the way they were running around like crazy ants, I looked for a space to sit to continue watching the show.

Finally, I was able to find a space on one of the benches, located in the hallway. Just as I began walking toward it, Idalma came walking out of the courtroom. Changing course, I disregarded the bench and met with her. "Is everything okay?" I asked.

"Oh, Yeah Pepi, everything is fine. Lena is calm and so is Floria," she replied. That was a relief, so long as everyone was calm, I was calm, we did not need additional drama at this point. As Idalma began walking toward the escalators, she informed me that she needed to return to her office but would return shortly. Just as she disappeared while descending on the escalators, Cecy came shooting out of the elevators.

"Hey Pep, people are stupid, they see that you're trying to get out and instead of opening a path they block you in," she argued. I began laughing because she had a short fuse for discourteous people and was having a minor fit, all by herself.

Realizing why I was laughing, Cecy stopped and simply said, "I must have sounded like a mad woman, huh?" I simply shrugged my shoulders and responded, "Only you. But no crazier than these people running like chickens without their heads."

I totally understood her, sometimes, people are ordered via subpoena to respond to the courthouse and are less than civil, especially if it is one of their cases. Unfortunately, it happens more than not. We just looked at each other and chuckled for a moment before she asked how the case was going. I let her know that closing arguments had concluded and a five-minute break was ordered by the judge. She let me know she was heading to another courtroom to drop off some documents for a judge's signature but would meet me in the presiding courtroom. As she walked away, I told her I would be saving her a spot. She gave an affirmative response while I reverted to being a social butterfly. Finding the opportunity, I mingled and spoke with a bunch of attorneys and officers that were hanging around the courtroom's entrance. That is when I took pause and realized, my nerves were back to normal, not a care in the world. This was going to be a day of redemption for Little Lena and her family.

In the middle of the hallway, a group of officers were huddled, distributing shots of Cafecito. My prayers were answered. Craving for the potent brew, I eased my way toward them to join in the Miami tradition. We greeted each other with handshakes and hugs. Then, I was given a small plastic cup, no bigger than a thimble, which was then filled with that dark black liquid. Bringing the cup to my lips, I shot its content down my mouth in one gulp. *Not Jack Daniels,* I thought but the next best thing. "I've always said it, there is nothing like it to keep you going!" I exclaimed to the guys. The group agreed and continued with multiple conversations simultaneously. It is amazing how anyone could understand who was talking and about what, with so many interruptions within the group. That is just a 'Cuban' thing. The way conversations are carried out, gives the feeling that courtesy goes out the window. Yet, everyone seems to know what each other's points of views are, even if one was not directly involved with the conversation. Now, how funny is that?

Between all of us officers and the media crews, much of the hallway leading to courtroom 2–3 was blocked. Those who attended the earlier session in the courtroom if they stepped out might lose their place in the gallery. The only ones assured of a reserved seat were family members of the victim and defendant. Even I, the lead investigator, was not guaranteed a seat but that would be highly unlikely. Still, with that in the back of my mind, I decided to make my way toward the courtroom.

Walking past a multitude of officers, attorneys and news reporters made me wonder what motivated them to stick around. I had no choice; I was fully vested in this case. For many, it must have been the curiosity and for some, it was a way to present this human-interest story to audiences across South Florida who watch the nightly news. Either way, I wished this day did not have to exist, with its sorrow and pain attached. Either way, it would soon be over.

Entering the courtroom, I looked to my left at the bench where I was seated earlier. There was no room to sit, every space was occupied by reporters. Several of them, having recognized me, smiled, and mouthed, "Good Luck." Returning the smile, I continued toward the first pew, sat, and scooted toward Lena. Moments later, Idalma returned and sat between Lena and Floria. "You okay my friend?" she asked.

"Just waiting, sweetie, hopefully we get started soon," I replied.

Just then, the bailiff opened the courtroom's rear door, entered the courtroom, and walked past the prosecutors and defense attorneys. Seeing that he had walked past the attorneys, he stopped, turned around and proceeded to inform them that the trial would be resuming in five minutes.

In harmony, the attorneys responded with "Thank You." The bailiff made a quick turn and continued toward the courtroom's double doors, pushed them open and entered the hallway. The doors shut quietly as he exited, but I could see him through the glass door pains giving instructions to those waiting outside.

Several minutes later, he reentered the courtroom and marched directly toward the judge's chambers. As he disappeared into the rear hallway, those who were left standing outside the courtroom began reentering, filling in all the available spaces on the pews. Within minutes, there was no seating spaces available and those left without a seat decided to take a chance by standing in the isle. *Standing room only I wonder if the judge is going to allow that*, I thought. That is when I felt Reid's hand on my shoulder. Turning around, there he was, standing confidently and in a low tone said, "We got this." *Gee, that's weird, Reid giving me a somewhat of a high-five. That was so unlike him*, I thought. I just smiled and shook my head in acknowledgement. He then returned to his chair and began staring at the door leading to the deliberating room. Maybe he was yearning for the jurors to begin their return to the courtroom or maybe not. Surely, I was not going to ask him what the hell he was doing.

These had been the longest five-minutes ever. Only twenty minutes had elapsed, but finally it appeared that this phase of the trial would be continuing. These are the times that drive investigators, prosecutors, and family members bonkers. The waiting is painful, it is like a perpetual dagger being driven into one's heart. Procedures and decorum, that is what our justice system is all about, although sometimes, one must wait longer than they want for justice to be obtained. Looking at Lena and her mother, they were silent and mummy-like. They showed no facial expressions, why would they, both had endured this long arduous trial. A process which had taken a toll on both, emotionally, spiritually, and physically. To relive an event as horrifying as this one is rough, but as a parent, I have no way of understanding such pain. Nor would I want to know.

Like an apparition, the bailiff entered the courtroom, walked toward the deliberating room door, opening it. He stood by as the jurors made their way out, one by one toward their assigned seats. Once they were seated, the bailiff motioned for the corrections officers to bring out the defendant who had been sequestered in the holding cell, located behind the courtroom speaking with his defense team. Moments later, I saw Erin George entering the courtroom followed by the corrections officers who were escorting Laudin Matte to his chair. As Erin walked past Reid, she looked toward him, gave him a cheap smile but said nothing.

There were no words that could be uttered at this point. Both attorneys stepped into this courtroom days ago prepared to execute their duties. One had to defend a monster who had committed an unspeakable act while the other was responsible for presenting the state's case on behalf of a murdered child. Trials such as this one can make or break an attorney's reputation if they fail to perform in a manner that is less than outstanding. Certainly, in this case both attorneys were well prepared. They matched each other's wits and professional prowess, except, my investigation was solid and well executed which the Erin could not match.

I glanced at my watch, *Damn, it was already 4:00 o'clock and the jurors haven't started deliberating. How much longer was this going to take*, I thought. Like any other homicide case, one never knows what happens behind closed doors when jurors discuss the facts of the case, or review pieces of evidence. Maybe they have additional questions or request, who knows. At this point and time, it is a crapshoot. All juries are different in their approach, hopefully this one is quick.

# Chapter 20

The jurors returned to the jury box and were now seated. They were deathly silent, except for the occasional creaking of their seats while they were being adjusted. With the seat adjustments out of the way, each juror was upright and focused. Everyone in the courtroom noticed how intent these jurors looked, as if they were preparing to receive a life altering message. Truthfully, they were. Once the judge presented them with the jury instructions, the fate of Laudin Matte was in their hands.

Finally, the defendant was in his place, head bowed and absent of any emotion or facial expression. His attorney, Erin George, along with her team were conferring beside him but he did not move. Who knows what was going through his mind? Was he thinking of how the rest of his life would be, inside a prison cell, or the real possibility of being sentenced to death? Surely, Erin had gone over these possibilities with him. Besides these obvious possibilities, might he be thinking of Little Lena? The helpless little child, just two and a half years old, who succumbed to his wrath because of his anger against her mother on that fateful morning.

The longer I looked at him, the less emotional I became for whatever outcome would be thrusted his way. For in the end, nothing would ever reverse what happened on June 3, 1994 at 3:10 am. The lives of many people were forever changed. Yes, Little Lena's suffering and anguish lasted countless minutes that must have felt like an eternity. Minutes that are unimaginable for those who are present at this trial.

Fortunately, she is at peace, rejoicing in God's kingdom. Unfortunately, for those of us who were present on that fateful morning, the horror of such an act will last a lifetime. As for me, the emotional toll has been costly which is something that will never be repaid. Thinking back on that morning, we should have been the ones who put down that animal. Still, I thank God every day for not allowing me or any of the others who were with me to take matters into our own hands. Yet, in my solace, all I can do is watch this evil miscreant squirm in anticipation of the verdict. Though he justly might receive the death penalty, such a fate would be too quick and merciful for Laudin Matte.

Suddenly, the bailiff opened the door leading to the judge's chamber and sounded out, "All Rise!" In one fell swoop, everyone in the courtroom stood up simultaneously. Moments later, Judge Banks entered the courtroom, his black robe flowing like an English headmaster entering a classroom. He quickly ran up the steps of the judge's bench and without missing a beat, sat down in his chair.

He started by addressing everyone inside the courtroom, "Thank you, ladies and gentlemen for your patience. This has been a long and exhausting trial for many of you, especially the families. To you, my sincere apologies."

Judge Banks was extremely eloquent and thoughtful with his opening comments. He framed everything after in a manner that exuded compassion and fairness but with a strict rule of law. He thanked both the defense and state attorneys for their work, comportment and how they each presented their case. Pausing briefly, he looked out at the gallery, thanked them for their cooperation and courteous behavior during this trial.

Finally, he took a long gentle look at the only family member present of Laudin Matte. Then, looked straight at Lena and Floria, Little Lena's mother and grandmother. Softly, he began by expressing the sorrow that had engulfed the courtroom during this trial, how he could not begin to understand the grief befell upon each family. His words were soothing and comforting as he explained the judicial process and why it was important to our way of life. Also, he let them know they would be given a chance to speak at another time if they so desired. He concluded by thanking those in law enforcement who were part of this case for their professionalism.

Finally, upon finishing with his remarks, he turned his attention toward the jurors. With a sincere tone, he thanked them for their diligence, patience and for the judicious questions they asked during the course of this trial. Judge Banks impressed upon them of their solemn responsibility to perform their civic duty to the absolute best of their ability. This moment and his comment struck at the core of our system of justice and fairness.

He continued to lecture them on how crucial it was to review any or all pieces of evidence, as well as testimonies presented to render a just and impartial verdict. Prior to introducing the jury instructions, he completed his comments and again thanked the jury.

Now, the courtroom was completely silent, as if a funeral were in-progress. I had never witnessed such a show of courteous behavior or reverence. Usually, one can hear the low murmurs of people sitting in the gallery, but not today. As it was throughout this trial, such comportment was not always present. There were many occasions when visitors would annoyingly cause interruptions by their untimely comments or low conversations. Still, this trial for the most part had been very civil, even though there were times when behaviors were less than acceptable. Not that people were unruly, just very opinionated during various points of the trial. Fortunately, the bailiff kept order while the judge conducted his responsibilities as if no interruptions were occurring.

As the minutes ticked away, anxiety was setting in just wanting Judge Banks to get on with the jury instructions. Hell, there came a point, when I felt like saying, "Dude, just get on with it!" That would have been the end of my career, not just as an investigator but probably as a police officer. For sure, it would have been professional suicide. Thinking back on that moment, there must have been bouts of apprehension, with case exhaustion being at the forefront. Thank God, cooler heads prevailed. Honestly, I just wanted the trial to come to its conclusion. It had been hard and arduous on everyone involved. The toll of this trial was going to be measured sometime in the future.

Each juror stayed in their statuesque position, sitting upright without moving a muscle in anticipation of the instructions they were about to receive. At long last, Judge

Banks cleared his throat, took hold of some papers that had been placed on his bench by his secretary and turned once again to the jurors. "Now, we have arrived at the most important juncture of this trial, the jury instructions. I want all of you to pay close attention, for these instructions will guide you on how to proceed during your deliberation. Take nothing for granted and if you have any questions or requests, make them known immediately," he stated. He continued by asking the jurors, "Do you understand what I have just stated?" In unison, every juror nodded their heads up and down, acknowledging what the judge had explained. Everyone was now on pins and needles waiting.

Judge Banks then proceeded by saying, "So, now that we got that small matter out of the way, let's talk about the jury instructions." He briefed the jury on what he was about to explain regarding jury instructions and why it was so important to fully understand them. His tone was low, almost monotone but steady. Surely, he did not want the jurors falling asleep on him during this phase, one of the most important of the trial. But he still had to articulate precisely what they needed to understand about jury instructions and its significant role in the judicial process. Just then, I felt Lena tapping me on my arm. I turned my head to look at her. That is when she asked me what was going on, since she did not understand why the judge was speaking so much.

I smiled at her and told her not to worry, this was how the judicial system functioned. One could see fatigue and desperation permeating about her face. She did not want to be here any longer than necessary but was putting up a good front in support of her daughter. "It will soon be over, once the judge finishes, the jury will begin to deliberate," I explained. She kindly thanked me for my patience, then whispered that she did not know how much more she could handle. Gently, I took hold of her hand, told her that everything was going to be fine and soon it was going to be over. Letting go of her hand, I could see Idalma smiling at me as if to say, good job. A sense of peace came over me knowing that my words had just comforted a mother, one who has been through hell in a hand basket. *Only a mother could endure such trials and tribulation*, I thought. My attention returned to the judge as he was finishing his explanation. Soon after, he filled his glass with water and took a sip.

"Well, let's get started, shall we!" Judge Banks exclaimed. With those words, he began introducing the jury instructions. Now, I do not remember verbatim how these instructions were presented to the jury, but to the best of my recollection, it went something along these lines.

"Ladies and gentlemen of the jury, you must base your decision on the facts and the law. You have two duties to perform. First, you must determine the facts from evidence obtained during the trial and not from any other source. Remember, facts are proven directly or circumstantially by evidence or by stipulation between the attorneys. Second, apply the law that I state to you to the facts, as you determine them to arrive at your verdict.

"Accept and follow the law as I stated to you, whether or not you agree with the law. Do not be biased against the defendant because he has been arrested for this offense, charged with a crime, or brought to trial. You should not be influenced by mere sentiment, sympathy, passion, prejudice or public opinion. Statements made by attorneys during the course of the trial are not considered evidence, unless stipulated. Then, you must regard that fact as conclusively proven."

"Decide all questions of fact in this case from the evidence received in this trial, not from other sources. Motive is not an element of the crime charged and does not need to be shown. However, you can consider motive or lack of as a circumstance in this case. Remember, a defendant in a criminal trial has a constitutional right not to be compelled to testify. So, do not draw any inference from the fact that the defendant did not testify.

"No person may be convicted of a crime unless there is some proof of the elements of said crime, independent of any admission made by the defendant outside of this trial. A defendant in a criminal action is presumed innocent until proven otherwise. If reasonable doubt is satisfactorily shown, the defendant is entitled to a verdict of Not Guilty." The tension was off the charts.

Everyone in the courtroom was on the edge of their seats, filled with anticipation. Knuckles could be seen turning white as those in attendance squeezed their hands against the backrests of the pews. I was not far from that, except I was clasping my hands together, tight enough that the friction was causing my hands to perspire. I was excited listening to Judge Banks going over the instructions but at the same time, eager for him to finish. Unwavering, he continued speaking.

"Do not discuss this case with no one except fellow jurors. But you cannot discuss this case with fellow jurors until the case is submitted for your decision and only when all jurors are present. Remember, evidence consists of testimony by witnesses, written, material objects or anything offered to prove the existence or non-existence of a fact."

"If you have understood these instructions, then momentarily, you will be asked to convene to the deliberating room to render a verdict. If you have any questions during this process, the foreman will provide the bailiff with the question in written form. It will then be given to me. Should you desire to review any testimony or evidence, then you will follow the same procedure as previously stated. You can take as much time as you need. Do not feel that you are being rushed. Take your time! If you cannot come to an agreement today, then we will reconvene tomorrow. It is now 4:30 pm, the bailiff has your orders for dinner. Bailiff, please escort the jury to the respective deliberating room." The judge concluded his reading and immediately dismissed the jury to perform their duty.

With that, the bailiff walked and stood at the end of the jury box. He motioned with his hand for the rear row to stand, then motioned for the front row to stand. With the jurors standing, he had them walk to the door that led to the deliberating room, opened it, then signaled for the jurors to walk single file through the door. Watching them walking in a single file reminded me of my time in the military. We would stand and line-up in single file, then proceed in an orderly manner. Once all the jurors entered the room, he closed its door behind them. With the door closed, he returned to his post near the judge's bench. Judge Banks then had both attorneys approach the bench. They exchanged a few words before returning to their respective tables. While the attorneys remained standing along with their staff, the judge informed everyone present that the court would be in recess until the jury was ready to return a verdict. Hearing this made me wonder, how long the jury was going to be out? There was no telling, I just had a gut feeling that a verdict was going to be handed down today. For some reason, I was certain that if the jury were close to a verdict, one way or another, Judge Banks would keep them late.

Finally, Judge Banks stood up, struck his gavel, and said, "Court is in recess until further notice!"

The bailiff cried out, "All rise," as the judge walked out of the courtroom. Now that the judge was gone, the courtroom immediately irrupted into a loud murmur. Every person present could be seen speaking to those around them, possibly opining about the trial. Maybe, even guessing how long the jury was going to take in rendering its verdict. While standing, I could hear the comments being made by those in the gallery. Many were convinced that a judgement of guilty was going to be pronounced soon. That would be a welcomed result.

While walking out of the courtroom, I could not help but wonder how easy it was for those in the gallery to think that way. I, on the other hand could not afford to lay down my guard. With jury's, one never knew how they would decide. Lastly, there I was, standing in the hallway in front of courtroom 2–3 almost in a trance. Slowly, I turned and looked down the hall. I noticed the local news reporters who were covering this trial begin trudging their way toward their respective positions for the cameras. They needed to make sure that the live report was aired at 6 pm. This was the time when everyone in Miami was home from work and watched the news.

While they were setting up, I scurried passed them, definitely not wanting to be stopped for a quick sound bite; this was not the time. Upon reaching the escalator, I could hear my friend calling out, "Pepi wait for me." Immediately, I froze in my tracks, turned around, watching as Idalma speed walked toward me with Lena and Floria. Just like me, they too managed to escape the carnivorous media without being peppered with questions. Once they arrived where I was, without saying a word, we stepped onto the escalator and worked our way down, leaving the buzzing sound of people on the second-floor hallway behind.

We reached the first floor in no-time. The only person who was somewhat short winded was Floria, but then again, she was older. Leaving the hallway that housed the escalator, all four of us walked straight out of the courthouse. Once outside, we silently began walking toward the State Attorney's building. The sky was purplish blue as the sun was beginning to set, its rays shimmered from the buildings that surrounded the courthouse, casting a beautiful glow. We walked in cadence, stopping momentarily to cross the street that led to the State Attorney's building. Oddly enough, the only sound I remembered hearing during our walk was that of the alarm bells ringing from the twelfth avenue bridge. Looking toward the bridge, I could see the guard rails begin to lower, a barrier to stop traffic before the center strands were raised.

Soon, the bridge was out of my sight. Idalma, Lena and Floria were trying to keep up with me as we approached the building. Before entering the building, we stood underneath an overhang that provided refuge from the elements. Surprisingly, Idalma asked me if I was going to her office. Without responding, I opened the building's glass door and held it until everyone entered. By the time each of us past through the security check point, one of the elevator doors opened. *Great, as if on que*, I thought, there was no time to sit around waiting for an elevator.

Our silence continued throughout our short ride up to the second floor, where Idalma's office was located. She led us out of the elevator, taking her key card from around her neck, she immediately opened a secured door. Somberly, we followed her into her office. Once inside, she began preparing a pot of coffee. "I know you need some of this, Pepi," she remarked. By the time she turned to ask Lena and her mother if they wanted coffee, they had already made themselves at home, sitting comfortably on a green leather couch. Any more comfortable and they would have fallen asleep. I knew exactly how they felt. The couch was so comfortable, that on many occasions it provided me with a great alternative to take naps while waiting countless hours to attend a deposition, pre-file, or trial.

As they lounged on the couch, I sat on a stiff, uncomfortable chair situated next to Idalma's desk. She dropped/flopped on top of her desk the load of files she had been lugging around. Then, with one swift motion, she twirled and landed on her comfortable chair. This was a very awkward moment, for no one was speaking. The exhaustion must have been creeping in on everyone. Finally, I broke the ice, by asking Idalma if Reid was going to join us. "You know what, I am not sure, he didn't tell me," she responded.

"How strange," I retorted. He must have had his reasons, so I left it at that.

With the ice now broken, we began chatting about our kids, their ages and how they were doing. Idalma and I had worked together for so long, she pretty much knew everything that was going on in my kids' world, just like I knew about hers. During our brief conversation, the coffee began to percolate and with a distinct awesome aroma that penetrated one's nostrils. I could not wait to pour a cup and frankly, it was needed right about now. Glancing over at Lena and her mother, reminded me of the great Roberto Duran, yelling, "No Mas, No Mas!" Floria was seated with her head laid back while Lena was using Floria's shoulder as a pillow. Who could blame them, they had been through so much? It made me wonder, how much more they could endure.

Standing up to allow blood to flow, I made my way to the coffee pot and began to pour myself a cup of java. Without spilling a drop, I turned to Idalma and said, "Look at them, they can't last much longer."

She gently shook her head saying, "I know, they've been through a lot." Before returning to my uncomfortable chair, I asked them if they wanted anything.

They shook their heads no, then in anguish Lena exclaimed, "I just want this to be over!" How does one respond to a comment like that? You cannot, there is not much one can say. While we drank our coffee, Idalma and I continued our lighthearted conversation. We had heard and seen enough gore for one day.

Just then, Reid walked into the office. grabbed another chair that was located behind the door, brought it next to me and sat down. "Everything okay?" I asked.

"Yeah, everything is fine, I had a few things to attend too before coming here. I also left my secretary in the courtroom, just in case," he responded. I congratulated him on his closing argument and let him know it was one of the best I had ever heard. Smiling, he thanked me, then stated that he was not sure how long the jury would be deliberating. Did he know something and was unwilling to share? Why would he make such a comment? Surely, he understood just like I did that the jury was going to at least eat their dinner before concluding.

He stood up, walked over to Lena and her mother, and told them to keep their spirits up. He explained to them that everything was done to ensure a positive outcome, but now it was up to the jury. Knowing Reid as I have gotten to know him during this trial, he was not going to give the family any false hopes. Yeah, he was confident, but he was not about to take a chance. There was no telling with a jury, they could go either way. Strangely enough, after witnessing today's closing arguments and how attentive the jury was, I had an exceptionally good feeling right about now. As Reid began to walk out of the office, I told him to let me know once he heard anything from the courtroom.

While the office door was slowly closing, I could hear him saying, "Will do Pep." Anxiously I glanced at my watch, it was still too early to check on my daughters, most likely they were being picked up from school right about now. Taking traffic into consideration, I would have to wait until 6:00 pm to call them at home.

While enjoying my coffee, Idalma looked at me and asked if I wanted her to bring me something from the cafeteria. That was sweet of her, God only knows I was hungry enough, but now was not the time for food. "No thanks," I replied. With that, she stood up, called Lena and Floria who continued to be in a daze, with their eye's half closed but not asleep. Upon hearing Idalma's voice, both perked up, sat straight on the couch while listening to her. She told them that they had to eat something, if not they were going to faint. Reluctantly, both agreed to accompany her to the cafeteria to eat.

It was moments like these when one appreciated the professionalism and caring of a good victim advocate. Idalma knew precisely what she needed to do to keep both women motivated, engaged and upbeat. This was not the time to allow them to feel downtrodden. She knew just like I did, that juries would take whatever time was necessary before rendering a verdict. We also knew that a rendering of guilty was not guaranteed. History had taught us that lesson.

All three women left the office. Feeling better that they were going to make their way to the cafeteria and grab a bite, I relaxed. With the office empty, it was the perfect opportunity for me to sit on the couch, close my eyes, get comfortable and take a ten-minute nap. This was a common routine, surely, knocking out would not be a problem. A homicide investigators' burden, work a case, capture the bad guy, prepare for trial, follow-up on any request made by the prosecutor, testify, sit with the next of kin and prepare for the outcome. It is funny, how people think homicide investigators work their cases like a television show. If they only knew the number of hours spent on each case, time that is not spent with family and will never get back. Many investigators end up with broken homes because of this job, still they go out every day and perform at a high level to bring about justice to a grieving family.

Suddenly, voices were heard coming from the hallway outside of Idalma's office. Unconsciously, I checked my watch again, *Damn, 6:50 pm already,* I thought to myself. The voices were getting louder, so I hurried to get off the couch and fix myself. I had taken a 45-minute nap and felt great. By the time the office door opened, I had already settled back into the chair next to Idalma's desk. "I thought we were going to find you sleeping," she declared.

"Are you kidding me, there was no way I could fall asleep," I sheepishly replied.

Idalma began laughing, then proceeded to inform Lena and her mother how I was known for being able to fall asleep anywhere. She would know, haven woken me up on many occasions from different offices within the building while waiting to attend a deposition or pre-file conference. This was the only way to get some rest, if not, investigators would mentally and physically break down. As it is, breakdowns still occur because this type of rest was not good for one's health.

"Have you heard anything from Reid?" I asked.

"No," she replied and continued telling me that his secretary was in the courtroom and would notify him as soon as anything happened. With that, I informed her that I would be in the next office to call my house. While exiting the office, I turned, letting Lena and Floria know that I was going to be nearby and not to worry. A common courtesy on my part that did not require a response, but they thanked me anyway for informing them. *Such kindness or humility is unheard of during moments like these*, I thought.

Walking toward the nearest office, I ran into several secretaries in the hallway. They were on their way home and wished me good luck with the case. This was the biggest trial of the day, possibly the year and everyone in the State Attorney's Office understood the jury was currently deliberating. Finally, I made it to Cecy's office, her door was open, which gave me access. Working my way around her desk, I sat in her chair. Taking a deep breath, I picked up the receiver, a dial tone could be heard, so I began dialing home. After about three rings, one of my daughters picked up the receiver, "Hello," she said, in a child's voice.

"Hi, sweetie, how are you and your sister doing?" I asked.

"Hi, Daddy, good," she replied. "How are you doing, when are you coming home, do you want to speak with Mommy?" She just blurted out a barrage of questions in less than ten seconds.

"No, sweetie, tell Mommy I will be home later, I love you," I responded.

"Love you too, Daddy," she replied, then unexpectedly hung-up the receiver. Typical child, she finished what she had to say and 'click', end of conversation. I laughed while slowly walking out of Cecy's office. Alone in that section of the building, knowing that everyone had gone for the day, afforded me the luxury of laughing out loud without people looking at me funny. It felt better knowing that everyone got home okay, so I hurriedly returned to Idalma's office.

Upon entering her office, I immediately asked if Reid had informed her of any new developments. She gently responded that no word had come down from the courtroom regarding the verdict. Lena and her mother remained uncomplainingly seated on the comfortable couch, where not long ago I had dozed off. While giving Idalma a crazy look, one that questioned, how much longer would it be before a verdict is rendered? Suddenly, I found myself looking past her shoulder glancing at her desk clock. It was now 7:40 pm. *Unbelievable! The jury couldn't be taking this long*, I thought, *how much more did they need to convict this monster?* For me, Father-Time was playing tricks by not allowing time to move. This unknowing was driving my impatience, but then, I heard Lena whisper something to her mother. The unintelligible words caused me to turn and, in that moment, upon studying both women I realized it was not my place to be impatient.

Still, the jury had everything required to render a decisive verdict and bring this case to a close. In reality, and for selfish reasons I wanted this case to end as much as Lena and Floria. Its haunting images were part of my daily life, and not a day goes by without me thinking of Little Lena. Still, this trial had reopened my barely healed wound. As for them, it is about attempting to bring some sort of resolution or maybe not. Can a mother ever attain full closure for a brutally murdered child? Right now, I just wanted a verdict or at least an inclining of what was going on in the deliberation room. To be a fly on the wall.

Considering the elapsed time, it was possible these jurors were just finishing their dinner. Maybe their decision had already been made, in essence, this waiting was an exercise in one's mental anguish and discipline. Sitting down again on my designated chair next to Idalma's desk, gave way for me to ponder; "Investigators must have unwavering inner fortitude when conducting any Major Crime investigation, especially a brutal murder. Because there are so many facets to successfully closing a murder investigation, one must be prepared for anything, one being the trial phase. But this one had been testing my inner core as well as my belief in how one can overcome evil." Hopefully soon, everything that I hold true and dear will come to pass. A part of Evil will be pummeled, if only for today, but beaten none the less. Only a guilty verdict can validate my mission of bringing bad people to justice, even if at the cost of personal sacrifice.

While deep in my thoughts, the telephone suddenly rang. In that one moment, it sounded like a train horn blurting out the alarm before crossing an intersection. Jumping up, my first instinct was to grab the receiver, but my friend beat me to it. Why wouldn't she, it was her office not mine. Both women who had been comfortable on the couch were now standing as well, inching their way toward Idalma. We were all standing so close, the voice on the other end was heard clear as a whistle, saying, "The jury is ready."

"Who was that?" I asked with excitement.

Idalma looked at me saying, "Reid's secretary, they want us in the courtroom." While she started collecting her things, I was informing Lena and Floria of what had just taken place. We quickly grabbed our belongings and began making our way out of the office heading toward the elevators. How strange that Reid had not called himself, maybe he was already heading to the courtroom. Besides, he had a million things on his mind. This is when a little knot began swimming in my stomach, anticipating what was about to happen.

# Chapter 21

Arriving at the elevator first, I forcefully pressed the button with the arrow pointing down, as if this were going to move the elevator any faster. Just as the doors began to open, Idalma and the others arrived. Holding the doors open, all three women entered, each found a niche toward the back wall of the elevator. Within seconds, the doors closed, a sudden bump jarred the elevator as it began to descend. The one-minute ride in this silo felt like an eternity, with no one daring to speak or make a sound. We were on autopilot, deep in our thoughts, just wanting this day to end. After exiting the elevator, we took our solemn walk across the parking lot. It felt the same as a funeral procession, no one uttering a word. The apprehension could be felt protruding from Lena, it was thick and visible to those who knew her. Finally, we reached the marble steps of the courthouse building. As we hurried up the steps, the shoes made a clicking sound, causing our approach to seem as if we were tap dancing. Once at the top, I headed straight for the only entrance with a security guard. We showed our identifications, walked through the turnstile, and hurried toward the escalators.

The escalators were moving slowly, so we decided to step our way up instead of standing still. This allowed us to make it to the second floor faster. The buzzing sound was still emanating from the hallway but not as loud as it had been several hours before. Most of the curious visitors had left for the evening. The only ones remaining were the local news outlets with their reporters. A lone, independent, news photographer took several photographs of us as we walked past him. Immediately I thought, *Surely, one or two would be making its appearance on one of the local newspapers. If the verdict is brought forth tonight, certainly, one of those photos taken would make the front page.*

We slowed our cadence while approaching courtroom 2–3. I made sure to walk ahead of the others to open the courtroom's door as a courtesy. While reaching for the door handle, I paused, finding myself hesitating in my task. My reluctance, though not noticeable to those in the immediate vicinity, was noticeable to me. While standing still, my outstretched arm attempting to grab the handle seemed as if it was suspended in the air. A deep bag of emotions lined the pit of my stomach as I finally pulled on the ornate brass door handle. This was no time for uncertainty, I had to appear resolute in my conviction that tonight a guilty verdict would be handed down. One must have trust in the system and understand that hard work and dedication will bring about positive results, even under these trying circumstances.

Pulling on the cold handle, I held the door open for the others to make their way through the threshold. A burst of cold air covered us while walking down the aisle toward the first pew. I spotted Reid standing next to the prosecutors' table. His assistant was already seated, not paying attention to the surroundings. Idalma darted straight for him, uncharacteristically, leaving Lena and Floria behind. I chuckled inside thinking how crazy it would have been if Lena were holding Idalma's hand and she was dragged to the ground. Picturing that scene in my mind allowed for a moment of levity. There were very few such moments, but this one came at the right time.

As Lena and her mother made their way through the aisle, I noticed the bailiff and several Correction Officers escorting Laudin Matte. They were slowly walking a monster toward the defense table, with him waddling like a penguin and sporting the traditional jewelry, shackles, and handcuffs, tied to a waist harness. The gray suit he was wearing did not hide the fact as to why he was here. *A wolf in sheep's clothing. A monster will always be a monster*, I thought. Monsters were meant for nightmares and movies, but not this one. This one was alive and kicking right before our eyes.

Lena and Floria were oblivious to him, as he was to them since he did not bother looking in their direction. Although they had been within fifteen feet of each other throughout the trial, not once did their eyes make contact. I always wondered if that was collateral damage from his abusive treatment and historical demeanor toward Lena. Now, he was sitting between Erin and her assistant while they conferred quietly. I observed their demeanor, and surely, they were not discussing the trial. Most likely, they were deciding where to have dinner. In either case, it did not matter to me what they were planning. Like a chess match, I felt this one was Check-Mate.

279

Reid and Idalma concluded their conversation, when suddenly he turned to me and said, "Sorry, Pepi, for not calling you, I took off from the office once I received the phone call." I nodded my head, completely understanding his reasoning, what else was I going to do? Turning my head to scan the courtroom, it felt eerie seeing it so empty, except for those that mattered.

The large throngs of onlookers from early in the day were now gone, probably seated at a dinner table or in front of their television watching Jeopardy. Whatever the case, this earnest location was now free of distraction, leaving space for us who toiled to bring this case to justice for Little Lena. Would she have been satisfied with me? Would she be a lasting memory for her mother, or will she eventually fade away after time? Suddenly, I felt a deep sadness unlike any other. Yes, this whole case, from its inception, has brought out many dark and sad emotions that I am unable to purge.

It has always been my hope that she is continuously looking down on us, smiling, knowing we worked relentlessly to bring this case to trial. In my heart, she is in heaven rejoicing without pain, but always on my mind. My memory of her remains vivid in my head. Grotesque as that night was, this little girl inspired me to perform my job to its highest level and to be a better man. There had been times when I felt down or worn out, oddly enough, it was during those moments I could hear her laughter and it encouraged me to press forward. To say such a thing or even suggest it, is crazy, considering there is no plausible explanation since I never heard her laugh. Inexplicably, to me, it feels as if it is her essence. Soon, this will all be over and maybe we can all gain some sort of closure. I have often wondered if each person will be able to go back to being normal. After being a part of such a case, there is no way I could ever use the word normal during the remainder of my career. Death has become a part of who I am, a chosen path that few dares to travel. It is a burden for which only a very select group have the fortitude to handle.

It could not be much longer, we have been here for almost fifteen minutes, everyone was present except for the judge and jury. Unintentionally, I glanced at the courtroom's clock, which showed 8:10 pm. Unexpectedly, out of the corner of my eye, I spotted one of the reporters entering the courtroom. The reporter found a space to sit without effort, removed a notepad from her briefcase and began writing God knows what. Looking up at the clock again, I wondered, *Damn, how much longer.* Certainly, this judge wanted to go home as much as the rest of us. Turning to Lena, she was surprisingly showing no signs of emotion or expectation. Idalma had prepared her well, not to be overconfident to avoid a possible letdown. Understanding that a jury, at a drop of a dime, could destroy any family's expectations.

Suddenly, the door leading to the judge's chamber opened. *It was judgement time,* I thought. The bailiff hurried to his post and as Judge Banks entered, he cried out, "All rise!" Judge Banks took up his position on the bench, emitted a few pleasantries to those of us in attendance, then sat down. His secretary stepped away from her desk, which was in front of the bench. She proceeded to hand the judge several pieces of paper, documents, I surmised. He reviewed their contents, then placed them in a designated basket. He looked up at the bailiff and asked, "Are they ready yet?"

The bailiff answered, "Yes judge."

With that, the judge instructed the bailiff to escort the jurors back into the courtroom. Immediately, the bailiff went to the secured door leading to the deliberating chamber and opened it. He could be heard telling the jurors, "You may return to your seats." The courtroom was silent, except for the pitter-patter emitting from the juror's feet as they shuffled, single file, through the door until they were seated inside the jury box. This being a Capital Murder case, all twelve jurors took a moment to adjust their seating positions, mostly getting comfortable for the homestretch. Once the chairs were adjusted, without saying a word they each sat down.

Tension and anticipation were felt throughout the courtroom, for those of us remaining. How were these jurors going to decide, for the victim or the defendant? The prosecutors presented an excellent case, much of it based on the investigation and witness testimonials. They were powerful in and of themselves, but to see the graphic photos of how Little Lena met her fate – well, that should have sealed it for any normal human being. As for the defense, they performed their job to the best of their ability. But their best was not going to be enough on this night.

While seated in this cold, morgue like courtroom, I felt comforted by a sudden warmth and peace. No longer anxious or consciously optimistic. A renewed sense of favor lifted my spirit in a way that could only be explained as celestial. While the judge continued performing his duties, I sat back in my space on the pew. I looked to my left watching Lena and her mother, motionless and silent. What were they thinking? They had endured this dramatic, emotional ordeal with grace and resilience. For some unexplainable reason, I slid my left hand along the pew, where it eventually encountered Lena's right hand. Without saying a word, she took hold of my hand. It might have been an unconscious gesture, an act to sooth her through this period or maybe, she felt comfortable and reassured by my presence. But then again, it might have been therapeutic for me. Then, with her hand in mine, I closed my eyes and silently began reciting the Lord's Prayer and a Hail Mary.

Unexpectedly, the bailiff cried out, "Silence in the courtroom."

*Why the drama?* I wondered. Since the courtroom was noiseless. That is when I turned around and looked at the clock, this time, it showed 8:30 pm. It had been over two hours since the jury was last seen. Finally, we were about to cross the finish line. Then, Judge Banks again began the proceeding by thanking those of us in attendance for our patience and diligence throughout the judiciary process. He commented on how this process was a cornerstone of our democracy and its importance to preserving the rule of law. Everyone in the courtroom was hanging on every single word he spoke. As if he were a minister during a homily; every word was being mentally and thoughtfully digested. His eloquence and phrasing during his final oration were to be envied.

True enough, he was an articulate speaker who kept all of us engaged while presenting a very sincere and empathetic antidote to all parties involved. Certainly, he was not going to bring back the victim or heal the suffering

283

of her family. Neither would he be able to roll back the hands of time so that the defendant could reconsider his actions. The atrocious deeds of that fateful morning were done, sending everything in motion, which got us to where we are today. Now, his voice began to slowly subside until he stopped speaking.

He reached for his glass, brought it to his lips and took a quick sip of water. After returning the glass to its proper place, he cleared his throat. I Lowered my head, listening to my inner voice saying, "Dude get this over with." I looked up quickly, as if someone heard what I had just thought. Man, that would have been something, had that comment were blurted out loud. Alas, it was all in my head and everyone around me was still focused on the judge. My impatience was getting to me, it had been a long trial, and this had been an exceedingly long day. Hopefully, my endurance would last, it had too.

Slowly, I let go of Lena's hand and placed mine on my lap in anticipation of the judge's utterance. The judge did not disappoint, as if on cue he entered the final stretch. He began by asking the defendant to stand. Laudin Matte stoically followed the instructions along with his defense team. Reid and his assistant also stood, as per courtroom decorum. With all participating parties standing and slightly fidgeting from obvious nervousness, the judge continued.

Looking intently at the jury foreman, who was now standing, he asked, "Mr. Foreman, have you reached a verdict?"

The foreman replied, "Yes we have your honor." Once the foreman answered, Judge Banks ordered the foreman to hand the document with the decision to the bailiff.

With document in hand, the bailiff turned to the judge. Without hesitation, the judge said, "Bailiff, please give the document with the jury's decision to the secretary, she will mark it and enter it as evidence." The bailiff walked to the secretary's desk and handed her the document.

Cautiously, she looked over the document, stamped it, then placed a designated tag with a number on it. Once she concluded, she turned and handed the document to the judge. With document in hand, he reviewed it, then slowly looked up. Undeniably, the suspense was noticeable throughout the courtroom. All eyes were as wide open as an owls', just waiting. Again, the judge continued, "The jury having been duly sworn and after deliberate consideration of the facts – state the following: We the jury find the defendant, Laudin Matte, guilty of 1$^{st}$ degree murder, guilty of one count of kidnapping and guilty of one count of aggravated child abuse."

Upon hearing the verdict, I turned to Lena, who was in Idalma's arms and said to her in Spanish, "We did it." Lena, with tears flowing from her eyes, looked at me but did not respond. I looked across and noticed Floria, she was still seated and crying just as much.

Watching these two brave women gave me a moment for pause to reflect on what had just occurred. A sagacity of accomplishment, not so much because of the verdict but despite it, knowing all the hard work, dedication and personal sacrifice made it worthwhile. While surveying my surroundings, a lot of smiles were seen, when suddenly an outstretched hand appeared, it was Reid's. We shook hands, exchanged congratulatory remarks, followed by small talk. Again, he complemented me on my work before returning to his chair. Now it was my turn to sit back down. Once seated, I felt a sigh of relief, a yok of stress had just been removed from my shoulders.

The judge continued speaking, but I was not paying attention after hearing those profound words, "Guilty as charged." Upon regaining my composure, the judge was concluding by asking Erin George if she wanted the jury polled, immediately, she responded, "Yes."

Moments later, Judge Banks stated the following: "I want to thank each of you for your service during this trial, we will reconvene for sentencing in two weeks. The defendant will be remanded to the Dade-County Jail until sentencing. Officers remove the defendant." The officers, who had walked the defendant into the courtroom earlier were now escorting him out. His gait was one of defeat. Upon reaching the door, leading to the holding cell, the judge struck his gavel and exclaimed, "Court is adjourned!"

Once the judge stood, to make his grand exit, the bailiff cried out, "All rise." Those remaining in the courtroom stood and watched as the black rob disappeared into the rear hallway. The reporters began writing last minute notes and collecting their personal belongings to quickly exit the courtroom. While watching them hurriedly make their way toward the main hallway, outside of courtroom 2–3, Idalma tapped me on the shoulder.

When I turned, she gave me a hug and whispered, "Great job, Pepi, this case was meant for you and no one else." Not that I would ever want such a case again, I half smiled and thanked her. Her kindness and dedication were always on display during this long ordeal and it was greatly appreciated. Our friendship grew a lot during this trial. A friendship that would last for many years.

Slowly, I stepped away from the pew and into the aisle, allowing for Idalma, Lena and Floria to exit. They walked past me; we did not look at each other as they made their way toward the courtroom's door. Thinking nothing of it, I remained next to the railing that separated the gallery from the main section and took a long hard look at courtroom 2–3, soaking in the moment. The courtroom was now completely silent, everyone was gone, leaving me alone where justice had just been served. I placed both hands on the railing, took a deep breath and exhaled. I turned around slowly and began making my way toward the door.

*How many reporters would be standing outside?* I wondered. Hopefully, Idalma was able to whisk Lena and her mother away from the cameras. Surely, the last thing they wanted was to be the center of attention.

Upon reaching the doors, I glanced up at the clock, it was now 8:55 pm. While slowly pushing the doors open, my mind picked up a sudden, faint sound of a child's laughter. Quickly, I turned to still find an empty courtroom, with its lights now dimmed. *Just like at the medical examiner's building*, I thought. Deep in the recesses of my mind, I felt Little Lena's presence once again. Maybe this was her way of thanking me or maybe it was my own belief that willed a moment such as this one. Either way, I kept staring into the courtroom until its doors closed. Once shut, I entered the second floor's hallway. Surprised, I watched as all the local media outlets were breaking down their equipment, *Thank God, I wouldn't have to stand here to give a statement*, I thought. I continued watching until the last camera crew exited the hallway.

The second floor was now completely dark except for the section where the escalators and elevators were located. Making my way past the remaining reporters, I heard several of them saying, "Nice work, detective." My Joe Namath moment, as I raised my hand in acknowledgement of their comments while continuing my walk toward the escalator that would take me down. A lone, courthouse security guard was standing by until everyone was out of the building. Finally, I stepped onto the descending familiar escalator, taking the slow ride. Once on the main floor, I began making my way toward the exits, that is when I noticed Idalma, Lena and Floria. They were huddled around each other talking while waiting for me. "Hey, what are you guys still doing here?" I asked in Spanish.

Idalma answered that Lena wanted to wait for me so we could leave the building together. Well, maybe she did not forget about me after all. I hurried my steps and as I approached, their huddle broke-up.

By the time I reached them, they began asking a million questions and talking about the trial. They wanted to know what would happen in several weeks, during the sentencing phase. I explained to them that since Laudin was found guilty of all the charges, under Florida law, he could be sentenced to death. The judge would review the recommendation but could impose his own. Lena shrugged her shoulders without saying a word. There was no need, she knew very well the death penalty was not going to bring back her little girl. She looked at me and for the first time I truly felt what a physical toll this tragedy had taken on her.

Her face was withered and drawn; her frail body was vividly pronounced through her inexpensive but presentable dress. This once very good-looking young woman was now a fraction of what I remembered from that frightful early morning. There is no price that could be associated with what this young mother has had to endure. Lena had put on a great front throughout this whole ordeal, a testament to her will of survival, a mother's love.

Looking at all of them, I asked in Spanish, "Are you ready to leave?"

They all nodded yes as we began our slow walk toward the exit. Suddenly, Lena, who was a few steps in front of me turned around and stopped, blocking my path. That is when I noticed her lips quivering, and her eyes began to welt. *Damn, I did not want this to happen*, I thought. She began thanking me with raw emotions pouring out, while simultaneously extending her hand, as if wanting to shake mine. Automatically, my hand moved forward to meet hers. As our hands met, I felt an object being placed in the palm of my hand. Lena kept a firm grip on my hand, gave me a hug worthy of a long-lost family member and gently kissed my cheek. She let go of my hand and stepped back, that is when I noticed the object in my palm. It was a small gold medallion of a cupid's heart. "Please keep this in memory of my little girl," she said in Spanish. What could I do? Such a gesture should not be rejected, that would be cruel. I found myself gazing at this small piece of metal which stirred up my emotions.

My eyes began tearing, and felt the tears trickling down my cheeks. Then, uncharacteristically, I opened my arms and hugged her. We hugged each other as we cried. Those few moments felt like an eternity. Lena again thanked me for what I had done. At that moment, like a shot of adrenalin, I felt validation like never before. Slowly, we let go of each other, turned and without saying a word headed through the exit door. We walked down the marble steps of the courthouse, Idalma continued toward the State Attorney's building with Lena and Floria while I detoured toward my parked vehicle.

Walking toward my vehicle, inexplicably, I began crying again. The surge of emotions was running high, each tear was a cleansing of my soul, a purging of all the negative feelings I had been harboring inside. *How can man be so evil and cruel, to harm such an innocent child for revenge?* I wondered. Death would be to merciful and swift for that monster. He will never suffer as Little Lena did or feel the emotional pain of her mother. Finally, I reached my vehicle, opened the driver's door, removed my jacket, and threw it on the back seat. *It was finally over*, I thought.

I entered my car and began loosening my tie while sitting down behind the steering wheel. Once the engine was turned on, the illuminated clock on the radio display read 9:10 pm. I deliberately leaned my head back against the headrest. Soaking up the cold air from the air-conditioner, it gave me time to pause, thinking, *This turned out to be a good day. Now it was time to go to work. My guys will be waiting at the station, and another night has begun. Besides, I needed to write up my report, inform my bosses of how the trial concluded and make sure that my case file got properly filed away in the bowling alley.* Just as I pulled out of the parking lot, an image popped up in my head, Cafecito. The lifeblood of a homicide investigator in Miami.

Several weeks later, Laudin Matte was sentenced to death in Florida's electric chair. His defense team immediately prepared for his appeal. After the sentencing hearing, I took a long drive to Woodlawn South Cemetery, stopped at the florist stand near the entrance and purchased a dozen pink roses to match the pink shoes Little Lena wore for her funeral. I remember her mother telling me that she bought them the day before her murder. She was going to wear them for a birthday party.

Driving through the grandiose gates of the cemetery, I looked across the garden of stones and colorful flowers. The sky was a beautiful light blue, cloudless, with the sun shining as bright as I have ever seen. Minutes later, I parked my vehicle next to a section filled with small bronze and marble markers on the ground. While making my way between the headstones, it saddened me to see so many markers for children. Many of whom were no older than five years of age. Some markers had angels, little bears, flowers, and religious symbols. Finally, roses in hand, I reached a gray marble marker with a bronze heart, figures of angels on either side were noted as if watching over this sacred ground. The marker read, L M.M, January 8, 1992–June 3, 1994. I Stood in front of the marker for several minutes with my rosery in hand and prayed.

Upon concluding my prayers, I bent down and removed the flower vase attached to the marker, placing the pink roses inside. They stood out like a fresh painting, the pink against a backdrop of blue skies and freshly cut green grass. That is when I noticed an inscription in Spanish taken from her favorite song, it read, '*Nunca Voi a Olvidarte*' (I will never forget you). Upon reading those words, I teared up knowing her memory would always stay with me. I placed two fingers to my lips, kissed them, then placed those same fingers on her name. I remained for a few more minutes thinking of what could have been of her future and thanking God for each of my own children.

Retreating to my vehicle, I began to wonder angrily why we arrived at this moment in time where I was placing flowers on the grave of such a beautiful little girl. Upon entering my vehicle, inspired by the moment, I picked up my notebook and began to write. My writing was a part of my self-prescribed therapy. After several minutes, I looked down at the paper which read the following:

'For the desperate man that you took in…Your child became the sacrifice of your sin…Battered and agonized by his evil games…You suffered through the tortures without shame…With his twisted mind, he went after the tame…He ended her life to cause you pain…Your suffering is now endless and who is to blame…This little girl was sacrificed for you, to end his pain…'

Driving away from the cemetery, I felt at peace and headed home. Thanking God for his mercy.

Four years later, the death sentence was overturned at the appellate level stating that L M.M death did not cause her undue or aggravated suffering. The aggravating factors were overthrown, and the monster's petition was granted. He escaped the death penalty but will live out his natural life in a hellish environment, behind bars, reminded each day of his misdeed. Maybe, this was justice after all.

This book was based on one of my investigations and names were changed. It was written exactly how the incident occurred with several creative differences. It was a way to assist me in healing. The stresses placed on investigators across America who investigate violent crimes are immeasurable and throughout a career can cause tremendous emotional, physical, and spiritual damage. One's psyche can fray and morph into PTSD if not properly treated. Therefore, this was part of a process in an attempt for me to reconnect as a human, to be normal once again. A small measure of repent for unwillingly causing harm to those I love and inadvertently affected. "The course for cleansing one's soul is long and arduous after facing the acts of evil."